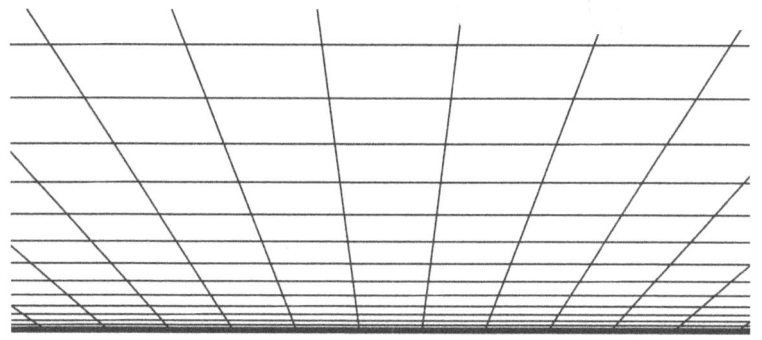

REVIVING GRAHAM
PROJECT DEEP
BOOK FIVE

BECCA JAMESON

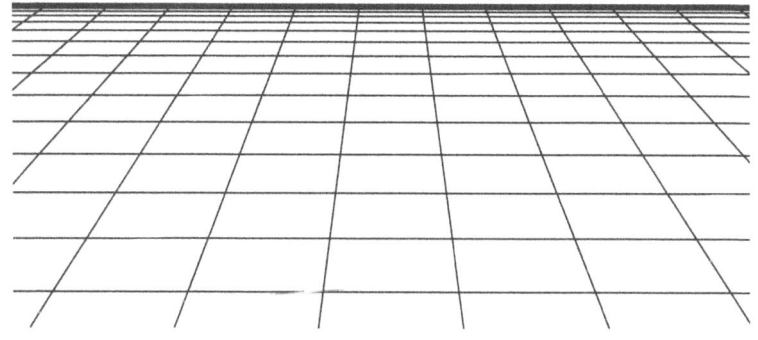

PROLOGUE

Dade Menke ran his hand absentmindedly through his hair as he stared at the computer screen. He did that often, and as was customary, it was Blair's gentle hand landing on top of his over his thick hair that made him aware of his actions.

Blair threaded her fingers with his and pulled their combined hands down to his shoulder, leaning into him from behind until her chin rested on his opposite shoulder. Her lips landed on his ear. "You need to take a break," she murmured. "You've been working for hours."

He leaned his cheek against hers, closed his eyes, and sighed. "It's so frustrating, and the clock is ticking. Every time I stop to eat or sleep or laugh or shower or exercise, I feel guilty. People are counting on us. People are living in limbo. I hate that six members of my team aren't even reanimated yet. Especially Graham Wentz. The thought of him halfway through the process, in a coma, in hiding, makes me incredibly nervous."

"I know, babe. And you're doing the best you can. But you're working too hard." Her gentle hands slid down his chest, and she held him tighter. "You left out sex," she whispered directly into his ear.

He reached behind to wrap his hand around her neck, twisted his face toward her, and kissed her. He did leave sex off the list, but he never left it out of their day. Even if all they had time for was a quickie before they got up, while showering, or right before they fell asleep, he never left out sex. And he'd never feel guilty about that.

He was clear on the fact that he'd been given a second chance at life, and he wasn't about to squander it.

No. To be honest, he'd been given a third chance at life. The first life had been cut short ten years ago when he and the rest of the team working in the government bunker in Falling Rock, Colorado, contracted a rare form of viral-onset anemia—AP12. All twenty-two people in the medical wing of the bunker were cryonically preserved—the entire team of twenty-one plus General Winston Custodio, who had been the one to arrive with the disease in the first place.

For Dade, it seemed as if he woke up the next morning, when the reality was ten years had passed. But he quickly found he'd been reanimated into a tumultuous world where all hell was breaking loose in the bunker.

His second chance at life had also been cut short when he found out he had the genetic marker for yet another form of anemia, AA2, that would kill him if he received the cure that had been developed for AP12.

And yet, he had lived. An experimental stem cell transplant had saved his life, giving him opportunity number three to make the most of it.

He smiled at Blair, the woman who'd left the bunker with him as his security guard. The woman who'd shaken some sense into him and forced him to adopt a positive attitude when he'd wanted to crawl into a hole and die. The woman he'd fallen in love with. The woman who was now on the run with him while they secretly tried to figure out what the hell was going on inside that bunker.

Except for a few people—Ryan Anand, Emily Zorich, Zeke Holleran, and Michelle Houston—no one knew Dade was going to live. They all thought he was somewhere dying a slow death with Blair by his side.

Blair pointed at a plate on the table. "I made you a sandwich." She slid around to his front and lowered herself onto his lap, cupping his face. "At least take a break to eat lunch. You can't solve the world's problems if you don't eat."

He set his hands on her waist and slid them up and around to her back. "Thanks for reminding me how damn lucky I am." He kissed her again, lingering longer this time, loving the feel of her lips on his. She made him feel alive. She gave him hope.

"You are pretty lucky," she teased as she leaned back, separating their lips.

A knock sounded at the door, making them both freeze as they turned to stare at it.

"You expecting anyone?" Dade asked.

She shook her head.

It wasn't as if no one ever came to the door. It happened. Deliveries. Management. Neighbors. But it always made the hairs stand up on the back of Dade's neck.

He grabbed Blair's hips and moved her next to him before standing and heading toward the door.

They had been renting this furnished apartment in a small town in Montana for a few weeks. They relocated often. It was almost time to move again.

A peek through the peephole gave Dade no information. A young man stood there, ball cap shadowing his face. His brown hair was a bit too long and curling around the edges of the cap. He wore scruffy tennis shoes, worn jeans, and a *Dark Side of the Moon* T-shirt that couldn't have belonged to him originally. The kid wasn't born when it was made.

Blair set her hand on Dade's back. He hadn't even heard her

approach. She was getting good at stealth. "Who is it?" she whispered.

"No idea," he whispered back.

The kid stuck his hands in his pockets and rocked forward and back on his feet. He tugged one hand out to knock again while Dade watched.

Blair nudged Dade out of the way and lifted onto her tiptoes to look through the peephole. Her brow was furrowed when she turned around. "He's just a kid," she pointed out.

He lifted his brows. The two of them had been on the run for weeks, living under the radar. They didn't take chances.

She rolled her eyes. "He probably lives below us or something. Or he's looking for a job. Or he's at the wrong address. We'll look like idiots if we ignore him and then he sees us leaving later." She murmured all of this while shoving Dade out of the way.

Dade swept out a hand. "Fine. Open the door."

Blair unlocked the door in two places and opened it about six inches. Dade stood behind her, his foot at the base of the door, ready to kick it shut.

The young man lifted his gaze. He was frowning. He cocked his head to one side and rolled his eyes in the same way Blair had just done. "You two are the worst secret agents on the planet."

Dade jerked in his spot at that opening line. "Pardon?"

"Can we help you?" Blair asked, her spine straightening so that she stood taller. She also held the door with a death grip under Dade's hand, just as ready as he was to slam it shut.

"My name's Spencer. You're Dade Menke and Blair Rollans," he stated as he glanced from one to the other.

Not a soul had their real names. They hadn't gone by Dade and Blair since they'd left Colorado.

Dade was fucking nervous as he licked his lips and

responded, "No idea who that is. I'm John Jones, and this is my wife Stacey. You must have the wrong apartment."

Now the kid chuckled. "That's the best you could come up with? John Jones? How cheesy."

Dade's heart rate picked up by the second. He leaned into Blair's back, feeling her tension.

"How about you let me come inside so that everyone on your floor doesn't hear us, and I'll tell you who I am and why I know who you are."

Seconds ticked by.

So much anxiety. Deflation. Frustration. Dade's worst nightmare.

Spencer lifted both hands in the air. "I don't have a weapon. You can frisk me if you want." He winked. The kid fucking winked. And then his cocky eyes went wider as if to taunt them. "I don't have much time. Take a chance on me. I promise I'll make it worth your while."

Blair glanced at Dade, and he nodded before stepping back and opening the door wider.

Spencer slid into the apartment as Blair shut the door.

"You might be unarmed, but I'm not," Blair stated. "So, you better talk fast before I lose my patience." Yep. That was Dade's woman. Badass and feisty when circumstances called for it.

Spencer pointed at the couch and armchair in the small living room that also served as a kitchen and dining room. The super had referred to it as a great room, but that was comical considering how small it was. "Let's sit. I'll talk."

Dade took Blair's hand and led her to the sofa while Spencer took the armchair. He had an air of confidence that far exceeded his years. "First of all," he began, "let me start by saying that your hacking skills suck royally, and you need to stop it before you get caught."

Dade narrowed his gaze but said nothing. It was obvious denial wasn't going to be effective. This kid knew stuff.

Blair set her hand on Dade's thigh and gripped it.

Spencer sighed and slouched back in the chair as if he had permission to get comfortable. "Quick synopsis. Four years ago, a covert government organization approached me to work for them."

That was the end of Dade's silence. "Four years ago? Were you twelve?"

The kid laughed. He took off his ball cap, ran a hand through his hair that was too long on top, and put it back on, seemingly adjusted. "I'm twenty-two. I was eighteen at the time. Just out of high school."

Dade suddenly felt much older than his thirty-five years if this was what twenty-two looked like.

Spencer continued. "I'm a computer hacker. A genius by most people's standards. I was still in high school when I started digging around in places I shouldn't have." He laughed as if it were cool to fuck with other people's computers. "Mind you, I never did anything to get people in trouble. I just hacked into mainframes because I could. I get a thrill out of the challenge."

"Speed this up," Dade stated between gritted teeth.

Spencer rolled his eyes yet again. "I was hired by a group called Blue Cell."

"Never heard of it," Blair said.

"You wouldn't have. It's top secret. Operates below the radar. Way below the radar."

"Go on," Dade encouraged. His entire body was stiff. He had a feeling his world was about to be upended. His and Blair's.

"I've been assigned to hack into every detail of Project DEEP. I need you to understand that I'm fucking smart. I know where every damn member of your team is, both the first team that was preserved ten years ago and the second team headed up by Ryan Anand. I've known every move you people have made from the moment you were reanimated."

Dade flinched, unable to hide it. What the fuck did this kid want?

Spencer held up a hand, palm out. "Don't freak out. I'm not going to turn you in. I want to help you."

Dade leaned forward at those words. He set his elbows on his knees. Blair did the same at his side.

For the first time since he'd arrived, Spencer fidgeted and looked slightly less confident. Chagrined. "At first, I thought I'd hit the lottery when I got this job. A foster kid who'd lived in seven homes in eighteen years. A high school diploma with grades that would make most parents cringe. An ability to decode things that were a bit morally ambiguous. No college education. No prospects at all.

"I was hotheaded and full of myself when Blue Cell approached me and offered me the world. I knew they were a government organization. I didn't know much else. I had no idea they were not on the up and up. How the fuck could a branch of the government be dirty?"

A chuckle slipped from Dade's lips. He knew better than most people alive how dirty the government could be. He'd been digging around trying to figure out what the hell their aim was for weeks, knowing someone or a pile of someones were working hard to undermine everything that Project DEEP did.

"Yeah," Spencer continued. "I get it. Preaching to the choir. But here's the thing: Your people are in danger. You need to move them. All of them. ASAP."

Dade hesitated. How the fuck was he going to find and move the twenty-one members of the first team—the reanimated group—as well as the twelve members of the second team—those who worked their asses off to return the first team to the living?

Dade was supposed to be dead. He didn't have the manpower or the time to hunt people down and move them.

And where would that be? "Where the hell am I supposed to move everyone to?"

"I have some suggestions."

Dade cringed. "And you expect me to trust your suggestions?"

"My God." Blair looked like she was going to rush across the room and strangle Spencer. She gripped her thighs with both hands as she straightened. "How could you possibly know where everyone is? And why?"

He shrugged. "I'm that good. And it's my job. At this point, Blue Cell is keeping tabs on everyone to make sure they stay split up and out of the way."

"Wait," Dade said as he lowered back to sit next to Blair, "are you saying Blue Cell orchestrated that bombing at the bunker a month ago?"

Spencer nodded. "The goal was to disperse everyone. That's always been the goal. It finally worked."

"So all the crazy shit that happened was caused by this Blue Cell group?"

"Yep. Everything. Even the kidnapping of Ryan's girlfriend, Emily Zorich. It's amazing what a desperate father will do. A few suggestive nudges, and the man was convinced Emily was the key to reviving his daughter."

"Jesus," Dade muttered.

"The messiah hasn't been involved yet, but you never can tell. As soon as I manage to hack into His website, I'll let you know," Spencer joked, laughing as if any of this were funny.

"Why are you telling us this?" Blair asked.

Spencer sobered and rubbed his forehead with one hand. "Several reasons."

"Let's hear them," Dade prompted, growing annoyed.

"Like I said, I'm a decent guy, in spite of my past record. I had no idea when I started working for Blue Cell they had bad intentions and would stop at nothing to get what they wanted."

"And what is it that they ultimately want?" Blair interrupted to ask.

Spencer sighed. "Unfortunately, I don't have the answer to that. I get my assignments, and I do them. If I ask questions about other aspects of the organization, people will get suspicious."

"You're a hacker," Blair pointed out. She was glaring at Spencer when Dade glanced at her.

Spencer nodded. "Yeah, well, I can't hack brains, just computers."

"Great," Blair stated sarcastically. "Continue. Why are you really here?"

"I don't want to have anything to do with people dying. So far, you've all been relatively safe, but if anyone gets too close to the truth—whatever that might be—I'm afraid Blue Cell will stop at nothing to take you all out one by one. I want to help. I've already tried to help as best I could, but it would be easier if I had you two as a liaison. Your team isn't going to listen to me directly."

"I'm not sure *we're* willing to listen to you either," Dade pointed out.

"I can appreciate that."

"How have you tried to help?" Dade asked, eyes narrowed. "We've had nothing but problems for months. I don't see what you've done to help things."

Spencer squirmed before responding. "I've sent anonymous texts to some of your team members, warning them to get out of the bunker."

Blair flinched. "That was you?"

"Yes. Obviously I was too late. Two men followed them away from the bunker, but I tried."

Dade rubbed his forehead. "This is ludicrous."

Spencer sighed. "Listen, the reason I'm here now is because you have an urgent problem. I've dug around in the data you all

9

keep for DEEP. I understand the meaning of that acronym perfectly well. Disease & Epidemic Eradication & Prevention. The data from over thirty years of cures and treatments is stored on the servers in that bunker. Millions of lives would be lost if that data disappeared."

Dade sucked in a sharp breath. "Who the fuck would do that?"

"Apparently...me."

Blair shook her head. "It's backed up. Multiple times. In clouds."

Spencer stared at her. "I'm super-clear on that. And I have access to all of it. I can and will make it disappear."

"Jesus Christ." Dade leaned back. "Why the fuck are you telling us all this? Quit your job. Tell them no."

Spencer narrowed his gaze. "I value my life too, asshole. I'd be dead before I left the room. Besides, it wouldn't do any good. They would just hire someone else to do the job. Wiping data is not that difficult."

"So, what the hell are we supposed to do?" Blair asked.

"I have a plan. One that keeps me alive and allows Project DEEP to carry out their mission at the same time."

"Great," Dade returned sarcastically. "And what do you get in return?"

"The satisfaction of having done the right thing and protection so that Blue Cell can't get to me."

"And you think I have the power to make that happen?" Dade asked.

"I'm hoping you will when this is over. After you've taken down at least a fraction of this organization. Surely, your people will have the clout to get me into witness protection. Blue Cell is huge and powerful. You'll never be able to destroy them. Even if you expose this plot and win this battle, there will always be someone watching me. I need to know that the good guys will have my back."

Dade found himself nodding. "Okay. If you're telling the truth, I'll make sure it happens. Now, tell me this plan of yours."

"Well, it starts with Graham Wentz…"

CHAPTER 1

"Kate?" The weak voice coming from across the room startled Kate so badly she nearly stumbled as she spun around to face her patient.

Graham Wentz. The man she had kept under constant observation for a month while his organs returned to full function was finally awake.

She rushed to close the short distance between them and set a hand on his shoulder, smiling. "Welcome back."

He frowned, glancing around the room. "Where am I?"

"A clinic in Colorado. Long story." *Very* long story. She knew from witnessing the reanimation of over a dozen other coworkers how confused he would be this first day. He would need time to shake the cobwebs and get his brain to fully absorb everything he'd missed.

His gaze came back to hers. Intense. Too intense for the fact that he'd just woken up moments ago. She shivered. "Where's everyone else?"

"Another long story. The important thing is that you're awake, and all your vitals are good. Don't rush things."

The look on his face suggested he might argue. Not

surprising. After all, she'd always known him to be inquisitive and sharp. Kate herself had only been pulled out of preservation three months ago. The first few days were a foggy memory.

Kate schooled her face, forcing a friendly smile. Inside, she was nervous. Her heart was racing and the tight ball she'd had in her stomach for weeks squeezed harder. He was back. Those pale green eyes she remembered were staring up at her. His thick strawberry-blond hair was longer than normal after spending a month in this bed. She kind of liked it.

It took every ounce of energy to keep from reaching up to smooth her hand over his hair or cup his cheek or lean in closer and set her lips on his forehead. But those hadn't been mannerisms she'd used with him a decade ago, and she didn't want to startle him. She had no idea how he might respond to her doting over him anyway.

The entire situation was crazy since she'd been nursing him back to health now for weeks. Alone. She'd seen every inch of his body. But now he was awake. It would be awkward to continue to ogle his facial features or set a hand on his arm the way she had every day.

Graham sighed and then drew in a long breath. "Start talking."

She stiffened. "How about a drink of water? You need to get your organs to fully wake up and start functioning." His organs were fine. He'd had an IV for four weeks. Everything was in working order. Nevertheless, she picked up a cup and filled it with water.

When he tried to lift his head, his eyes widened. "Holy shit. How long have I been asleep? My head feels like it's not even connected to my body."

"That's normal. Physical therapy will help. I'll get you started." She tucked her hand under his head and helped tip him forward so he could take a sip of water.

He swallowed and then dropped back down as if he'd gone

for a run. He lifted one shaky hand up swipe it over his face and into his hair. His eyes were closed when he dropped his hand. "Kate. Talk to me."

She pulled a chair up closer and sat, ignoring the awkwardness and grabbing his wrist. For a moment she stared at the contrast of his lighter freckled skin against her more naturally tanned fingers. "Maybe you should try to sleep a bit longer, and then we'll talk. Anything I say to you right now will be forgotten."

He slowly turned his face toward her, meeting her gaze. He searched her face, probably trying to read her expression. "My memory has always been one of my best assets. I don't think I lost it in the cryostat." His gaze was intense, never wavering, eyes narrowed slightly.

She returned a similar stare and asked him a tough question as a test. "What was your diagnosis before you were preserved?"

He rolled his eyes as if he were bored. "Viral-onset AP12. Happy?"

Damn. He did seem sharper than she remembered feeling when she'd awoken. She realized she was gripping his wrist too tightly and eased up. Naturally, Graham wasn't the sort of person who was going to be placated. It would be easier to give him an overview now even if she had to repeat it again later today and then tomorrow.

She studied his face. She'd done so many times over the past few weeks, but he wouldn't know that. She needed to remember she didn't have the freedom to stare at him or hold his hand now that he was awake.

A new reality was descending, one in which her fantasies about Graham were about to go up in smoke. The truth was she'd been half in love with the man before they were preserved, but she'd never told him. She'd never told anyone until recently. He hadn't known her from Adam, of course, but she'd been attracted to him anyway. In fact, her last regret before being preserved had been that she'd never had the guts to so much as flirt with him.

Now, he didn't move an inch. Not even to blink. He was staring at her, having paid more attention to her in the last thirty seconds than he had in years. He'd spoken more words to her cumulatively also.

She took a breath. "There was an explosion at the bunker about a month ago. I've been here with you ever since. We're a few hours south of Falling Rock."

"An explosion?" His body jerked.

"Yes. You're one of the last of the original team to be reanimated. The new team has been bringing us all back as fast as they can, but there are a lot of people who aren't pleased with our existence." She really wished he would go back to sleep. She'd known she would need to tell him all of this, but she hadn't counted on it being today.

He frowned. "Why?"

She sighed. "Who knows? Religious zealots think the government shouldn't be playing God. The media wants a story. You name it." She didn't even give him half of it, but good Lord, he needed to rest more.

"Did someone find a cure for AP12?"

"Yes." She smiled. This was the best part of the story. "Remember Tushar and Trish's son? Ryan Anand?"

He nodded. "He's about twenty, right?"

She chuckled. "He *was*. But he aged while we didn't. He found a cure and put together a new Project DEEP team with another doctor, Damon Bardsley, a cryonicist. They've successfully brought us back."

Graham licked his lips and then slowly asked his next question in a shaky voice. "How long have we been vitrified?"

"Ten years."

CHAPTER 2

The next time Graham woke up, he found Kate curled on her side on a cot several feet from him. She was sound asleep, her face relaxed, her brown hair with blond highlights fanned out around her. Her hands were tucked under her chin, and she looked younger than usual. Peaceful.

He stared at her. Kate. Kate Bauer. He tried to swallow and found his mouth too dry again. How was it that the very woman he'd had a serious crush on for three years had been assigned to nurse him to health? A woman he'd been too timid to approach. A woman who'd made his heart beat faster every time she was in the room.

He'd never had the guts to stare at her this long, not even cumulatively over the course of three years. How long could he watch her sleep without her waking?

He barely had enough energy to turn his head toward her, so it was easy not to disturb her. Though his mouth was dry. In a minute, he would try to reach for the water.

He felt more alert this time. His brain was less foggy, and he tried to piece together everything she'd told him.

Damn. Ten years. He hardly understood what the hell was

going on or why they were hiding in a clinic. She needed to explain that part better.

And he needed to get his shit together and get out of this bed.

There were only twenty-one members of his team, and they spent years working together every day before the last few months, not leaving the bunker, so he knew most of them as well as he knew anyone. He'd always been an introvert, however, so that wasn't saying a lot.

Except for Kate. He'd paid closer attention to her over the years. He knew her mannerisms. The way she laughed. The serious expression she wore when she was deep at work. He even knew the look of deep sadness she'd carried when they all realized they would not live.

He was a geneticist. He'd spent long hours buried in his own research. All of them had worked hard around the clock in their final months before succumbing to AP12 one by one and being preserved. Tushar and Trish were the team leaders. They'd taken on the task of preserving everyone. Someone must have figured out a way to preserve *them* in the end, as well.

Still staring at Kate, he managed to lift one hand across his body and touch his wrist where she'd held on to him earlier. He wondered if she realized she'd been touching him. She definitely hadn't ever touched him before. Though, he'd wished she had.

She had stared at him too. Hard. Really looking into his eyes as if they'd meant far more to each other before they'd been preserved than they actually had. Like they knew each other better. As if she could read his thoughts. They hadn't exchanged more than a few cordial words in years. Because he was a chicken.

Kate was younger than him. She'd been one of the last people to join the team. He thought she might be about twenty-seven. Though he also remembered her to be a whiz who graduated high school ahead of her class and then gone to West Point. Then she'd gone to medical school at Stanford. Like most of the team, she'd been handpicked out of college by the government to serve her country in the bunker.

Not that he was a slacker. He knew he was bright. He'd gone to Auburn through their ROTC program and then Yale medical school. He'd also been handpicked by the government several years before her.

She shifted slightly in her sleep, and he swore he could inhale her scent from the few feet of distance between them. Or perhaps he was imagining it. Lavender. Her shampoo, maybe. Or body lotion. He remembered the scent from before they'd been vitrified, which in his mind had been just yesterday.

No, he hadn't spoken to her often, but he'd noticed her. He'd also done his best to ignore the fact that he'd noticed her. She was fun, bubbly, outgoing. Way out of his league.

No way in hell would he have ever risked flirting with her. For one thing, he would never ask out someone he had to see every single day. He would have felt like a total jackass for the rest of forever working in such a tight space with her after she turned him down.

Instead, out of self-preservation, he'd outwardly ignored her. Sure, he'd watched her when she wasn't looking. But he'd never made eye contact any more than necessary. Didn't sit near her. Rarely spoke to her.

He was incredibly surprised to find her with him wherever the hell they were. Not just surprised. Shocked. Intrigued. Had she been assigned? Or volunteered? Probably she'd been pawned off on him because she was an MD and would know how to take care of him. He needed a hell of a lot more answers.

He also needed water.

When he rolled his body slightly to the side to reach for the cup, his fingers refused to close around the side of the glass, and he ended up knocking it on the floor instead. "Shit," he muttered as Kate jumped to her feet.

"Graham. I'm so sorry. I fell asleep."

"*You're* sorry?" He frowned at her. "I'm the sorry one. I was trying not to wake you. My damn hand wouldn't take orders from my brain."

She reached for a fresh cup, filled it with water from the pitcher, and tucked her hand under his neck as she'd done earlier.

He considered pretending he never got his mobility back if she was going to touch him often and lean so close.

When the cool water his lips, he sighed. Who knew water could be so refreshing?

"You want more?" she asked as she eased him back to the pillow. "Or something else? Soda? Ginger ale? I don't want you to overdo it today, but I can get you something from upstairs."

"Upstairs?"

"Yes. We're in the back of a clinic. Dr. Marcie Brown runs this clinic. She has living quarters above us."

"Ah. Have you been staying upstairs with her, then?"

He was certain Kate's face turned several shades of red. "Not exactly."

His gaze darted to the cot as it dawned on him. "You've been sleeping in here with me for a month?" *Holy shit.*

"Mostly." She looked away from him, busying herself with the cup and his IV and then the sheets around his legs.

He grabbed her hand, something he'd never done before. *But holy shit. Holy. Shit.* Not only had she stayed in his room, but she was nervous about it.

She looked flustered when she met his gaze, and then she rushed to speak again. "This entire situation made me uneasy. I was only marginally qualified to monitor all the equipment. I didn't have the luxury of last-minute instructions. And I had to worry constantly about your safety. So yes, I slept in here."

He gripped her fingers tighter, his throat clogging with emotion. Finally, he managed to whisper, "Thank you."

"Anyone on our team would have done the same," she murmured, not drawing her hand away from his grip.

He shook his head slowly. "Maybe. Maybe not. But they weren't here, and you kept me alive."

She nodded and looked down at their entwined fingers. "You should get some more sleep."

"I've been asleep for ten years. It sounds to me like I should get myself completely up-to-date and stronger as fast as possible." How much danger were they in?

"I'm going to need to start physical therapy with you to help get your limbs to cooperate."

He narrowed his gaze, confused. "Did the world stop using physical therapists while I hibernated?" He tried for a teasing voice, but the truth was he had no idea what the world might have done in the last ten years. Nor was he accustomed to teasing anyone. It felt awkward.

She smiled. "No, but I don't trust anyone. Very few people know you're here. I'm going to manage things myself."

"Where is everyone else?"

She shrugged. "Honestly, I have no idea. I came here with Michelle Houston and Zeke Holleran. They left the next day for wherever Temple sent them. We're scattered all over now, and as far as I know, no one is privy to much information about anyone else."

"Every time you speak, I come up with ten more questions." His brain was rushing to catch up, but it was hard, and the holes were making it harder. At least it sounded like Temple Levenson was still the general in charge of the bunker.

"Yeah, I'm sorry. I can shut up and let you rest. I'm sure it would be better. You don't have to commit piles of information to memory so fast."

Graham shook his head again, gripping her fingers tighter as

21

though he'd woken up in another man's body. A man who was outgoing. Someone who touched women's hands and made eye contact with them. He was way out of his comfort zone.

But, it felt so good to touch her. Her hand was soft, smaller than his, smooth. And in an interesting twist of fate, she didn't try to pull away. He shook the errant thoughts from his head. Maybe this less timid side of him was born of necessity. He needed answers. "It sounds like it would be best if I *did* actually rush to catch up. First, tell me who Michelle is and then give me a rundown on the rest of the team."

She lifted a brow. "You're never going to be able to remember any of this."

He smiled. "Try me."

She tipped her head to one side, chewed on her lower lip, and then blew out a breath. "Okay. I'll say one thing—if anyone can jumpstart their brain quicker than should be reasonable, it would probably be you."

He smiled broader. Smiled. At Kate. "I'll take that as a compliment. My body might need some help, but my mind is growing clearer by the minute."

"Right. So, Michelle is on the second team. After everyone but Tushar was preserved, Temple had someone from another bunker come in and preserve Tushar last. His son, Ryan, made it his life's mission to reanimate all of us. He's damn smart."

"Apparently, he succeeded."

She gave a quick nod. "Damon Bardsley helped develop the reanimation chamber. There have been others, but ours was the first to be fully successful."

"Wait, other what? Other people besides the DEEP team have been reanimated? You mean like at another facility?"

"Exactly, but only two survived reanimation in the Arizona facility, and no one lived longer than a few weeks."

Graham's memory kicked in fast. "I have to assume no one else in the world was preserved before fully succumbing to their illness." This fact was highly classified and would need to go to the grave with all of them, especially if a bunch of religious zealots were already making noise about them playing God.

She tipped her head back and forth. "I'm not sure I would assume that anymore. I'd believe anything these days. I'm pretty sure there are other bunkers with other preserved people. But, you're undoubtedly right about the Arizona bunker. People who died of any illness can't readily be revived. They were too far gone."

"Got it. So, how does this reanimation process work?"

"Can't help you much there. Each person goes into the chamber for four weeks to essentially thaw. After that, we get a total blood transfusion and are put into a four-week coma to let our organs resume function."

"Damn. That's a long process. How many have been revived and how long have they been working on it? It must have been years."

"Emily was first. Ryan wanted her to be able to look over his notes before giving her the cure for AP12. She was the most knowledgeable about the virus, and he followed her notes when developing the cure."

"Makes sense. When was this?"

"Almost a year ago. Tushar was next. And then Trish. Dade was fourth. While he was in the chamber, however, the government built three more. Then things sped up. Zeke, myself, Grayson, and Colton were next. I've been awake three months. To make a long story short. Four more followed us and then four more before your group. That leaves two after you. They both should have come out of their chambers today and started the coma phase."

"Got it. So, a month ago there was an explosion at the bunker?"

"Yep. Someone decided to run a truck into the front gates, hoping to make it all the way to the bunker, but the car exploded on impact. The gate was compromised, and Temple went into action evacuating the majority of us to different locations."

Graham closed his eyes and tried to absorb everything. There was no doubt he was getting tired again. No matter how hard he fought the pull to go back to sleep, he was losing. "Temple Levenson has been in charge for all these years?" he asked, fading.

"Yes. She's still in charge."

"How many people are on Ryan's team?" Graham struggled to stay awake. He wanted more information. He wanted answers. He didn't want to sleep another minute. He wanted to continue listening to Kate's voice, holding her hand, feeling her warmth, absorbing her gaze. She was a life force. An angel. He had no idea what new version of himself had taken over his body and turned him into someone extroverted enough to touch a woman, let alone look into her eyes and hold a conversation, but he hoped the new Graham stayed for a while.

"Twelve."

He tried to lick his lips and focus, but the world disappeared again.

CHAPTER 3

It was dark when Graham woke up the next time. The blinds were closed, and the only light in the room came from flickering machines and the faint stream of light sliding across the room from under the door.

He hoped it had only been a few hours since he last awoke and not days. He felt marginally stronger as he turned his head toward the cot and found Kate once again sleeping. She was on her side facing him like last time too.

He had to wonder if her need to be not just near him but in the same room as him was purely professional and out of fear for his safety against an unknown enemy, or if it was more. The idea that she might feel something for him was preposterous, of course, but it was a nice daydream.

He had to admit to himself he was shocked to wake up a third time and realize he hadn't imagined anything. He had indeed been reanimated, and the woman he'd had a crush on for several years—the woman he'd hardly spoken to and rarely made eye contact with was in his room. Not only that, but apparently she was the only person around he even knew.

Graham felt completely helpless. Contrary to Kate's

assumption, he could remember everything she had told him so far. And it would seem the situation with both his team and the new team was a disaster. He desperately needed to pull his shit together and find a way to start helping out. Lying in this bed another day or hour or minute was unacceptable.

So far he hadn't gotten his hands on a computer or even a book. Items he was comfortable with. For his entire life, he'd managed to hide behind reading or research. He'd realized he probably looked like a total nerd with his head always buried in a book, but keeping himself occupied had always helped him hide his shyness.

He would ask Kate for something to read, but first, he needed to start moving. He wasn't at all sure his arms could lift a book yet.

After giving his strength a test by lifting his head, he decided he could surely pull himself to sitting and maybe even stand. He pushed on the mattress at his sides with both hands, lifting his head and then his shoulders. It took several tries and so much energy that sweat formed on his brow by the time he managed to sit fully upright.

For a moment, he felt victorious, and then the room started to sway and he instantly realized he was going to topple. The question was: which direction? When it became clear he was going to fall to his right, he reached out with a hand to grab the edge of the small table where the water sat. He needed to steady himself. The last thing he wanted was a concussion from hitting his head on the floor in his mad attempt to force himself to go too far too fast.

Unfortunately, the table was on wheels, so the moment he braced against it, it slid away from him. The pitcher and several other items on the top tumbled to the floor. The only thing that kept Graham from joining them was the fact that the cot blocked the table from moving more than about six inches, which left Graham holding himself up by his hand braced on the table.

In seconds, his arm was shaking from the exertion. But that was all the time he needed because Kate was out of bed and at his side before his arm gave out. She grabbed him around the chest in a bear hug and hauled him back to sitting before easing him onto his back.

He sucked in long breaths as if he'd been exerting himself for hours instead of taking less than a minute to attempt to sit.

Kate leaned over him, her arms still wrapped partly around his back, her cheek resting on his chest. She was also breathing hard. Before he could manage to apologize for once again yanking her out of sleep, she spoke against his chest. "You are a stubborn man, Graham Wentz."

He lifted one hand and slid it up her back, though he had no idea why he would do such a thing. "Sorry I woke you," he managed. "Again."

She lifted her face finally and met his gaze in the dim light. "Did you think you might be able to jump up and go for a stroll?"

He took a deep breath. "I was hoping." He gave her a lame smile that felt like it only lifted one side of his mouth. She was so close. Inches from his face. And she smelled wonderful. Her eyes... Even in the near darkness the deep blue penetrated him. He wanted to stay like this for as long as she'd let him. Where was his shyness?

She shoved the rest of the way off his chest and set her hands on the bed at his side, still leaning over him. "Okay, see, apparently I didn't explain how this works yet. You're not the first member of the team to be reanimated. You're the seventeenth. I personally witnessed the four who awoke after me, and I studied the files of all those before me. Not a single one of us has jumped out of bed the same day and gone for a jog."

He winced. "I don't want to be like everyone else. Besides, it would seem it's imperative that I get my shit together and start helping out. I'm not used to lying around doing nothing. I like to work."

"Well, you don't have superpowers, so you're going to have to give your body time. Your mind seems to be sharper than anyone else's was, but your damn mind was probably sharper before we were all vitrified too."

Heat rose in his face. Was she complimenting him? Yes. Yes, she was. He realized his hand was still resting on her back. He'd never let his hand linger like this on a woman. Part of him started to panic, but the other part insisted he enjoy the moment. It felt nice. It wasn't appropriate, but she wasn't complaining, nor had she seemed to notice.

"Can you perhaps trust me on this issue and let me help you get to a point where you're physically able to get around?"

"Maybe. If you promise me you'll speed up the process so we can get the hell out of this clinic as soon as possible." He glanced around the small room. "I already feel claustrophobic." Even though this was essentially a hospital room, it was filled with her scent—lavender. It overpowered the antiseptic and bleach he should be noticing.

If he didn't get himself together so they could get out of this clinic, he was liable to make a complete ass of himself soon. Because he enjoyed her presence far too much. For a guy who'd been conscious less than a full day, he was beyond aware of the woman caring for him, and he didn't have the first clue what to do about it.

She laughed, but not in a good way. "Please. Don't go there. You've been awake a total of about thirty minutes. I've been cooped up in here for a month, and I wasn't sleeping the entire time."

Judging from the bags he'd seen under her eyes, he would guess she hadn't slept enough during that month, which made little sense since she could have spent every one of those days resting. He hadn't even been awake. Nor had he been in any real danger as far as he could tell.

Again, he wondered what her motives were. "Why?" he asked. If he pushed her for answers, she would be able to shatter his growing daydream that she felt something for him. He had some sort of ridiculous fairy tale going on in his mind where Kate had come to his rescue because she secretly had a crush on him. He needed to dispel that absurd myth fast. Self-preservation.

"Why what?" She tipped her head to one side.

"Why did you stay so close? It doesn't sound like I needed around-the-clock medical care. You could have slept in the clinic's living quarters or even gotten a hotel or something."

"Yeah, well, first of all, apparently you *do* need around-the-clock care, seeing as that's the second time you nearly fell on your head. And besides, I'm not that kind of nurse." She patted his chest and rose more fully next to him.

His hand slid down her back, and he inadvertently stroked her butt before jerking his arm around to set it across his belly. "You're not a nurse at all. You're a doctor."

She grinned. "You're alive, aren't you? I must have done something right."

"I'd say you did a lot of things right, but that's not the point." Why the hell was he pushing this issue? *Because her hands are on you and she's holding your gaze. Again...*

But what would he do with the information if she did admit she had a thing for him? He wasn't prepared to hear something like that. It was preposterous anyway. He just needed her to give him a logical secondary explanation so he could move on before he made a fool of himself.

"I'm pretty sure it is."

He closed his eyes and inhaled deeply. She wasn't giving him anything. "I'm sorry. If I promise to be a good patient and do what you say, will you find a more appropriate bed and get a real night's sleep?"

She scrunched up her face and glanced away. Was she flushed? "You trying to get rid of me?"

He frowned and shook his head. "No. Not at all. I just don't like being responsible for the bags under your eyes." He lifted a hand and stroked a finger over the dark shadows below her deep blue eyes. He couldn't see their color with her head turned to the side, but he didn't need to. He had them filed in his memory.

She stood motionless while he touched her with such familiarity.

If he wasn't mistaken, she sighed as her eyes slowly closed and her lips parted, her cheek tipping more fully into his touch. It only lasted a moment, and then she jerked herself out of whatever place she'd gone and took a step sideways as if it were suddenly super important that she tuck the blanket around his knees and calves.

"You should go back to sleep," she murmured.

"I'm not tired."

"Well, you should try. The reanimation will give you a sensation much like jet lag. It will last for about a week. It's best to force yourself to sleep during the night and stay awake as long as possible during the day."

"'Kay." He would agree with anything if she would lie back down. Not because he didn't enjoy talking with her, but because she needed sleep far worse than he did, and he needed to rein in his thoughts before he said something stupid he wouldn't be able to take back and embarrassed himself.

His tongue seemed to be a bit loose. He was afraid he might blab random things like how good she smelled or how soft her hair was or how much he liked looking at her perfect heart-shaped mouth.

In his past life, he'd never allowed himself to entertain

thoughts like that. If he'd ever let his mind wander so thoroughly in that direction, he surely would have ended up tripping over himself. Instead, he'd dedicated himself to his work.

Work he could handle. It was not subjective. It was real. Specific. It kept him even. He'd often bury himself in data and spreadsheets and test samples for over twelve hours a day. Work fulfilled him while he accepted the fact that he would never be the sort of guy who could look into a woman's eyes and articulate anything that made sense.

He wondered if all the others had awoken to amorous thoughts about whoever was first to encounter them or if he was just a pervert. Probably the latter. Probably because he'd gone into the cryostat thinking similar things about Kate.

Actually, it was worse than that. He'd gone into preservation kicking himself for not having ever once had the balls to even make eye contact with Kate, let alone tell her how he felt.

The honest truth was that a sadness had overwhelmed him as he succumbed to the drugs that put him to sleep, and he'd made a promise to himself that if they were ever reanimated in the future, he would not squander his second chance at life.

Once upon a time, he hoped if he ever had the opportunity again, he would get over his terrifying shyness and tell her how he felt. He couldn't believe he was just now remembering that vow. Maybe this new Graham had known it from the start. A part of him was petrified of her rejecting him, but this was different than before they'd been preserved. She was different, and he hoped maybe he could be too.

But at this particular moment? Dammit. He was tongue-tied. There was no way he could proclaim he'd had a thing for her all those years ago, years that to him were seemingly yesterday.

Graham had been preserved before Kate, but he suspected only by a few days. And here he was, alone with the woman he'd last thought about. She was doting on him and seemed genuinely interested in his well-being. As a doctor? Or more?

No, in spite of his promise to himself all those years ago, he wasn't bold enough to declare his feelings for her. He needed more evidence he wasn't crazy.

His eyes slid closed, and Kate set her hand on his forehead and stroked his skin. "Sleep," she whispered. "I'll be right here."

Those words were comforting, and they lulled him into resting. Maybe he could tell her how he felt tomorrow when the sun came up...

CHAPTER 4

Kate lay awake for a long time after Graham finally fell back asleep. Damn, he was stubborn. She shouldn't be surprised. He was a workhorse. It probably infuriated him that he hadn't woken up able to jump out of bed and resume his work curing diseases.

She was certain even before he could stand or walk, he would want to get his hands on a computer and get back to what he did best. How many hours a day had he worked before they were preserved? He'd often be the first one in the lab in the morning and still be clicking away on his computer when everyone else had left.

He either loved his specialty—genetics—that much, or he simply had no need for human interaction. She suspected it was somewhere in the middle. Other members of the team were also introverts, but none compared to Graham.

Wait until he found out how many advances there had been in medicine and technology in the last decade. Enough changes that none of them were able to rush into the lab to resume their old jobs.

The truth was, the process was slow, and all of them would

need refresher courses on medicine and technology before they could reenter the workforce. It didn't matter if they decided to stay on with the government or move to the private sector. They no longer had the skill set to jump right back in.

She stared at the ceiling and smiled. Somehow she imagined Graham, with his superhuman abilities, could defy all of them. It was incredibly attractive that he was so pigheaded and sharp already. He'd probably pick up the latest medical journals, flip through the pages, and declare himself up to speed in a week.

If he didn't kill himself beforehand.

She closed her eyes and took slow deep breaths, hoping to fall back to sleep. She could hear Graham's steady breathing, however, and it both soothed her and reminded her he was only a few feet away and just as attractive as he'd been when she'd been preserved. Ten years. It seemed like months to her, probably the three months she'd been awake in a world where Graham had not been with her. Not consciously anyway.

Tomorrow, she would get him started on physical therapy. Obviously the man had no intention of being held back, so she needed to pick up the pace and ensure he didn't fall on his ass in his haste.

Sleep in another room... Yeah, right. If she'd been in another room tonight, he might have been badly injured. Though it was difficult to admit the reason she stayed so close to him was far more personal than professional. She'd lusted after him for three years without ever saying a word. It felt like divine intervention or something that she'd been randomly chosen to see him through this process. She certainly didn't want to take any risks with his life.

Not that she would have taken any chances with anyone's life. Not even a stranger's. But would she have left the room more often if it had been someone else? Probably. But it hadn't been someone else. It had been Graham. And she preferred to be close to him. Even while he was in a coma.

34

She worried that she'd gotten attached to him and wondered what sort of weird routine they might fall into now that he was awake. He was definitely more alert and his mental acuity had returned much quicker than anyone else's. Assuming he indeed remembered everything that had transpired each time he'd awoken.

Deep breaths.

She hadn't known what to expect when he awoke, but not this. Not a man who looked her in the eye, touched her with a familiarity they weren't accustomed to, and had emerged from preservation with conversational skills. She didn't know how to process this new Graham.

He'd been so timid before, never looking directly at her. She had assumed he considered himself far superior to her in the field of medicine. Hell, *she* agreed. Not because she wasn't capable of attaining great things in life but because he had seven more years of experience then her, and he was far more dedicated. He'd seemed to have devoted his life to the job.

While she'd always loved her work with Project DEEP, she'd had other dreams too. Dreams of a family. A husband and kids. A life outside of work. She'd used Graham as her muse for that daydream for years. Now that he was awake, she needed to pinch herself to remind herself he'd never shown any interest in her.

Kate had gone through a strange period of time before the team had been preserved when she mentally kicked herself for never attempting to get him to *see* her. If it weren't for the occasional team meetings over the years, she couldn't even have been certain he knew her name.

When they'd gotten sick with AP12 and she'd realized she was going to die, she'd played the *what-if* game in her mind for weeks. What if she'd put herself out there and asked him out? What if she'd at least spoken to him? Life had seemed so futile as it slipped through her fingers, making her regret three years of hesitation because she hadn't had the courage to force him to notice her. She'd carried that pride to her early grave, kicking herself until the end.

When she'd woken up from that presumed grave three months ago and then had Graham handed to her on silver platter to care for and bring back to life, she'd taken a vow that she would not squander the opportunity. No matter what happened, even if he laughed in her face and turned her down, she would let him know her interest this time around. Make him see her.

She was so intensely aware of his presence next to her. Far more so than before he'd awoken. Even though he was asleep again, he was a vital life form in the room.

Not that she intended to dump her heart at his feet while he couldn't even run from her in his current state, but she would put herself out there, drop hints, touch him, look him in the eye. One day in the near future, she would tell him how she felt. Soon. When he was well enough to stand on his own and could consider her as more than just a random woman who'd helped him back on his feet. She couldn't pressure him while he was reliant on her. It wouldn't be fair, and it could result in some very uncomfortable days.

Putting herself out there for men was a foreign concept because she'd never met one she liked enough to do anything about it. Except Graham, and with him she'd kept her feelings to herself because she didn't figure it was worth putting herself out there for someone who didn't even know she was alive.

The few times in life she'd made an attempt to flirt with a man, she'd been disappointed. Years ago, she'd stopped the charade, deciding it needed to happen organically or not at all.

She would not settle. She'd watched her friends in college and med school settle, dropping one by one into the category of married as if it were a rite of passage or something, and the men waiting for them at the end of the aisle weren't nearly as important as the act itself. It felt like people conformed to societal norms all around her while she sat on the sidelines with some strange old-fashioned belief that she would not waste her time on anyone until sparks were flying and electricity sizzled in the room.

She never told anyone why she rarely dated. It sounded ridiculous even to her own ears. Not even her parents would understand.

It wasn't that anyone had instilled some sort of purity expectation in her mind. She wasn't a prude in her heart. It wasn't a religious thing either. It was personal. She'd rather go to the grave alone than spend her life with the wrong man. Settling.

There was no guarantee that the right guy could be Graham either, no matter how much her stomach flipped when she was around him. How would she know until she put herself out there and stuck her toe in the water? What she *did* know was that he was the only man she'd ever met who'd repeatedly made her heart beat faster and her blood pump.

She'd ignored both for three years. Why? Because he'd never given her any signal he knew she existed, much less that he was interested.

Until today.

It took a while for her to calm her racing heart and fall back asleep, but when she did, she slept hard and deep, bolting awake to find the room bathed in light. She jerked her head to the side to find Graham wide awake and sitting upright.

Somehow he had managed to find the controller for the bed and prop himself up without falling on the floor. He was also staring at her. His mouth was turned up just enough to indicate a slight smile. "You must have been in desperate need of rest. You slept so hard I was starting to wonder if you were alive over there."

She swung her legs around and pushed to sitting, running

her hands through her hair. She wore the same navy scrubs from yesterday, and she needed a shower. "I guess I don't snore then, huh?"

He shook his head. "You don't even breathe. Or twitch. Or move. It was kinda eerie."

"I don't think I usually sleep that well. I guess my body shut down."

"Does anyone else even come in this room?" he asked.

"No. Not unless I ask them to. Marcie sometimes helps me out, and she has a nurse who checks on me every day, but we're inconveniencing them enough as it is by taking up a room in their clinic for a month."

"So you're saying we need to get out of here." He pointed at his IV. "If you disconnect me, I bet we can make that happen. Where exactly are we going?"

"I don't have a clue yet. I'm waiting for instructions. No one would expect you to leave this clinic for at least two weeks. That's been the average time everyone has needed to have the strength to stand and walk and get around safely."

"Two weeks?" His eyebrows lifted. "Yeah, that's not going to work for me. How about we bump that up to two days and count yesterday as one and get the show on the road?"

She stood, slid her feet into her tennis shoes, and padded over to his side. After checking his pulse, she looked into his eyes. "How about we compromise? I'll disconnect everything and get you started on solid food if you promise to stay in this bed for another week while we get your legs stronger."

He reached across his body and grabbed her hand, which was still on his wrist. The number of times he'd touched her in the last twenty-four hours was quickly reaching double digits. She couldn't remember him ever even grazing against her in the three years she'd known him before they'd been preserved.

Her heart rate kicked up again, and she had to remind

herself he was completely out of sorts. He probably didn't even know he was reaching for her.

"A week?" He shook his head. "Not a chance. I've never sat that long in one place. Hell, I've never stayed in bed a full day before. I'm breaking records here," he joked. "There must be work I should be doing. Diseases to cure. How about you disconnect everything, I eat something, and then you help me get to the shower?"

She laughed. "That is *so* not going to happen. Not today, big guy." She patted his hand on top of her. By now they had a double-decker sandwich of hands.

"We'll make it work."

She shook her head, still laughing. "Your legs would buckle as soon as you set them on the floor. You're stuck with sponge baths for another week. We can reevaluate then."

"Hmm." He sat up straighter.

She flinched at the tone of his voice, and she narrowed her gaze. "What are you plotting now?"

"Not plotting. Just realizing two things."

"You can keep those thoughts to yourself." She so totally didn't want to hear what might come out of his mouth to go with the devious look on his face after the mention of bathing him. There was no way the damn blush she felt on her cheeks wasn't giving her away.

His smile spread. In addition to touching her more than he would have in his previous life, she also didn't think she had seen him smile more than a few times either. And when had he gotten so chatty? She'd rarely heard him communicate with anyone before they'd been preserved. Especially with her. Quiet. Shy. Kept to himself. Very reserved.

This man staring at her and talking, possibly even joking with her, was a foreigner. If it weren't for how incredibly sharp he'd already proven to be, she would think his brain had been completely scrambled or he'd had a lobotomy.

"Too bad," he proclaimed. "Gonna tell you anyway."

She tipped her head to one side and bit the inside of her cheek. "Fine. What did you realize?" She held her breath. For one thing, he appeared to be teasing her. Graham Wentz. The man was not a comedian. For another thing, when she'd gone to sleep vowing to lay her feelings for him on the table in the near future, she had not meant today. She was far from ready to face something like that. So, discussing his sponge baths was not on her short list for the day. And the way his eyes danced with mirth made her want to run from the room to catch her breath.

"One, now that I'm awake, it would be rather mortifying for you to bathe me. And two, I'm equally mortified that you have been doing so for a month."

Another flush raced up her cheeks, and she glanced away. "I'm a doctor, Graham. It was necessary and clinical. Don't lose any sleep over it."

He wasn't wrong. She'd seen every inch of his amazing body. Even after ten years of vitrification, he was attractive. She had done everything in her power to shut her brain down and take care of him as clinically as possible, but she'd seen him. He was right about that.

"You could have hired a nurse or something," he pointed out.

She lifted her gaze to him, her face heating further. "Jesus, Graham. Are you angry about this? So what if I've seen your body? I've seen lots of bodies. I'm a medical professional. I'm surprised it bothers you this much. I did it to keep you safe. The less people involved, the less our chances were at being found." Her protest sounded a little too exuberant.

She tried to tug her hands back to get away from him, but he held tight. "You misunderstood me." He gripped both her hands in his now. "I never said I was angry. Nor do I think you would ever entertain an unprofessional thought."

Oh, he was wrong. She'd entertained a lot of unprofessional thoughts. That was why her face was now beet red.

He released one hand and reached for her cheek, tipping her chin up in the most intimate gesture. He searched her eyes.

She shuddered under the intensity of his gaze. "Maybe you've kept me a secret from other patients coming and going from the clinic, but you didn't keep me from the staff. Not for a month. Not a chance. Anyone could have been assigned to care for me.

"Instead, you've taken on the entire burden on your own. You've slept in this room on that uncomfortable cot for a month, making sure I was completely safe and healthy. You didn't have to do any of that. So, stop bullshitting me, and tell me what's really going on."

For a moment she thought he was insinuating that she was keeping some deep dark government secret from him, and then she realized he was pushing her to admit something entirely different.

He held her chin and leaned closer.

Her face grew incrementally hotter. She was not ready to discuss her reasons for caring for him so intently. Not today. Not tomorrow. Why did he have to be so damn insightful? And how had he been so completely aloof for the three years before they were preserved if he was able to so easily nail her down on his second day of reanimation?

"Under normal circumstances, I would point out that I wasn't born yesterday. But in this case, I was actually born yesterday. It would also seem I've woken up in an alternate universe where the pretty girl from my first-grade class actually likes me."

She flinched. "Of course, I like you. Why wouldn't I like you?" She really needed to weasel out of this situation before she made a fool of herself. How the hell had she woken up in an alternate universe where the hot guy from *her* first-grade class actually noticed *her*? "I've always liked you. Now, let go of me, and I'll go find you some breakfast."

Instead, he pulled her hand closer and set it on his chest, his other fingers still on her chin. He shook his head. "You're deliberately changing the subject."

"You've lost your mind," she pointed out.

He chuckled. "There's no doubt about that, but if I'm dead or still in that cryostat, I'll take it if it means…" he swallowed visibly, "…if it means you might be a little attracted to me."

She froze. He was hitting way too close to home now. No longer skirting the edge of the subject. She said nothing. If she wasn't mistaken, he'd just implied he would be pleased that she liked him.

"I…" She swallowed. Tried again. "Um…"

"Now I feel like an ass. How long have you been interested in me?"

She tried to turn away again. She wasn't ready for this sort of confrontation. How the hell had she managed to reveal her feelings for him so blatantly in two days? "Graham, your brain is scrambled. Let me go." How did he have the strength to grip her like this?

"There isn't a damn thing wrong with my brain. Except it obviously wasn't firing with all cylinders before I was preserved. There's no way in hell you decided you liked me while I was lying here in a coma, so it had to have been before that. I'm not always so great with people, especially women, particularly when it comes to reading signs. It takes a lot for me to just look at people sometimes. But I'm paying attention now."

She glanced away, tucking her lips between her teeth. Her total lack of protest was giving her away. But, anything she might say would come out all wrong. If only he would let her get out of the room, then she could regroup, take a few deep breaths, and make a plan for what to say to him. This was embarrassing.

"Judging by your reaction, I think I'm right. Now, tell me. How long?"

"Jesus, Graham. Let it go. So what if I was attracted to you? Who wouldn't be? You're off-the-charts intelligent, cute, talented, and dedicated. The list is long."

He flinched, his entire body jerking back. "Wow. How did I not know this?"

She shrugged, still not meeting his gaze. *Please, God, let me get out of here. This is so humiliating.* No woman wants to have her crush brought to her attention and voiced out loud like this. Her mouth started running anyway to answer his question with the same words she'd just tossed out a moment ago. "Probably *because* you're off-the-charts intelligent, cute, talented, and dedicated to your job. I was just some girl who happened to work in the same lab."

He gasped. "Some girl who worked in the lab?" His voice rose. "Kate, you are not some girl at all. Not even close. First of all, you're a woman, not a girl. Second of all, you act like you were the janitor. You're a doctor. You graduated from Stanford, for God's sake. And thirdly, before you let your mind wander one more second in these ridiculous fake murky waters you've stirred up, let me point out that the reason I never permitted myself to glance your way is because you are way the hell out of my league."

That got her attention. She jerked her face back to meet his gaze. "Out of your league? That's the dumbest thing I've ever heard."

He shrugged. "Kate, have you looked in a mirror?"

She blushed on top of the heated flush. He must have hit his head on the corner of the little rolling table before she got to him last night.

He smirked. "Apparently not. You should do so. Three years ago, this amazing, sexy, smart, funny, well-rounded woman with big blue eyes and gorgeous long thick hair joined the DEEP team and knocked me on my ass. I could barely speak to you for fear I'd choke. So, yes, way the hell out of my league," he added.

She flinched. "That's pure shit." She'd known him to be shy, but had she misinterpreted his total lack of interest in her when really it had all been a result of timidness on his part?

He shrugged again. "Maybe, but it's true."

"How the hell could I be out of your league? I'm just a person like anyone else. Your intelligence leaves me in the dust. As do your looks and your body." She jerked back a few inches, finally breaking free of his grip and waved a hand through the air in the general direction of his torso.

She continued, rambling on, unable to stop herself. "You're buff like you live in a gym even after ten years of preservation. Your hair is the most amazing color of strawberry-blond that most women would give their right arm for. And those clear green eyes are currently drilling a hole in me as if you can see inside my soul. If you'd ever looked directly at me before we were preserved, I might have fainted. You never gave me a single second of indication you thought I was anything more than a colleague. Hell, I'm pretty sure you went out of your way to ignore me."

"Jesus," he whispered, snagging her hand again and drawing it up his chest before pressing the back of her fingers to his lips. He kissed her knuckles gently, and her knees nearly buckled.

"Graham..."

His voice was softer when he spoke again. "I noticed you. Of course I noticed you. Every man with a pulse notices you. I kept my awareness to myself because you're...well, *you*. And I have absolutely no game when it comes to talking to someone like you. But I've been astutely aware of your presence from the moment you first joined the team. Now, tell me how long you've been interested in me."

"Ten seconds longer than that. I saw you first." She had no idea how she managed to admit such a thing, but there it was.

He continued to hold her hand against his chin. "Apparently we had a misunderstanding. Let's fix that, starting now."

"Okay, but let's get you fed and cleaned up and then work on physical therapy first," she suggested. Anything to get out of this room before she fainted. This was not happening. It was like a dream. A good dream, but unnerving at the same time. And so totally unexpected. She needed to pinch herself.

It was one thing to lust after the man from afar. It was another thing entirely to admit it out loud, have it reciprocated, and then process that mutual attraction. She hadn't planned for this. She wasn't at all sure what to do next.

Except run. So she could think clearly.

He squeezed her hand, pressing it against his lips as if he were afraid to let her go. His eyes drifted closed. Finally, he leaned back against his pillow and released her. His mouth had that little tip at the corners when he spoke again, softly. "I swear to God if I wake up from my nap and don't remember every single detail of this conversation, I'm going to be extremely pissed."

She found herself speaking without thinking again. "I'll be far less embarrassed."

She started to back up, but he opened his eyes and grabbed for her hand yet again. "You have absolutely no reason to be embarrassed. It's clear we both let our assumptions control us in our last life in equal measures. We won't do it again." His body relaxed after that final burst, and he slid back into sleep.

Thank God.

Could it really be that easy?

CHAPTER 5

Kate was still shaking as she made her way upstairs and into Marcie's guest bathroom. She closed the door and leaned against it, replaying everything that had transpired.

Was it really possible they'd both carried a silent torch for three years and hidden it so well that neither of them was aware?

On the one hand, she was mortified to have been called out like that, but according to Graham, he had been interested in her too. Game changer. She had no idea how to process this new information. She had visualized flirting with him mercilessly until he noticed her. Instead, it would seem they were going to leap over the flirting part and jump right into...

Right into what?

Kate flipped on the water in the shower while she removed her scrubs. As the water heated, she looked at her reflection in the mirror. She looked tired, even after a good night's sleep. Her hair was a mess. She had on no makeup. And there were bags under her eyes.

He was insane to think she was out of his league. This was indeed an alternate universe. With almost no contact with anyone from the outside world, she was beginning to think if she opened the door and stepped outside, she would find them on another planet.

When she stepped under the spray, she closed her eyes, letting the water sluice over her body. Her heart was still racing from the weird conversation she'd had with Graham.

She shuddered as the water hit her nipples, her body coming alive in a way she hadn't experienced before. Would he still think she was out of his league if he found out how ridiculously inexperienced she was with men?

It was downright embarrassing. She was twenty-seven years old—thirty-seven according to her birth certificate. The years when most girls would have been experimenting with sex had been awkward for her because she'd graduated high school a year early.

At seventeen she'd gone to West Point. She'd been young and never stepped out of line. At twenty-one, she'd gone to Stanford. It was during her first year of med school that she met an undergrad who was her age and they'd gone on a few dates. He was nice enough. Cute. Fun. Considerate. The full package.

But he didn't make her heart beat faster.

On their first two dates, he'd kissed her chastely at her door. No tongue. Just a kiss. No sparks.

On their third date, she'd let him take things further, beginning to think maybe she needed to round a few bases in order to feel the sexual urge most girls spoke of. It didn't work. They'd sat on her couch, fumbling awkwardly, while he put his tongue in her mouth. His hand slid down to her breast over her sweater. Nothing. Literally no sparks.

Needless to say, she'd wormed her way out of the tangle of arms and given him some lame excuse about needing to be up early the next day. He hadn't asked her out again.

After that disaster, she'd decided to concentrate fully on medicine. Every once in a while she dated, but the guys she met in her early twenties had been too boring. Usually other med students would set her up with their friends, but no one ever captured her attention enough to hold it.

She could have slept with any number of men. It wasn't as though they weren't willing. Guys found her attractive. That was obvious. But somewhere along the line she'd made a vow to herself, deciding it wasn't worth it to fuck for the sake of fucking. Until she met the *one*, she wasn't interested.

If people knew this about her, they would probably laugh or think she held very traditional religious beliefs. But people didn't know. No one did.

She shuddered under the spray of water and reached for the shampoo.

She had to wonder what Graham would think when and if he found out how incredibly inexperienced she was. She had never faced a situation like this. Until now, no man had made her nipples tingle and her sex tighten. It both scared her and titillated her at the same time.

She had no interest in telling him anytime soon, however, so she needed to slow this train down significantly.

The longer he thought she was out of his league, the better. At least it gave her an advantage. If she had to admit she'd had very few dates and no experience in bed... Yeah, no. She couldn't do it. Not yet. Platonic was her best defense for now. Not only had he been awake just one day, but they would need to sort through their feelings for each other and lay all their cards on the table later, after he was back to his usual self.

There was no way to trust his crazy foreign feelings at the moment. The two of them were trapped together in near isolation for the time being. What if circumstances were causing him to feel things more intensely than he normally would? They needed time to get to know each other before they got into all the intimacy stuff. See if their feelings could last. Maybe many of the others had woken up feeling more amorous. Hell, evidence would suggest they had. Several of her team had immediately entered relationships.

But this was uncharted territory for her. She'd guarded her heart close for a reason. Perhaps a silly one. Maybe she was ridiculously sentimental or something. But she didn't intend to break her vow to wait for the perfect man now. Nor did she have any way of knowing if Graham *really* could be that man so quickly, even if she had been lusting after him from afar for years. There was a difference between what-if daydreams and reality.

The reality was she knew she was intelligent, and that's where all her energy had gone for many years. If she hadn't been book smart, the government wouldn't have handpicked her out of West Point, paid for her medical school, and hired her to join Project DEEP.

She technically owed the government more than the three years she'd worked at the bunker, but essentially dying from a lab accident had wiped her slate clean of any future obligations.

Kate didn't have a single clue what she wanted to do next with her life, but whatever it was, it would involve medicine. She'd spent the first two months after her reanimation regaining her strength and getting a handle on technology.

The truth was for the past month, while she'd been on vigil in the back room of this clinic, she'd also spent countless hours studying the latest advances in medicine so she could get herself back up to par and return to practicing what she loved.

She was not, however, certain she wanted to stay with the Project DEEP group. Maybe. She wasn't closing any doors. But so far, things had been nothing but disastrous. In the three months she'd been awake, she'd seen her parents only one time when they'd come from Atlanta to Falling Rock for a few days.

She hadn't seen her sister at all except by FaceTime. She'd never met her sister's husband. They had a six-year-old daughter she'd never seen. Instead of reacquainting herself with her family, she'd spent months sequestered in the middle of a fight she wasn't sure she had the energy for.

Temple had offered her a new identity and a new life, but that would have meant severing ties with her family, so she'd turned it down, hoping things would calm soon and she'd be able to take a few weeks to go home.

The clock had ticked as the days went by. And then the explosion. And then four weeks in this clinic with the only man she'd ever felt something for. And now what?

She wasn't sure. That uncertainty was an important factor in her life and her decisions. Part of her wanted to run from her problems and those of Project DEEP. It wouldn't be safe or prudent, but it lingered in her mind.

It wasn't that she didn't still have a huge love for medicine. She did. But she wasn't fond of continuing to work for an organization that had her scrambling around hiding from an unknown enemy day after day. Week after week.

What would Graham want to do with his life? It was too soon for him to make any kind of decision like that.

The good news was she knew him well enough to guess he would hound her for educational resources right out of the gate. She was no expert on the latest technology, but at least she'd played with the newest computer software and internet services and could fill him in on what she knew and where he could find more information.

Realizing she was still standing under the spray of water, she quickly finished washing and got out. After hurrying to dress in another pair of scrubs, she rushed back to the bathroom and glanced in the mirror. Would it be weird if she put some effort into her appearance today?

Graham had never looked at her long enough to know how much makeup she'd worn in the past. Nor would he probably have noticed her hair.

Except apparently he had.

She opted to grab the hair dryer and blow her thick locks straight. And then she applied mascara and lip gloss. Nothing overboard.

When she emerged from the guest bathroom, she found Marcie putting dishes in her dishwasher. She lifted her gaze. "Hey, I met your patient. I hope you don't mind. I didn't intend to interrupt, but he called out to me as I passed his room. He's a gem. I can't believe how alert he is. I expected him to be groggy or something. He's charming."

Kate realized how long she'd been gone.

"Oh, and I fed him. I hope that was okay?"

"Of course. I'm not surprised. He's already been hounding me to get him on his feet," Kate responded as she reached for a mug and poured herself a cup of coffee. "I'm surprised he hasn't asked me for a Farmer's Almanac or the latest stock market statistics. He always liked to keep his mind occupied."

Marcie laughed. "You were close. I did give him a book."

Kate smiled at that as she rolled her eyes. She wasn't shocked. As long as Graham could lift his hands, he would find a way to bury himself in the comfort of a medical journal. He'd probably read a phone book if it were the only thing around.

"I also fed him scrambled eggs and toast. He wanted me to remove his IV, but I figured that was stepping way over the line, so I told him he had to wait for you to make that decision."

Kate chuckled. "He's a handful." She leaned against the counter, procrastinating. Needing another minute before she faced him again.

Marcie lifted a brow. "A handsome handful."

Kate flushed as she nodded. "Indeed. But he doesn't know it, so don't tell him. It will go to his head."

Marcie tipped her head to one side, her eyes narrowing, a small smile on her face.

Kate groaned. "Okay, okay. He's gorgeous. I get tongue-tied just looking at him."

Marcie laughed as she shut the dishwasher. "Are the two of you an item? You never told me that."

Kate shook her head. "No. I mean, we never were in the past."

"Ah, but you wish you had been."

"Something like that. What are you, psychic?" She smiled at her new friend, the woman who had harbored her and Graham for four weeks. Apparently she couldn't hide her feelings from anyone. Not even the recently revived guy downstairs. How the hell had she managed to keep such a secret from people before she'd been preserved?

Of course, she hadn't done a fantastic job of it. Emily had known. Not because Kate ever told her but because they were friends and Emily had been observant. They'd had more than one discussion since being reanimated.

Marcie tucked her dark wavy hair behind her ear as she laughed again. "I'm not sure how observant I needed to be, but you just fixed your hair, put on mascara, and stepped out here looking a little flushed."

Kate cringed. "Yeah. I guess that made it a bit obvious."

"Well, good luck. From my brief interaction with Graham, I'd say he's a real catch." She shoved off the counter and headed for the stairs. "I need to get back to the clinic before my staff sends up smoke signals. Let me know if you need anything."

"Thanks." Kate followed Marcie down the stairs and then took a deep breath before walking back into Graham's room.

He was still awake. In fact, he had his head buried in Marcie's book already, though he lifted his gaze as soon as she entered. He held up the book. "Marcie gave me this. A little light reading," he joked.

Kate looked at the cover. "*Genetics and the Future.* Riveting." She was kidding. It would be riveting to him, especially since genetics was his specialty and he was ten years behind.

He closed the book and set it on the table at his side. "She also fed me."

"I heard." Kate closed the distance between them. She busied herself removing his IV first, and then she picked up his wrist to check his pulse, out of habit. Or perhaps as an excuse to stand that close and touch him.

He ignored her attempts to set her first two fingers on his pulse point and instead shook her free and reached to touch her hair. "You fixed your hair."

She couldn't stop the flush, but she did inhale deeply. Part of her was pleased he noticed. She might have even self-consciously gone to all the trouble to see if he would notice the effort she'd made.

"I like it. I also like it when it's wavy. Or when it's pulled into a ponytail. Or even when it's wet because you didn't have time to fix it."

Yeah, more heat suffused her face. Was she ever going to stop reacting like that to him? She was just so shocked at this total about-face in their relationship. After never meeting her gaze or even seeming to know she worked in the same small bunker as him, suddenly the man woke up from a coma and openly flirted with her?

His hand eased around and he stroked her cheek with his thumb. "You blush easily." He was smiling.

She grabbed his hand and jerked it away from her face, clasping his wrist and holding it against the bed at his side. "I need some time to catch up with this new, not-at-all-shy Graham."

"That works out splendidly with my current timeline since I'm unable to stand, let alone anything else."

She swallowed. "Okay, stop flirting with me. You're making my head spin."

He flipped his hand over and threaded his fingers with hers.

How the hell was he so much more in control of his fingers today? "Yeah, that's not going to happen."

"Why not? Just… I don't know. Slow down. I can't keep up."

He squeezed her fingers. "I'm lying in a hospital bed in the back of a clinic with almost no muscle strength. I've been slow enough. I'm totally at the mercy of my body at whatever pace it decides to start receiving messages from my brain in a timely fashion.

"I just found out the sexy woman who's way out of my league actually likes me. I've been in a cryostat for ten years. I got a bonus run at a second chance at life. Mysterious people are apparently not happy I'm getting that second chance. And for once, I'm not too terrified to go after something I want. So, no. *Slow down* is not really one of my options. I'm going to mentally chase you around the room until I can physically do so, and then all bets are off."

She swallowed. She seriously didn't think he'd spoken that many words total to everyone in the bunker combined in the three years she'd known him. "You sure you didn't hit your head?"

He smiled wider. "For the first time in my life, I'd say my head is screwed on perfectly straight. Now, what's the plan? Let's get this physical therapy going so I can stand."

She nodded slowly. That was the plan, though she considered telling him he needed to wait another week to start it just to buy her some time to acclimate to this situation. The room was spinning.

Yesterday, she'd been unattached and pining after a man she wasn't positive knew her name. Today, he was hitting on her so hard he practically had them married.

As if he read her mind, he dipped his face closer to hers. "If you think I'm going to dawdle around and waste time when I should be pursuing you before you change your mind and get away, you're crazy."

He left her speechless. Again.

"Also, peeing into a plastic container is going to get really old, and there's not a snowball's chance in hell you or anyone else is going to be washing me on this bed anymore, so I'm gonna need to get strong enough to stand to use the bathroom and take a shower super-fast." He rubbed his chin with his free hand, brushing his palm up and down his cheek next. "I could use a shave too. This is going to get itchy soon."

She smiled. "You're in luck. It turns out I was a bit of a beautician in high school. I find it soothing. I can still cut and style hair, and I've shaved plenty of faces." Though offering to do his was probably a bad idea. She prayed he didn't make her so nervous she ended up slipping.

He tipped his head to one side. "You're full of surprises. Okay, I'll let you cut my hair and shave me, but only because my arms don't work, and the idea is incredibly erotic."

She groaned. "Stop that."

"What? It is. Gorgeous woman shaving me? Every man's dream."

"Great. I've created a monster." She yanked her hand out from under his and grabbed the remote for the bed before he could stop her, lowering it so he was flat. "Exercises first. Then I'll consider switching from physical therapist to beautician."

"Deal."

"I'm going to stretch your legs and show you some lifts you can do to get the blood flowing and awaken your muscles."

He yanked the sheet off.

She nearly gasped before she realized he had on gray workout shorts and a T-shirt. "When and how did you change clothes?"

"You were gone a long time. Marcie gave me everything I needed. Food. Drinks. A pan of warm water. Clothes. I managed."

Lord, he was going to enter a marathon tomorrow. And then she wasn't going to be able to run fast enough to avoid him.

After years of wishing she'd had the gumption to force him to notice her, now that he had, she felt rushed. No part of her had mentally prepared for this eventuality. She'd pictured weeks or months of thwarted efforts that would probably produce no results. She wasn't ready for this new Graham who not only saw her but wanted her. Now. Today.

It was exciting, but also scared the hell out of her. She should just tell him she'd had no experience with men, and then she could stop worrying about it. Except she wasn't prepared to have that conversation. How did a twenty-seven-year-old woman tell a man in his thirties that she was a virgin?

She didn't even know how to flirt. Nor did she know how to date. And the thought of having sex made her both nervous and excited at the same time. Every time she stepped into the room and saw his smile, she felt even more drawn to him.

Forget sparks. He was lighting her on fire.

It was too soon for this to be happening. She felt like she was in a made-for-television movie in which the hero and the heroine had to solve their differences and get into bed in under two hours.

Unnerved and totally out of her element, she ignored her concerns and went through a series of exercises with him. The fact that he was so fit would have shocked her if she hadn't already seen everyone else, including herself, come out of their preservation with the same surprisingly maintained muscle tone.

Of course, he needed therapy to get back to where he'd been ten years ago, but a lot of the work had more to do with getting the brain to fire messages than muscle tone. In addition, she remembered feeling dizzy and out of breath more often once she started walking around.

While she worked, her previously timid, serious, quiet, stoic, unattainable heartthrob kept talking. "Tell me about the threats. Why are we hiding?"

"Okay. So, Emily was the first to be revived. I told you that, I think."

"You did."

"Anyway, she went to her parents' home for a few days to get reacquainted."

"Shit." He winced. "My parents. What do they know?"

"They would have been given a vague notice that you would be reanimated in the near future and that someone would contact them with specifics. Temple doesn't like to jump the gun, just in case. You'll be able to contact them soon."

"Has anyone not survived?" He stiffened as he asked.

She set one leg down and picked up the other. The good thing about his running dialogue was that it kept her mind from wandering to his body. "Well, kind of. I'll get to that in a minute."

He frowned. "I keep interrupting. Go on."

"I'm going to give a summary. We can expand later."

"Sounds good." He winced as she pushed his leg higher, stretching the back of his thigh.

"Okay, here's the Cliff Notes version. Try to keep up."

He shot her a goofy glare. "I think I can handle it."

"You say that now," she teased. And then she set his leg down, looked him in the eye, and launched into the condensed version. "So Emily was the first to be revived almost a year ago. She and Ryan fell in love. She got kidnapped by a madman who wanted his daughter revived.

"Blair Rollans was her bodyguard. Emily had a tracker in her arm. The military hunted them down and saved the day."

"Jesus."

She narrowed her gaze at him. "Don't interrupt. I'm on a roll here."

He grinned and made a sweeping motion with his hand. "Please continue."

"Next to be revived was Tushar who then waited for Trish and the two of them went into hiding at a ranch in Montana run by an organization called SURVIVE. But the two of them had trackers also, and someone got their information, hunted them down, and tried to kill them. The bad guys are now dead for their efforts, and Trish and Tushar went back to the bunker."

Graham's eyes were wide, but he pursed his lips and nodded for her to continue.

"Dade Menke was the fourth to be revived. Blair took him to her cabin in the mountains outside of Falling Rock to sequester him. Ryan got wise and deactivated Dade's GPS tracker that time. But, unfortunately, Dade had a dormant form of aplastic anemia that took over his body as soon as he received the cure for AP12."

"Son of a bitch."

"Yeah. That part sucks. He had an inheritance from his grandfather, so he and Blair took off to God knows where so he could live out the rest of his days in peace."

Graham closed his eyes slowly. She couldn't blame him.

She took a deep breath and kept going. "Next to be revived were me, Zeke, Grayson, and Colton."

"Right. You said that yesterday."

She rolled her eyes. "I hate how quickly your brain is working. I want to slap you."

He scrunched up his face. "Sorry. Can't change that. Go on."

"Zeke hit it off with Michelle Houston, an immunologist from the second team, and the two of them traveled here with us after the explosion at the bunker. They left the next morning for God knows where."

"I'm seeing a theme here. Is God seriously the only one who knows anything?"

"It's possible. Though I do believe Ryan is privy to most of the information. He's the leader of the second team. He and Temple are making most of the decisions."

"I can't believe Ryan Anand is a grown adult who cured a disease and made it possible for me to be here today."

Kate took one of Graham's arms and started stretching it over his head. "Wait until you meet him."

"And he's with Emily? She's ten years older than him."

"Not anymore." Kate chuckled. "They're the same age."

"Right. So we didn't age…" Graham lifted his free hand and held it in front of his face as if examining it for signs of aging.

"Not a single day. No one has shown any indication they aged at all."

"Crazy. Hard to wrap my head around."

"Agreed. Once you get over the technological hurdle that made up the past decade, you'll start to forget time moved ahead of you."

"How much change could there possibly be in ten years? We were already moving at lightning speed."

Kate laughed. "You can't even begin to imagine. Turn lightning into warp speed and you'll be close."

"And the rest of the team?"

"I can't tell you much about anyone else because four had only been awake a month and four had only been awake a few days when the explosion happened. We all got scattered. I don't know where a single person is right now."

"But you're in contact with Temple, right?"

"Marginally. I use a burner phone. Everyone is just trying to stay hidden and alive right now."

"Have you called her yet?"

"No. I'm sure she'll contact me. She knows the date you would have been awake, and she also knows how long it takes for each person to be reasonably coherent." She shot him a wary look. "It's not two days."

He grinned. "I like to defy the odds. Now, about that shower…"

CHAPTER 6

Kate didn't grant him the shower request, but she did leave for a few minutes and come back with everything she would need to wash his hair, cut it, and shave him.

She unlocked the wheels on the hospital bed and pushed the head of it away from the wall. Next, she sat on a stool behind him, lifted his head, tucked a towel under his neck, and proceeded to wash his hair.

He thought he'd died and gone to heaven, unable to speak while she massaged the shampoo in and then carefully rinsed it over and over into a plastic tub. She left a few times to get more warm water until she was satisfied.

While she propped him up farther, he watched her closely. She was all business, every move sure and precise. How had he let three years go by without telling this incredible woman how he felt about her? He was a fool.

He also didn't recognize himself. He knew he'd been quiet and focused before they were preserved. Studious. Introverted. Shy. Somehow he'd never taken the time to live his life outside of medicine. He was thirty-five years old, and he'd never been in a serious relationship with a woman. Or any relationship.

The truth was that he was a virgin. He wasn't embarrassed about that fact, but he was concerned about disappointing her with his lack of knowledge. Somehow he doubted that any amount of clinical data or online research had prepared him for the real-life experience.

It had been three years since Kate had joined the team and he'd become enamored with her. Before vitrification, he'd never had the balls to put himself out there. He hadn't been kidding when he said he believed her to be out of his league.

But something in him had changed. Snapped into place since he'd awoken. He felt a sense of urgency to seize the day, emboldened by the fact that he'd learned the woman he'd lusted after had done the same from her side of the room for three years also.

They were both foolish.

She leaned close to him to snip away at his hair. Every time she reached for the top with one hand and cut with the other, her breasts came within inches of his face. He had to hold his breath a few times to keep from making a noise that would embarrass him and probably piss her off. The last thing he wanted was for her to stop.

When she was satisfied with his hair, she grabbed another basin of warm water, settled on the stool at his side, and proceeded to lather and shave his face. The woman knew what she was doing. "Tip this way for me," she whispered a few times.

She took her time, smoothing her hand over his chin and then his cheeks as she worked. Finally, she was satisfied, and she sat back with a smile. "Not perfect, but good enough, considering the position you're lying in."

He grabbed her hand before she could move away. "Thank you." His voice was gravelly. Unrecognizable. He was both humbled and enchanted. He would never forget this as long as he lived. "You've spoiled me. Now that I know what you can do, I'll be expecting this treatment all the time."

She rolled her eyes, her face turning red, but she didn't argue the point, which he considered a win. "You need to rest. Sleep is the only thing that will help you get stronger."

He held her gaze, still gripping her hand in his with the waning bit of his energy. He knew she was right, but he hated the idea of closing his eyes. Every time he did, he feared it would all prove to be a dream and he would not wake up again.

She smiled and leaned closer, stroking his face with her free hand. "I know that look. I remember that fear. I woke up in a panic for weeks and still do so occasionally. But I promise you this is real. I'm right here. You've been revived. And you need sleep."

It was difficult, but he did manage to rest off and on that day. Now, it was late. After midnight. Kate was curled on her side on the cot, facing him, her expression peaceful in slumber.

Graham's internal clock was totally out of whack. His circadian rhythm acted like he'd gone through fifteen time zones and hadn't fared well. He didn't care at the moment because he'd been gifted with the opportunity to stare at Kate's features at rest and memorize every nuance.

It was only fair. She'd had the ability to stare at him for a month.

He still couldn't believe she had considered him for even a moment in their past life. He was shocked by her assumption that he hadn't been at all interested in her.

For as much as she'd insisted she was into him, she was also incongruently skittish, which was not at all like her. He had no idea what that was about, but he intended to find out. Maybe she simply had his health in mind, but he thought it was something more complex.

It seemed like even though she obviously harbored feelings

for him, she in no way had expected them to be reciprocated and found herself stepping back out of shock. At least he hoped that was all it was. If she'd decided now that she'd been handed the prize, she didn't want it as badly as she thought, he would be fucked.

It was also possible she'd been lusting after a man she knew very little about who'd turned out to be quite different from what she expected. There was no doubt about that. Even *he* didn't really understand how it was possible that he'd awoken with a seemingly altered, more courageous personality.

In his mind, he was the same guy. And he reasoned that circumstances were affecting his behavior. For one, he was emboldened by the fact that the woman he'd been attracted to had feelings for him too. That was huge and gave him courage he didn't ordinarily have.

However, there was more to his shift in personality than just Kate's returned feelings. This was the first time in his memorable life that he didn't have specific responsibilities demanding immediate attention. All through school and college and his work for DEEP, he'd been under a constant time crunch. A race against the clock to study or memorize or solve something.

Having a to-do list he could never possibly accomplish was the only thing he'd known before now. In a way, it grounded him. He could always count on there being enough work to keep him busy. And the list was filled with subject matter he understood. Definitive responsibilities with definitive results.

Since they were in hiding and he had only a borrowed genetics book in his reach and his legs weren't cooperating, he couldn't change his circumstances if he wanted to. Forced vacation. Unless someone handed him a computer, he was totally at their mercy.

His work ethic had grown out of necessity. He'd used work to deal with his introverted personality. Work had allowed him to shut himself off from the world around him without having to awkwardly stumble through social interactions. It was comfortable.

Dating was not comfortable.

Admitting or acting on feelings for a woman was not comfortable.

The idea of putting himself out there to Kate had been the ultimate in discomfort for three years.

He'd noticed Kate. He'd *always* noticed her. Every time she entered a room he knew it. In fact, he probably overcompensated for his attraction by intentionally ignoring her even more than anyone else. He'd been too mortified for her to find out the quiet, introverted geek across the room would give anything to ask her out.

Two days ago, he'd woken up with no responsibilities and the object of his affection leaning over him with her lavender-scented hair, big blue eyes, and a smile that lit up a room. The prospect that she might also be interested in him had emboldened him and turned him into a man he'd never met. He kinda liked the guy, though, so he thought perhaps he'd let him squeeze in and share the space.

Inside, he was well aware of his shy personality, but maybe, just maybe, he could tamp that Graham down a bit, knowing that Kate liked him. It was no longer such a gamble to share his returned feelings.

For once in his life, perhaps he could give his full attention to something, or someone rather, that wasn't part of some bigger objective. Kate wasn't a stat or a list of data or a combination of chemicals. She was a woman. Where his work had always been precise, comforting in its specificity, relationships were assuredly not.

If nothing else, his newly found assertive personality left Kate flustered, and he totally enjoyed watching her squirm under not just his intensity but the fact that he had her constantly guessing.

She'd worked her ass off to ensure his safety for the last month, even going so far as to sleep in his room, and that meant everything. It meant he could and would lure her in, figure out what made her hesitate, and overcome it.

He just needed legs.

When Graham woke up next, the sun was streaming into the room and he was alone again. A part of him clenched to find Kate not in the room. It was day three, and he had to admit he preferred her close to him. Not just because he needed her help, but also because he liked having her aura in the room. She was vibrant and alive, things he wanted to feel too.

By the time he had himself propped up, the genetics book open in his lap, she returned. Her smile was golden. She had a tray of food, and she looked rested and rejuvenated. She'd showered. Her hair was almost dry. It was wavy this morning.

"How do you feel?" she asked as she set the tray on the table and spun it around so he could reach things. She yanked the book from him and set it out of reach.

For a moment, he felt that old sense of panic, and then he shifted his attention to Kate and took a deep breath. "Better every time I wake up. Today I'm going to shower."

She chuckled. "Today you're still going to lie here and work on your leg strength."

He narrowed his gaze as he took a drink of orange juice. "I'm beginning to think either you like keeping me under your thumb or you don't want me to see outside this clinic because the truth is there was an apocalypse and we got left behind."

She laughed.

"I'm imagining the world is actually destitute. Nothing is left but crumbling buildings."

"And chickens." She pointed at the eggs. "And pigs." She'd also added bacon today. "And fruit trees." Her eyes were twinkling as she teased him.

He tapped his lips with his fingers. "I also have no way of knowing if you're telling me the truth about how long I was preserved. Was it really ten years? Or has it been ten days or two hundred years?"

She laughed again.

Damn, he liked that sound.

"Hmmm. I guess you'll find out when you see Temple, or even your parents."

"I guess." The mention of his parents changed the tone to something more serious. "Are they still in Oklahoma?" he asked, referring to his parents.

She turned around and picked up a file from a stack he hadn't noticed sitting on the counter. This was an exam room, not a hospital room. It had a sink and counter for doctor visits. No bathroom. She handed him the file. "Latest info. Yes, they're still in Oklahoma."

He pushed the food aside and opened the file with shaky fingers. Susan and Richard Wentz. His dad was retired now. His mom had always been a stay-at-home mom. His two older brothers had families that had grown in number since the last time he'd walked the earth. Six kids between the two of them. One divorce.

He set the file down and looked at her. "It's so weird. This makes it seem so real."

"I know. It was very strange reconnecting with my parents. They came to Falling Rock for a few days, but I've had to rely on video calls since then. I keep putting them off until the insanity is over, but it never ends." She leaned her hip against the bed, her shoulders dropping. "I have a sister too. We were close when we were little."

He tentatively set his hand on her other hip. "You're from Atlanta, right? Is your sister still there?"

"Yes. She has a daughter too. I can't believe it. I've only seen pictures."

He tugged on her hip to encourage her to come closer. When she finally let herself sway his direction, he slid his hand up her back and pulled her down against his chest.

She nestled her face against his neck while he held her close. It felt so good. So right.

He really needed to get out of this bed. Playing the invalid wasn't working for him.

Suddenly, the door to the room opened and enough of a shadow fell across the room to indicate the person entering wasn't Marcie.

Graham lifted his gaze and jerked upright so fast he nearly knocked Kate on the floor. "Dade?"

CHAPTER 7

The first thing Graham noticed was the mixed look on Dade's face—both elation and concern. He was smiling as he rushed forward to give Graham a hug, but his eyes were frowning.

A blond woman hung back a few feet. She had to be Blair.

Kate's eyes were wide as she grabbed Dade next and hugged him just as fiercely. When she was finished, she held him at arm's length and looked him up and down. "You look fantastic. What's all this shit about you having aplastic anemia?"

Graham had to agree. Dade looked better than ever for a guy who was presumably dying. "What are you doing here?"

Dade reached behind him and pulled Blair up to his side. "Long story. This is Blair." He kissed her on the forehead and turned back to face Graham and Kate with the biggest smile Graham had ever seen on any human. It was obvious Dade was very much in love, and the way Blair was looking back at him told Graham she felt the same.

Graham sensed their connection filling the room as if it were palpable. He wanted that. He wanted it with Kate.

"Nice to meet you both," Blair said.

Dade nodded toward Graham. "Meet Graham Wentz and Kate

Bauer." He glanced back and forth between them. "Two members of my team who are unexpectedly standing very close together and touching each other. Interesting development, but we don't have time to dissect that right now." He released Blair and pulled a backpack off his opposite shoulder to set it on the bed.

"What's going on?" Kate asked.

"We're getting you out of here first. When we get somewhere safe, I'll explain." He opened the backpack and produced track pants which he tossed at Graham. "Kate, grab whatever you want to take. You ladies wait for us in the hall. I'll help Graham, and then we're out of here."

He was both talking fast and moving fast. In fact, he took Blair and Kate by the shoulders and nearly shoved them from the room.

Graham pushed himself to sit up taller. "I have zero strength and no ability to walk. But you know that, so while you help me get dressed, start talking. My brain is a hundred percent." Graham tossed the sheet off his body.

"Good. I knew I could count on your mind. You've probably read two medical journals and developed a better way to organize the app store already. But, I'm also fully aware of your physical state on day three. I've got you. You're going to have to trust me. I don't want you here in this clinic another minute. It's not safe. When we get to a safer location, I'll explain further."

Graham's heart was racing. He wasn't sorry to be leaving the clinic, but he was concerned about the state of the team. His mind was also working hard to keep up. "App store?"

Dade shook his head and chuckled, but he didn't answer Graham's question. He worked efficiently and fast, helping Graham into the pants and then pulling a pair of tennis shoes out of the backpack. "I'll get you to the SUV in a wheelchair and then lift you inside."

"Who knows you're here?"

"Blair. You." He grinned. "Oh, and Kate. You two seem awfully chummy."

Graham groaned.

Dade continued talking while he kneeled to tie Graham's shoes. "Serious shit has hit the fan. I know it's a lot to take in, and I'll explain everything, but you need to understand that I don't trust very many people."

"Maybe it would help if you informed me exactly who you trust."

"Ryan. Emily. Kate. Ryan's parents. Zeke. Michelle."

"Temple?"

"Nope."

Graham flinched. "Please tell me you're kidding." They'd worked for Temple for years. She was the general over the entire operation. She was a genuinely good person.

Dade stood. He set a hand on Graham's shoulder and met his gaze. "I'm not saying she's dirty. I don't know for sure. But everyone is guilty until proven innocent these days, and she's in the middle of the shit storm."

Graham stared at his friend. "You do realize I woke up three days ago. I haven't even seen outside directly yet. It's a serious stretch for me to believe Temple would ever do anything to harm anyone on our team."

"I know. And I'm sorry to spring this on you so fast, but there's nothing I can do to change the facts. It's possible someone higher up is either controlling Temple or using whatever information she reports to her superiors to sabotage us."

"Someone above Temple?" Graham said sarcastically. "You can't be serious."

Dade shrugged. "It's all we have to go on right now. Someone is getting information. Either they're passing it on directly or an innocent source is. We know they're getting a lot of it from hacking into the computers. But who's running this operation?"

Graham took a deep breath and ran a shaky hand through his hair while Dade spun around and then returned ten seconds later with Kate and Blair and a wheelchair.

"We have to go." He lifted Graham into the chair without a word and pushed him out of the room.

Marcie held the back door open. Obviously Dade had spoken to her before he entered Graham's room.

Kate had a backpack and a suitcase with her. She must have rushed upstairs and packed everything she could grab quickly.

Blair held several things also, probably whatever she had helped Kate gather.

The sun was bright, and it felt amazing on Graham's face. He squinted up at the sky as Dade wheeled him a few yards to an SUV that was not even in a spot. It was just haphazardly pulled up to the back door.

Blair opened the rear passenger door and then rushed around to the hatch to deposit Kate's things.

Dade lifted Graham easily and set him in the back seat. When he reached for the seat belt, Graham swatted him away. "I've got it. I'm not that helpless."

Dade nodded, his brows drawn together.

Kate spoke for a few more seconds to Marcie, and then she ran to catch up with them. She rounded the SUV and climbed into the other side next to Graham.

The entire thing took less than ten minutes from the moment Dade stepped into the clinic.

Dade twisted to face the back seat. He looked toward Kate. "Do you have a phone?"

She reached into the bag she'd set at her feet and pulled it out. "Yes."

"Turn it off."

Graham watched her fumble with the device with unsteady hands.

Dade nodded. "Good. Don't turn it back on. We can't take the risk that someone might track it."

"You don't have a GPS tracker, right?" Blair asked.

Kate shook her head. "Zeke took it out before we left the bunker."

"What about Graham?" Dade asked.

Kate shook her head. "Ryan didn't put one in him."

"Good." Dade turned back around and started the car.

The second Dade pulled out of the parking lot, Graham cleared his throat. "Start talking."

CHAPTER 8

It was Blair who spun partially around so she could see the two of them while she spoke.

Kate was shaking next to Graham. She looked as unsteady as he felt. His adrenaline was pumping so hard he felt like he could surely jump out and push the car. Who needed gasoline?

Graham let his gaze roam to Dade, but he was concentrating on driving. So, Graham spoke again. "Start with Dade. You don't seem like a man on his death bed."

"He's not," Blair conceded. "He had an autologous stem cell transplant. The chances of success were about forty percent, but it worked."

"And yet?" Graham asked.

Blair nodded. "It seemed safest to let everyone believe he wouldn't make it. Ryan was seriously concerned about the fact that someone has been selling information about all of you to anyone willing to buy it."

"Rightfully so," Kate added, "but how does it help that Dade pretended to be dying?"

"Because we've been working from the outside to track the mole, hoping no one would suspect us. We've inadvertently hooked up with a computer hacker. Name's Spencer. He's just a kid really. Twenty-two. Technological whiz. He showed up at our apartment to warn us.

"He works for an organization called Blue Cell—the group responsible for everything happening to you. He's capable of giving us a heads-up every time Blue Cell is about to act."

"Why would he do that?" Graham asked.

Blair sighed. "Apparently he grew a conscience. And he wants protection in return."

"Jesus." Graham set his hand on the seat next to him, but it was going to be impossible for him to remain upright for very long with Dade whipping around corners and changing lanes. He had enough strength to sit up in bed, but trying to hold his balance was pushing his limits.

Kate must have realized his predicament because she suddenly unbuckled her seat belt and moved to the center. As soon as she was fastened once again, she subtly leaned into him.

He could have kissed her. No one commented or even looked askance. Graham leaned against her and looked back at Blair. "Go on."

"The other three members of your team who were reanimated at the same time were sent to other locations for the last month. Someone found Josiah before he even woke up, and Khloe was located yesterday."

"Located by whom?" Kate asked.

Blair shrugged. "Whoever isn't happy you all exist. We don't know the answer to that yet. We don't even know if there's truly a connection between these incidents and the people who found Tushar and Trish or even Emily, though Spencer said Blue Cell was behind it all."

"Is everyone okay? Who else woke up three days ago at the same time as me?" Graham asked.

Blair nodded. "Besides Khloe and Josiah, Bianca. Colton was with Josiah. They were at a clinic about an hour from here.

Colton noticed two men lurking around outside about a week ago. We put surveillance on them. They must have been waiting for someone to leave the clinic. Dade and I swept in and grabbed Colton and Josiah yesterday. They're safe."

"My God." Graham couldn't believe how complicated this was.

"I know." Blair sighed. "Dalton Haines—a security guard—was with Khloe. He was diligent and overheard someone speaking in the hallway outside Khloe's room about her."

Graham's heart was racing. This was so insane.

Blair continued. "Long story short, Dalton grabbed Khloe right out of her bed, borrowed the doctor's car, and fled. They contacted Temple who called Ryan for assistance. Ryan, of course, called us, and we picked them up last night. They're safe."

Graham sighed. "It sounds like Temple is working as hard as anyone to keep the team safe."

Blair nodded. "Yeah. I agree, but Ryan doesn't want to widen our circle of trust, even to Temple in case she's unknowingly reporting to the enemy."

Kate grabbed the back of the seat in front of her and leaned forward. "You're running around picking all of us up and not telling Temple?"

"Exactly." Blair's face was stoic.

"My God," Kate whispered.

Dade inhaled sharply. "You have to understand, until yesterday, few people knew I was healthy or even alive. Temple is still not one of them. We can't take the risk that her knowing about me would cause dozens of other people to know, and compromise everyone's safety. It's easier to ask for forgiveness than permission. The less information Temple has, the safer we all are. Telling her the details of our locations puts her in a position to have to report that information."

Graham nodded slowly. He understood. He just didn't like it.

In fact, he hated it. The thought that Temple could be involved in anything that would harm a single hair on any member of his team made his stomach roil.

At the same time, he was itching to be helpful. He hated that his body was slowing him down when his team needed him.

Dade glanced at them. "Temple has a lot on her plate right now. She doesn't have time to check in with every one of you or even deal with the prospect of moving you yet. As far as she's concerned, you, Bianca, Khloe, and Josiah need about three weeks before you could even leave your various safe locations.

"So, that's our time frame. I can't stick around long, but there wasn't anyone else who could run down here and ensure all of your safety while remaining totally under the radar."

Graham's brain was racing.

Dade spoke again. "I hate to do this to you, but we're going to have to leave you two in a safe location for a few days and come back. We need to snag Bianca before someone finds her."

"Who's with Bianca?" Kate asked.

"Grayson."

Graham ran a hand over his face and then set it on Kate's thigh. He was holding on to the door with his other hand, doing everything in his power to gain stability. "My head is spinning." He didn't mean that literally, and no one took it that way either.

Kate set her hand on top of his as if it were the most natural thing in the world, as if they had touched each other like this for years.

It calmed him. She was an anchor to him in this tornado. He would be totally overwhelmed without her. He also wished he weren't so dependent on her, and he hoped to rectify that as fast as possible. He wasn't used to depending on other people. It made him uncomfortable.

Blair twisted to face them more fully. "I know it's a lot to take in, and we promise to bring you more up to speed as soon as we can get back to you." She reached over the back of the seat and handed Kate a phone. "It's a burner. No one has the number except us and Ryan. One of us will call you when we can."

While Blair spoke to Kate, Graham watched Dade diligently keep an eye on both the road in front of him and every single detail around them. Did he think they might be followed?

A shudder ran down Graham's spine.

Kate gave his hand a squeeze but didn't comment. How was she so in tune with him? It was illogical how the two of them fell into sync together as if they'd been married for fifteen years when really they'd barely spoken to each other until three days ago and had only acknowledged being interested in each other yesterday.

Graham shifted his gaze to Blair when he realized she was holding out a second phone. Her voice was soft as she said, "Use this one to call your parents. And then destroy it."

He nodded slowly, palming the phone. His parents...

In a few moments, Blair continued. "After we pick up Bianca and Grayson, our plan is to bring them to join you. It might take us a day or two."

"And then what?" Graham asked.

Dade glanced in the rearview mirror and smiled. "We have sanctuary."

"Where?" Kate leaned forward slightly.

"Montana." Blair handed a slip of paper to Kate. "If for any reason you run into a snag or don't hear from us, do what you have to do to head for this address."

Graham leaned toward Kate to see it was an address in Denver. "Did Denver move to Montana while I was hibernating?"

Blair smiled. "The organization helping us is called SURVIVE. They have an entire underground system to help people disappear all over the country. They're good at it. They were the ones harboring Tushar and Trish."

Graham turned his attention to Kate. "I thought you said

someone found them and tried to kill them at that ranch in Montana."

Dade responded. "They were wearing trackers. The man who tracked them—our new friend, Spencer—had access to the GPS coordinates. You're not wearing or carrying anything that can be traced."

"Can we trust this Spencer?" Graham asked.

Dade nodded. "Pretty sure. He's already helped a lot."

Kate tipped her head to one side. "But SURVIVE? We're going back to the same place where Tushar and Trish were attacked? Doesn't that seem obvious? Why do you even trust *them?*"

Blair shook her head. "We've set up a home base at one of their ranches in Montana. Not the same one where Tushar and Trish stayed. I know it seems irrational, but we thoroughly checked them out. The majority of their employees are former military. Their reputation is impeccable."

"I hate to point this out," said Kate, "but we don't have money."

Blair snapped her fingers and reached into a bag next to her on the seat. A moment later she handed Kate an envelope. "Cash. It's the only way to be sure you aren't traceable. Divide it up into several pockets and locations just in case."

"You're going to leave us at a hotel?" Graham asked. He couldn't imagine how they could possibly sneak him into a hotel without raising eyebrows.

"No. We're taking you to a SURVIVE safe house. I'm not kidding when I say they run an underground system you can't begin to imagine."

"Is it…legal?" Graham asked.

Dade chuckled. "We've got unknown enemies tracking us down all over the country. Right now, I don't give a fuck about legalities. I'm just trying to get my team to safety."

Blair shot him a look and then returned to Graham.

"SURVIVE isn't running around shooting good guys, if that makes you feel better. Do they skirt the edge of the law? Probably. They're like vigilantes. They take the hard cases like ours. But they also take government contract jobs. That's how Tushar and Trish wound up with them in the first place."

Damn, this was complicated. "What can I do to help? No way in hell am I going to hang around hiding while the rest of the team work their asses off to figure out who's trying to eliminate us."

Dade shot him a grin in the rearview mirror. "You haven't changed a bit."

Graham would beg to differ, but he didn't. "Not about my team, no. Did you think I would turn my back and crawl into a cave?"

Dade shook his head. "Nope. But I need you strong physically before you can be of help. We've got an essential role for you, but we need you physically and mentally fit first. Get your hands on Kate's computer and familiarize yourself with the latest technology too. It's imperative. We're all useless until we jump forward ten years."

Graham nodded and then turned his head to look out the window. He flipped his hand over on Kate's thigh and threaded his fingers with hers. She didn't object.

They were driving up a windy mountain road now. He hoped for his sake and Kate's that Dade and Blair were making the right choices. It wasn't as if Graham was in a position to argue with Dade. He needed to trust his team members. He also needed to bring himself up-to-date with technology. While he was waiting for his body to catch up with his brain, he could at least educate himself.

CHAPTER 9

When Dade finally pulled up to a rural mountain home, Kate realized she'd been sitting so stiffly for so long that she was exhausted and her body ached. Her tension had been half mental from absorbing so much confusing information and half physical from supporting Graham next to her.

A man and a woman came out of the house as Dade and Blair jumped down from the SUV. Dade shook the man's hand as he approached.

Kate was in the center seat, and she didn't want to leave Graham, so she waited. It was only a few seconds before Dade turned around and opened Graham's door.

Now that the man was closer, Kate could see he was older, perhaps in his sixties. He had gray hair and a nicely trimmed gray beard and mustache. The woman also had gray hair that hung in a bob at her shoulders. They looked like the average retired couple who now spent their days hiking and enjoying life.

Apparently they also ran a safe house.

The older man dipped his head to smile at Kate and Graham. He held out a hand to Graham. "Jerry Kobrick." He pointed to the woman behind him. "This is my wife, Eliza." He reached across Graham next to shake Kate's hand.

"Kate Bauer," she informed him.

Graham cleared his throat. "Graham Wentz. Thank you for your hospitality."

Jerry smiled broadly. "Let's get you inside, shall we?" As if it were no big deal, he gripped Graham's forearm and helped him slide down from the SUV.

Kate held her breath out of fear that Graham would collapse. She didn't trust his legs at all, and she knew Graham's pride would prevent him from pointing out how weak he was.

But she needn't have worried because Dade was at his other side in an instant, and the two men supported the majority of Graham's weight as they helped him into the house.

Eliza followed Blair to the rear of the SUV and by the time Kate joined them, they had all the bags out. Kate took one of them and followed the other two women inside.

In short order, Graham was situated on one end of an enormous brown leather sofa.

Kate eyed him suspiciously, watching for any sign that he was losing a battle to fatigue, but so far he seemed to be supporting his upper body fine.

Eliza rushed across the great room toward the kitchen area.

"Your place is stunning," Kate stated as she eased farther into the room and let her gaze wander. It was intentionally rustic with every modern convenience. The walls looked as though they were simply inside a log cabin. The floors were hardwood with throw rugs. The long dining table looked like it had been cut from the same tree as the rest of the home.

"Thank you," Eliza responded from the kitchen. "We built it five years ago to enjoy our retirement."

Kate wondered how often their retirement was interrupted by unintended guests. She wandered over to the fireplace and admired the artwork on the walls as well as the frame pictures in clusters on every surface—bookcases, mantel, and end tables. She ascertained quickly that Eliza and Jerry Kobrick had three adult kids and several grandchildren. In addition, Jerry had served in the navy. Several photos depicted a much younger Jerry in uniform.

When Kate turned around, Eliza handed her a glass of water. She had already served everyone else. "Please feel free to sit if you'd like," Eliza said.

Kate took a drink of water and then smiled at her. "I've been sitting for a while in the car. I think my legs would appreciate being stretched." She would also bet Graham's legs were in dire need of stretching. They hadn't done any physical therapy yet that morning.

When she turned toward him, she found him watching her. For the first time in her life, she felt self-conscious. Rarely had she found herself in a situation when she cared what she was wearing or what her hair might look like. Even though she'd taken the time to fix her makeup and straighten her hair the other day, today she could feel his gaze all over her body.

She was wearing scrubs. She was always wearing scrubs. They weren't flattering. In fact, there probably weren't many articles of clothing in the world that could be less flattering. Ordinary pale green today. For years her days of the week had revolved around what color her scrubs were.

Hell, she didn't own much else. She'd only been awakened three months ago herself. Emily had helped her order several things online, but they'd stuck to the practical. Jeans, tennis shoes, ordinary bra and panty sets. Nothing fancy.

And now Graham was watching her wander closer to him as if she were the most attractive person in the room, and he'd just noticed her for the first time. It was nice to feel his gaze on her after he'd spent so many years avoiding eye contact.

Dade had settled on the sofa next to Graham and was speaking to both him and Jerry. Blair was behind the sofa with her elbows on the back, leaning her cheek on one palm next to Dade's shoulder.

Kate realized she had been distracted by the cabin and then her own thoughts as she tuned back in to the conversation.

Eliza smiled broadly at her and set a hand on her biceps. "We built this house with two separate wings." She pointed toward a hallway on one side of the great room and then another at the far end. "Gives our children and grandkids some privacy and plenty of space when they visit." Still facing the second entry she'd pointed out, Eliza continued. "You two will be in that wing. I'll let you explore and figure out what rooms you'd like to use."

"Your home is gorgeous. And we can't thank you enough for letting us stay here." Kate swallowed through the emotion that climbed up her throat. The generosity of this couple was remarkable. Obviously they were employed by SURVIVE, but they did their job by choice. It had to be stressful taking in total strangers and keeping them safe.

Dade stood, leaned down to give Graham a hug, and then turned toward Kate. "I'm sorry. We have to go. Hopefully we can get back to you tomorrow, but plan for two days just in case. We'll either return or contact you on the burner phone. If you don't hear from one of us for any reason and you have to leave here, use the address I gave you."

Kate nodded. "Got it."

"In the meantime," Dade continued, "give Graham a tutorial on the latest technology. I need him up-to-date fast."

She swallowed.

Graham spoke next. "You haven't told us what you'll be needing from me."

Dade nodded. "I know, and I don't have time to explain it right now. I'll go into more detail later when we're sure of the plan. It's imperative you be physically stronger as well as mentally sharp, though."

"I can do that. Give me a few days."

Dade chuckled. "This is why I knew I could count on you."

Kate closed the distance between her and Dade and pulled him in for a hug. "Thank you. Please be careful." She lifted her face to his and smiled. "I still can't believe you're even alive, let alone standing vibrantly in front of me."

As she released him, Blair hugged her too. "I know we just met, but I want you to know we're working hard to make the world a safe place for both of you. Stay strong."

That lump returned to Kate's throat as she nodded again. She shoved away from Blair before her emotions could take over, and then she followed the two of them outside to their SUV. "How much do the Kobricks know about us?" she asked when the three of them were alone next to the SUV.

Dade responded. "Enough. They're well vetted."

Kate nodded. "Go. Get to Bianca and Grayson. I can't stand the thought of anyone in harm's way."

Two minutes later, Dade and Blair pulled away from the front porch, and Kate took a deep breath and returned to the house. She clapped her hands together and put on her business face for Graham. "Okay, let's get you stronger. Top priority."

He smiled at her as she reached his side. And then he grabbed her hand. "Go figure out where you want me, and then we'll get me flat somewhere. I need my legs to start cooperating ASAP."

She squeezed his hand, resisting the urge to lean down and kiss him as if they were an established couple before she walked away. It was uncanny how close they'd gotten in just a few days. It felt like the mere fact that they'd both verbally admitted their mutual attraction automatically made them a couple.

The truth was they hadn't discussed their relationship in those terms, and they really needed to spend some time getting to know each other first to see if their attraction existed on a level that wasn't just physical. But first, she needed to get him settled. And then he needed to start serious exercises. Little things that had to happen on the to-do list before they could even begin to define what they might be to each other in the future.

She had concerns. Namely that Graham had woken up gung ho about reuniting with the team, and now that he'd gotten caught up with Dade, she felt confident that as soon as he was physically able, he would take the next bus to Montana and jump into the fray. Twenty hours a day. Seven days a week. That was his style. She could tell he was fidgeting to get back to it.

Montana. Did she want to go to Montana and work in a secret location with twenty-some-odd people in hiding while life continued to go past her? She wasn't certain how she felt about that. Not that she needed to make any rash decisions today. First things first.

Kate released Graham's hand and followed Eliza toward the guest wing. Every item in the home had been lovingly chosen to give a welcoming ambiance. Just being inside the walls of this house was calming. Deep browns and rust and maroon made up the color scheme, and that extended to the guest wing too.

Eliza pointed to the first door on the left. "Guest bath. There's another larger one in the master suite on this hall, though. It might be easier for Graham." She kept walking to the second door on the right. "In here."

Kate followed her inside, admiring the furniture and the inviting feel. The master bed, dresser, and nightstands looked like they had been intentionally cut from the same wood as the floors and walls—same as the kitchen table and chairs had been.

The comforter was a thick fluffy maroon, as was the large oval rug on the floor next to the bed.

Eliza pointed to a door to the left. "Master bath. My husband can get him in and out of the bathroom or whatever you need."

Kate smiled at her. "I suspect Graham will be running circles around me before he should be. If Jerry can help me get him down the hallway, Graham will probably figure things out from there. His pride and frustration will give him the adrenaline boost to get back on his feet." Probably not in the few days they were be staying here, but she wouldn't be shocked if he was walking tentatively by then.

Eliza turned around and pointed out a linen closet inside the bathroom. "Towels. Shampoo. Soap. Anything you can't find, just let me know."

A noise behind them had Kate turning around to find Jerry assisting Graham into the bedroom. Not surprising.

She set her hands on her hips. "You're so impatient."

"You took too long," he teased.

She rushed forward to take the weight from his other side. "You'll be comfortable in this room. I'll take the one next door. Let's get you on the bed."

He shook his head. "Let's get me in the bathroom. I'm dying to take a shower."

Jerry took the bulk of Graham's weight and angled that direction.

Kate was impressed by Graham's apparent motor control. His legs were at least going through the motions. "How about a bath? Compromise. Then I won't have to worry about you falling."

He shook his head. "I've never had a bath in my life. Not starting today. I'll manage."

Jerry chuckled. "Can't blame you there."

Eliza rolled her eyes. "You're not helping, dear."

He laughed again. "The man wants to take a shower. There's a bench seat in there and a removable nozzle. I'm sure he'll figure things out."

"See?" Graham lifted his brows at Kate as Jerry lowered him to the toilet seat.

It was oddly awkward for all four of them, two sets of complete strangers, to be standing in the bathroom together.

Eliza opened the linen closet and grabbed a large towel, which she draped on a hook next to the shower door. Then she grabbed her husband's arm and tugged him from the room. "Come on. Let's let them get settled. Please let me know if you need anything at all." Eliza shut the bathroom door and seconds later Kate heard the door to the master suite also shutting.

Kate checked the shower. There was shampoo and soap inside. Then she turned toward Graham. "Seriously, this is crazy." She pointed at the tub. "The bathtub even has jets. Why don't you relax in there awhile?"

He reached out and grabbed her hand, pulling her closer. When he had her between his legs, he set his hands intimately on her hips and tipped his head back. "I'll be fine, Kate. My legs are rushing to catch up with the program."

"I don't want you to fall. A trip to the emergency room would totally blow our cover." She set her hands on his shoulders. "Let me help. Please."

"Are you trying to get me naked?" he teased, giving her body a slight shake. "Cause the idea is enticing, but I'm not strong enough to take that kind of step yet."

A flush rushed up her cheeks and she glanced away from him. She could get used to this new less shy version of Graham, but it still shocked her every time he spoke to her like that. And she had no idea if he was referring to mental or physical strength. Or both.

He was chuckling under his breath as he pulled her even closer. "I love the way you get all flustered. I wouldn't have pegged you as quite so…"

"Prudish," she offered as she tipped her head back down to meet his gaze again.

He shrugged. "I'm not sure that's the right word. Prudish is a word I would use for a sour old maid."

"Yeah, well…" No way was she going to point out that she

might not be sour or old but she was seriously lacking in the relationship department.

"Come on. You've always been a confident woman with your head held high. Outgoing. Funny. Friendly. If anything, I was the one who could barely string a sentence together. Ever since we established a mutual attraction existed, you've taken a step back. Sometimes I catch you staring at me in a way that makes me wish I were about three more weeks into this recovery, and other times you glance away, cheeks red, bottom lip between your teeth. Flustered. I'm really new to this and I'm having trouble reading you."

"Good. I like to keep you on your toes." It made her nervous that he read her so well. She *was* outgoing, funny, and friendly. But that was before she was faced with a man who seemingly was attracted to her. Now, she felt tongue-tied, awkward, and self-conscious instead. It was as if the two of them had reversed roles.

He twisted her words. "As soon as I can get steady on my toes, I'm going to want to explore this further."

"And that brings us full circle," she said to change the subject. "You're not yet steady enough to stand in the shower, Graham. I don't want you to fall."

"Compromise. You help me get inside. I'll sit on the bench seat. You hand me everything I'll need. And then you leave the bathroom until I call you back."

She eyed him, knowing it was the best she was going to get. "Okay, but please don't try to be a hero. I've seen you naked. It won't kill you to let me help if you get started and figure out you need assistance."

"Promise. Go get your suitcase and stuff and move us into the room while I shower."

She stiffened. "I'm not staying in this room with you. I'll take the one next door."

He swallowed. "I'd rather you stayed in this room with me."

"Graham..." No way in hell was she sleeping in the same bed as him. It was hard enough keeping her head on straight when she was in the same room. It was nearly impossible to think when he held her close like this. Sleep in the same bed? Not a chance.

"You've been sleeping in the same room as me for a month." He gave her hips a slight shake.

"That was different. You were unconscious and I had a cot."

"Well, now I'm far less boring and you have a bed. Think how much more comfortable it will be."

"Yep. Down the hall."

He shook her again. Where he was getting this strength, she had no idea. No way could she have sat upright as long as he had today and had the energy to grip anyone like he did on *her* third day awake. It was also an indication that he probably could take a shower alone without difficulty.

Which meant the clock was ticking. Soon he would want to start exploring this thing between them on a physical level.

Of course, who was she kidding? Her body came to attention every time she was near him. And when she wasn't near him too. And when he touched her and held her close. Was she ready for this?

It had only been a day since they determined they had been attracted to each other before preservation. Now they were moving at warp speed toward a relationship she wasn't entirely sure she was ready to face.

She'd had three months to consider her attraction for him. He'd had three days. Three days wasn't enough time for anyone to be so certain of something this important.

Could his attraction be trusted under these extreme circumstances?

Maybe if she was another sort of woman, she could rush forward and claim this prize. But she wasn't. She was the sort of woman who needed to be sure before she was all in. He didn't know that about her, and she had rationalized that she had plenty of time to tell him. But his clock was running much faster than anticipated.

Her body's reaction was nudging her toward him. She loved it when he touched her so intimately. She wanted to know what it would feel like to give herself completely to a man.

He was tempting her and teasing her because he didn't have all the facts, and she was too embarrassed to blurt out the truth yet. What she did know was that she would be devastated if she slept with him and then he left her.

People did that sort of thing. Most people did. Few women in her position would turn down a gorgeous, intelligent, sexy man who was offering her what she knew instinctively would be the most amazing thing she would ever experience. But she'd gone twenty-seven years without giving it away, and she wasn't about to throw that conviction in the trash now.

Call her crazy, but she wanted the world. And she wanted it with one person. She wasn't about to sleep with Graham while they were staying in this safe house. Certainly not before she admitted to him that she had no experience. She didn't want to blindside him. Her conviction was personal, and she needed to find a way to tell him. But definitely not until she was sure he felt as strongly about her as she did him. "I'm not sharing a bed with you," she repeated, her voice too soft and lacking vehemence.

"Are you worried about Jerry and Eliza? Cause they don't strike me as the sort of people who are going to question the status of two grown adults under their roof. They aren't even going to know what our sleeping arrangements are. I doubt they will even come down the hallway to this wing of the house again until after we've left."

She cleared her throat. "I'm not worried about the Kobricks. Just...no. Stop badgering me."

He furrowed his brow, impressing her with his

determination. Meanwhile, he toyed with the hem of her shirt between his fingers, a sign that this discussion pushed him a little out of his comfort zone. His determination was also an attractive attribute.

Even though the man she'd fallen for had been shy and reserved, she wouldn't want him to spend his life standing meekly beside her. He didn't back down. Impressive. "Give me something here, Kate. It's just a bed. It's not like I'm going to maul you. I'm not even sure all my body parts are receiving messages from my brain yet. I don't want you down the hall. What if I need you?"

She was certain he threw that last question in to get under her skin. She rolled her eyes, even though inside she was caving. "If you can shower alone, you can surely sleep alone."

He shook his head. "I'm certain I can, but I'd rather not be alone." His next words made her knees nearly buckle. His voice dipped to a softer, serious tone. "Kate, we spent three years skirting around each other because neither of us had the guts to admit our feelings. We're not wasting another minute playing that game. We've been given a second chance at life. I want to seize it. I want you next to me. Please."

She swallowed. How could she argue with that logic? He had reached into her heart and squeezed it. "Okay." It was just sleep. She could share a bed with him to sleep. He hadn't suggested they have sex. Right?

He smiled slowly as if slightly surprised she'd given in. "Thank you. Now, we're totally going to have another discussion about your hesitation later, but right now I'm going to shower, and you're going to go get your things." He eased her away from him a few inches.

She turned to his side as he put his arm around her shoulders and helped him to his feet. He had far more strength in his legs than she would expect, so it only took a few moments to get him in the shower. Fully clothed. Apparently he intended to handle everything from there.

She did, however, bend down and silently remove his shoes. If he objected to that minor assistance, she might growl at him. After setting them outside the shower, she stood.

"I'm good. I'll yell if I need you."

She held his gaze for a moment and then stepped out of the enclosure and left the room. When she had the door shut, she leaned against it and took a deep breath. This thing between them was happening fast. She needed to wrap her mind around it and figure out a way to respond.

This new Graham was determined and sure of himself, but underneath the more confident exterior, she could still sense the man she'd known for three years. The more timid one. The one who fiddled with the hem of her shirt nervously while asking her not to leave him alone.

Sure, he had more confidence. After all, she'd made it easy for him by admitting she'd been into him since she met him. Even though his nervous tension still showed through, at least her admission had given him a boost of self-assurance.

She needed to find her voice.

One thing she felt confident about was that Graham would be polite about her revelation. He might think she was odd, but he wouldn't make her feel like some sort of virginal unicorn.

There were only two possible outcomes from admitting her lack of experience to him. One, he would accept and honor her convictions, which would make her a lot less stressed around him. Or two, he would think she was too prudish to bother with and back off. If he did, he wasn't worth it.

CHAPTER 10

Graham closed his eyes and took several deep breaths, trying to pull some strength from someplace deep inside him that was totally depleted. He'd used every ounce of his energy trying to be stronger than he was, but after the trip in the SUV and then sitting on the sofa and making his way to this shower, he was empty.

And yet, he needed to find a way to get these clothes off and bathe. So, he tugged his shirt over his head and then lifted one hip and then the other to shrug out of his pants.

He was seriously frustrated as he leaned forward to grab the handheld showerhead and flip on the water. He held the spray away from his body until it got hot, and then he ran the warm water down his body for the first time in ten years.

Of course, it didn't seem like ten years to him. It seemed like three days, but three days was a long time to wash himself with a sponge and a bowl of water. A problem he created for himself when he stubbornly refused to let Kate bathe him.

Perhaps he was being irrational, but every time he pictured her running a washcloth all over his body, he shuddered. For one thing, it unmanned him. For another thing, he would either grow painfully aroused from her touch or worse—not have enough sensation yet to get aroused at all.

Judging by his reactions to her every time she'd been close—but especially fifteen minutes ago while he'd held her between his legs—he didn't have to worry about the functionality of anything below the waist. Everything was in working order.

He smirked at himself now as he glanced down and then took himself in hand and gently stroked from bottom to top and back down. Yeah, everything functioned just fine. Granted, the only hand that had ever touched his erection was his own, but as he closed his eyes and visualized Kate stroking him with her hand, or her mouth, or her tight warmth... *Damn.* He shuddered. None of those things had ever happened to him before, but he was beyond certain experience wasn't necessary in that department.

It took him longer than he would have liked, but eventually he was clean, hair and body. He turned off the water and grabbed the towel. Drying off and getting out of this enclosure was going to be a challenge.

Two seconds later there was a knock at the door and Kate spoke from the other side. "You okay?"

"Yep."

"Can I come in?"

"Not yet."

"I swear to God, Graham, if you try to stand alone, I will personally strap you to this bed and not let you get up again for a week."

He straightened his spine at her choice of words. He'd also been toweling his hair, but he stopped mid-stroke, eyes wide. It took several seconds before he could continue, and then he hastily wiped himself off and managed to lift his ass enough to slide the towel under him and wrap it around his waist.

"Can I come in yet?"

"You're so impatient. Yes."

95

She opened the door, eyeing him skeptically before relaxing. "Good. You didn't move."

"See? I can be a good patient."

She chuckled as she stepped into the shower, slid her hands under his arms, and helped him up.

As soon as he was standing, he wrapped his arms around her and both held her against him and leaned into her. At six feet, he was seven inches taller than her, so he rested his chin on her head as he spoke. "Just so we're clear, at no point in this relationship will you be strapping me to anything."

She giggled and then tipped her head back to meet his gaze. "You sure? It might be fun."

He lifted a brow. "Oh, I'm super-sure. If anyone's getting tied down, it will have to be you, if you like that sort of thing." He winced. "Jesus, that sounded cheesy. I have no game when it comes to lines. Unless, I mean, do you like that sort of thing?"

She shook her head. "I don't see that happening, but in your weakened state, I'm not sure you could stop me from immobilizing you if I need to."

From some strange store of energy he shouldn't have been able to produce, he managed to turn both of them forty-five degrees so that her back was to the wall, and he flattened her to it, his entire body pressing against hers. He lifted one hand to thread it up into her hair and tipped her head back again. "Do I seem weak to you?"

She visibly swallowed, eyes wide, face pale. And then she shook her head. "Irrationally, no."

God, he wanted her. He was in no way strong enough to think such thoughts, but it seemed like after years of pent-up frustration over her, now that the dam had broken, his libido had kicked into overdrive, and an urgency to fully claim her had taken ahold of him. His virginity was about to come to an end, as soon as he could hold himself up...and maybe walk.

The urgency wasn't rational. She wasn't going anywhere.

She'd made it clear that she'd also lusted after him for years. But for some reason, he felt like she wasn't fully his. She still had this hesitation that lingered on the edges. It bothered him. He needed to talk to her about it. Was her reluctance born from something he'd said or done?

He needed to show her how good they could be together. Erase her doubts. He wanted to do that with his mouth on every inch of her body. He wanted to make that hesitation on her face disappear. But he also wasn't strong enough yet.

"Let's get you to the bedroom," she murmured, her voice deeper than usual. She squirmed against the shower wall. "I'm soaked."

"Bummer." He didn't move yet. He wasn't done holding her like this. So close. So intimately. What parts of her were soaked?

"Graham..."

He finally eased back a few inches, and she wiggled around to his side and helped him out of the shower.

He clasped the towel at his waist with one hand to keep it from falling and draped his other arm around her shoulders.

It took several minutes and a lot of resting to get his legs to carry him all the way to the bedroom and over to the bed. When he finally got there, she tugged back the comforter, and he dropped onto his back, breathing far too heavily for a trip across the room—a combination of the effort it cost him and the arousal he felt.

Graham was working hard to tuck the introverted, timid, shy version of himself out of sight. A man who hadn't been able to make eye contact with a woman, especially Kate, for thirty-five years. In his place was a man who wanted this woman with every ounce of his being. He realized he couldn't fully transform his personality, but he found the will to put himself out there. For her. For them. For the possibility of a future he never dreamed might exist for him.

He watched her moving around the room, and prayed she

wouldn't notice the tent between his legs that pushed the towel away from his body. Or maybe he didn't care if she saw it.

He had no idea if he could have this same reaction to other women or not—this newfound ability to make eye contact, form sentences, press her body into the shower wall. Was it just Kate? He would never know, because he didn't intend to let her get away. After thirty-five years of shyness and ten years in a cryostat, it was time he manned up and made several changes.

Kate returned to his side and held out a pile of clothes. "Jerry said one of their sons is about your size. He found some clothes for you." She didn't glance down at his body as she spoke.

Graham swiped a hand down his face. He was seriously losing the battle to remain calm and not have a little tantrum over his lack of mobility. At the moment, he would give anything for this phase of his recovery to be over. Helplessness didn't suit him.

"I'm gonna change," Kate whispered. "Maybe you should take a nap."

He turned his face toward her and met her gaze. "Yeah. Give me a bit, will you?"

"Sure." She nodded and then fled the room as if she were scared of him. She probably was. He couldn't blame her. He was feeling rather curt and frustrated with his lack of mobility. Getting to the bed had exhausted him, using up the last ounce of his energy. And he hated it.

As the door shut behind her, he closed his eyes and let sleep take him under. He didn't care that he was lying there naked with nothing but a wet towel around him. He didn't have the energy for anything else.

Kate had grabbed a clean pair of scrubs on her way out of the room, and she headed for the guest bath to change before making her way to the great room.

Eliza was at the kitchen stove stirring something. Jerry was leaning against the counter near her, drinking a cup of coffee. He was the first to notice Kate, and he nodded toward the mug. "Coffee?"

"That would be wonderful. Thank you." She joined them, admiring the way they stood so close to each other. She'd give anything to have a man in her life who wanted to be near her even while she cooked after decades of marriage.

Could that be Graham?

He certainly acted like it. After three years of never showing signs he'd known she was in the room, he'd become a different human being. It was as if in hibernation he'd added new qualities. He was still the same shy man she'd fallen for underneath—the one who fidgeted a bit while trying to talk to her. The one who was aching to bury himself in a book. The one who thought he had no game, all the while not realizing that *was* his game.

She was certain underneath his new attempt to flirt and tease her was the same man who would do anything for his friends and fully intended to get back to working fifteen hours a day.

Was he intentionally trying to be someone he wasn't, thinking he needed to be a different man to impress her?

She was still reeling from the way he flattened her against the shower wall. He probably didn't realize it, but that was the singular hottest moment of her life. It had been spontaneous and sexy, even though he immediately stammered over his thoughts about being tied to the bed or reversing their roles in that department.

Not only was it adorable, but she had struggled to avoid pressing her body into his and rising onto her tiptoes to kiss him.

Sure, she'd played it off like there was no way in hell she'd ever let a man tie her up, but she'd lied. The thought was titillating. The earnest look he'd shot her made her panties wet and her knees buckle.

After doctoring up her coffee with cream and sugar, she turned around and found Jerry smiling at her. "Did you find everything you needed?"

"Yes. Thank you so much." She had no idea what the protocol was for how she was supposed to act in front of these kind people who were hiding her and Graham from God only knew who. "Graham survived the shower without falling, and he's taking a nap now."

"Good." Jerry nodded. "He'll be back to his normal self in no time. He's a strong man."

She agreed. Perhaps faster than she was ready for.

Jerry gestured toward the pot on the stove as Eliza stirred. "My wife's beef stew won't hurt either."

Kate inhaled the aroma. "Smells fantastic. We seriously can't thank you enough."

Eliza turned toward her and patted her arm. "You don't have to, dear. It's what we do. We help people when they need it."

"You don't even know us," Kate pointed out. The bravery of this couple astounded her.

"Don't need to," Jerry stated. "When someone from SURVIVE asks for our help, that's all the vetting we need."

Eliza nodded in agreement. "We weren't much older than you two when we found ourselves in a bind. A village of people helped us out. We always knew we would pay it forward someday. And now that we own this house off the beaten path, we can do just that."

Kate wondered how often they had random house guests, but she didn't ask.

"You're safe here," Jerry added. "The place looks innocent

from the outside, but it's a fortress. No one is getting in, and we'll know if they even approach."

Wow. Kate glanced around. There was nothing to indicate the house was that secure. They hid it well.

"I'll be going into town later today to get groceries," Eliza said. "Is there anything you folks need?"

Kate shook her head. "We don't need a thing. Time and physical therapy will have Graham running a marathon soon. Thanks for the clothes, though. That's our only issue. He's only been awake a few days. He has no belongings."

Jerry nodded. "Clothes won't be a problem."

"Again, I can't thank you enough."

Eliza patted her shoulder. "No thanks required. It's what we do." She nodded toward the back porch. "If you want to relax for a while, the view is amazing. I'll let you know if I hear movement down the hall."

Relieved, Kate took Eliza up on her offer and headed for the deck. She blew out a long breath as she took a seat, alone with her thoughts.

Her brain was running on full speed lately. She had never in her wildest dreams expected Graham to wake up and immediately profess that his feelings for her had matched hers all along. She'd spent the past month building up the nerve to tell him she was into him, but he'd blindsided her with his returned affection.

Did she really know him at all? The Graham she'd known had been timid and unable to make eye contact. This new Graham held her eyes and pushed her to acknowledge their relationship.

She sighed as she stared out at the gorgeous mountain view. If she were honest, she could see that he was both men. He still had a reserved side that was cute and sexy in its own way. But he also managed to find the strength to lay it all on the line for her. She smiled as she tipped her head back and closed her eyes against the afternoon sun.

The truth was that Graham was growing on her more every day. She might not be quite ready to totally give in to his rushed suggestion that they jump into a relationship, but she was getting there.

She just hoped to God he didn't test the waters and then change his mind. That would devastate her on a level he couldn't understand. Already she knew he could be the real deal for her. The first man she'd been this attracted to. Not just physically but emotionally.

He brought her to life. Not to mention what he did to awaken dormant body parts she wasn't sure were fully functional even before preservation. If she gave herself entirely to him, she would be a goner. He would hold her heart in his hands and have the power to destroy her.

CHAPTER 11

Graham awoke confused, blinking as he turned his head in every direction, trying to figure out where he was. Voices in the distance told him there were other people around. It took him a few moments to remember. The Kobricks. He was in hiding. With Kate.

He blew out a breath and glanced down. He was still wearing a towel. The sheets were pulled over his feet. Kate must have done that before she left. He'd been too warm for more covers. Somehow she'd sensed that and left him alone.

He reached out with one hand and patted the mattress, looking for the clothes he knew she'd left near him. The phone Blair had given him was sitting on the pile of clothes. She had been thoughtful. He should call his parents.

He needed to get dressed first and foremost. The idea of exposing himself to Kate before he was able to do anything about his attraction didn't sit well.

He understood rationally she'd seen him naked, but a man in a coma was just a body. She was a medical professional. Seeing him naked while he was awake was an entirely different story.

Feeling stronger after his nap, he was able to pull on underwear and black sweatpants. He would be much happier when he got his hands on a pair of jeans. But the easier clothing would have to do for now. He also managed to pull to sitting and shrug a T-shirt over his head. And then he flopped back down with a sigh.

This really sucked. He was a horrible patient and an impatient human being. He hated not being able to do things for himself. If he could fast forward a week, he would in a heartbeat.

He took a breath and picked up the cell, palming it for a moment before dialing with shaky fingers. He knew his parents' home phone by heart, assuming they hadn't changed it in ten years.

After three rings, his mother's gentle voice came through. "Hello?"

"Mom. It's me. Graham."

Silence. Several seconds of silence. What did he expect? "Graham?" Her tone was off, softer, questioning. "Is it really you?"

"Yeah, it's me." He smiled. It felt good to hear her voice.

Her breath hitched, and she let out a sob. "My God. It's so hard to believe."

"I know, Mom. I'm struggling to grasp it myself."

"I followed the news. I knew there was a chance. But, I refused to let myself hope."

His eyes slid closed. "I know it's crazy. I wanted to hear your voice. I don't have much time right now. Things are...hectic. But I wanted you to know I'm alive. I'm perfectly healthy. I haven't even aged. I'm still the same me. When things calm down, I'll get in touch with you again. Hopefully I can come visit soon."

"Oh, honey, we would love that. Can we come see you?"

"Not yet, Mom. I really want to see you, but the government is trying to handle this delicately."

"Okay, but soon?"

"Yes. How's Dad?"

"He's going to be furious when he finds out he missed your call." She let out a forced chuckle.

"Yeah, I'm sorry about that. Give him my love please. I can't use this phone again, so the number won't help you."

"Why? What's wrong? Are you in danger?"

"No, Mom. I'm fine. They're being extra cautious. I promise I'll be able to see you soon."

"I'm so happy. There are no words." She sobbed again.

"I know. I promise I'll call again as soon as possible, but it might take a few weeks."

"Okay. I love you, honey."

"I love you too, Mom." He ended the call and gripped the phone against his chest. Hardest call of his life. His poor mother. What she must have gone through, especially in the last few months. Waiting. Hoping. And now he'd just had to ask her to wait even longer until everything with this Blue Cell shook out.

A soft knock on the door was followed by Kate sticking her head in.

He rolled his upper body her direction and reached out a hand.

She came to him, sat on the edge of the bed, and threaded her fingers with his.

"Sorry I was short with you earlier." He handed her the phone.

"No problem. I remember vividly how frustrated I was for the first week. You're way ahead of me both physically and mentally. You'll be up walking around in no time. Did you call your parents?"

He nodded.

She disabled the phone and removed the battery. "Sorry. I remember how hard that call was."

He didn't deserve her, but he wasn't going to let her get away either. From the moment she'd revealed she'd been attracted to him, he'd vowed to himself that she would be his. It didn't matter that he'd thought she was out of his league, because it was apparent she didn't see it that way. So, he was not about to give her a moment to change her mind.

"Can I stretch your legs? We haven't done any exercises today."

He nodded and rolled back so he was flat and staring at the ceiling. "The lucky thing for you is that I'll never forget how well you took care of me when I needed it most. When you're ninety and you fall and break your hip, I'll dote on you like you're the queen." He shot her a grin.

She rolled her eyes as she lifted his closest leg and stretched it upward. "You're incredibly confident about us. It makes me nervous."

Bingo. "Why?" he asked. He would push her because he really didn't think whatever her hesitation was had anything to do with him.

She shrugged, not meeting his gaze. "It's just that we've kind of only known each other a few days, and we're living under seriously intense circumstances. I worry." She let that last word drop off as she bent his leg another direction.

He reached for her wrist on his leg and squeezed it. "We've known each other for years. I realize I was an idiot for all those years, hiding from you while thinking you were too vibrant and alive for me, but I know what your heart looks like."

She shot him a glance, frowning. "What does my heart look like?" She brought his knee to his chest and stretched his glutes.

He still held her wrist. "You're incredibly devoted to saving lives and work tirelessly to find a cure for any disease that hits your desk. You're funny, with a friendly disposition that makes everyone around you feel better no matter what kind of day they're having. When you laugh, the room lights up."

She didn't meet his gaze, but he could see the flush growing up her neck and cheeks.

He gave her arm a tug to make sure she was paying close attention. "I'm positive that when you love, you do so with everything you have and everything you are. I won't squander the opportunity to own that."

"I wouldn't know," she murmured, and then she climbed onto the bed and over his legs so she could work on his opposite leg.

"I get that. I'm sure you don't give your heart away flippantly. I'm humbled that you would give me this opportunity. I promise I will never for a single day in my life make you sorry you took a chance on me." Deep words for a burgeoning relationship that had no legs yet. They hadn't even kissed. But he knew. And he also knew she did too.

She didn't respond, and he let her continue working in silence for another ten minutes, though he watched her closely. When she finished, she surprised him by crawling up to his side and flattening her body along his, her head resting on his shoulder, her hand on his belly.

He held his breath, thanking God for this step, and gently settled his hand around her.

She lay there for several minutes before speaking against his chest. "There are things about me you don't know. I'm worried about what you might think of me after I tell you."

He swallowed. It was impossible to imagine she had deep secrets he wouldn't be able to live with. "I'm sure there are hundreds of things about you I don't know. Give me a chance. Maybe if you tell me a few important ones, I can put your fears to rest."

She sighed and hesitated a few beats before dragging her

fingers around his chest in an absent-minded pattern she was most likely unaware of. "You said you thought I was out of your league, when the truth is I have extremely limited experience with men."

He sucked in a shallow breath, not wanting her to notice any reaction from him. Inside, he was fist pumping. Damn, she was hot. If she thought her lack of experience made her less attractive, she'd lost a few marbles. What were the chances two grown adults would have an equal lack of experience? "Why would I be disappointed to hear that?" he finally managed.

She shrugged against him. "You're suddenly so confident and sure of yourself. And maybe you're too sure of me. I'm worried you've got some inflated fantasy about me as if I'm some sort of sex goddess who's going to rock your world."

He couldn't help it. The laugh bubbled out of him before he could stop it.

When she stiffened and then started to push off him, he grasped her tighter. "I'm sorry. I didn't mean to laugh. You just shocked me."

She stopped shoving, but she did lift her face to glare at him, propping her upper body off his torso. "Graham, this is the hardest conversation I've ever had in my life, and you're laughing. I'd rather take a verbal exam about human anatomy in front of a twelve-person board of professors than look you in the eye and explain my lack of experience."

He sobered fast, wiping the smile off his face. "Kate, I'm so sorry. It was a knee-jerk reaction to your concerns. It's physically impossible for you not to rock my world. I was shocked you would think so." He ran a hand up and down her back, hoping to calm her. "I'm truly sorry," he repeated in a lower voice.

Her face was red, and she looked away, pursing her lips. This was very serious for her.

He needed to tread carefully. His laughter hadn't helped. He reached up and tucked a lock of hair behind her ear. "Let's clear the air here. How many men have you slept with?" Did she think she might not be able to please him in bed? Because that was crazy.

She took a slow breath. "None."

Fuck me.

Graham seriously needed to choose his words carefully. They mattered. *She* mattered. A fuck of a lot. "Okay. Let me set you straight on a few things. One, that is the sexiest thing you could ever say to me. So, if you think I would be put off by that, you're wrong.

"Two, my understanding is that when you're with the right person, it all falls into place perfectly. It's instinctive."

She flinched. "How many *right* people have you been with?"

He smiled. "None."

Her eyes widened but then narrowed. "How many wrong people have you been with?"

He gave her another shy smile. "None. I'm a virgin."

He watched her swallow, eyes wide again. "Seriously?"

He ran a hand up and down her back again. "Yes. So we're in the same boat. I'm sure you're shocked about my lack of experience considering how smooth my game is. Ha ha. But we'll figure it out together."

She took a breath. "What a double standard. Here I've been worrying myself sick about telling you I'm a virgin, and all the time you had the same secret. You never even considered it might be an issue for me to find out you were a virgin."

He shrugged. "True. I didn't worry about *your* reaction to my innocence. Didn't seem like it would be a deal breaker for you. You seem like the type of woman who might find it endearing, but trust me, it's not like I didn't get harassed plenty by the guys in my gym class in high school."

She rolled her eyes. "Don't you want to know why I haven't lost *my* virginity?"

"I assume it's pretty much the same reason I haven't lost mine. No point just having sex for the sake of doing it with a random stranger. When the right person came along, you would know it. Right?" *And the right person is currently looking me in the eye, flushed and gorgeous.*

She chewed on her bottom lip, her face dipped toward his chest. "Yeah. But, well, I'm not ready to have sex, so I need you to respect that for a while. You're moving at a fast pace. I need more time."

He set his hand on the side of her head and stroked it down her hair. "Kate, look at me." He waited for her gaze to lock on his. "I would never do anything to intentionally make you uncomfortable. *Never.* We move at whatever pace you want."

"Thank you." She was trembling.

He would do anything to ease her fears. Her virginity was obviously not the deal breaker she had presumed, though he still found her concerns mind-boggling. It was sweet and would bring him to his knees if he could stand. But he did need to respect her wishes and act accordingly.

She nodded slowly. "For me it's just a personal decision. At some point along the way when I was in my early twenties, I realized I wasn't like other women. I wasn't made to jump into bed with random men and have meaningless sex. In fact, the idea does nothing for me. I want the world. The dream. And I won't settle for less."

He stroked his fingers through her hair, so endeared to her. "That's beautiful, Kate."

She flushed and set her cheek on his chest again, but she spoke. "Don't get me wrong. You're the first man to tempt me. But I want to be sure. And more importantly, I want *you* to be sure. It would destroy me if we gave that piece of ourselves to each other and then you changed your mind about us." She lifted her face again. "I need to feel certain, and I need to be assured you do too. Maybe that's corny, but it's who I am."

His heart leaped out of his chest. It was hers. Did she realize he was holding it in his hand, offering it to her to do with as she pleased? No matter what happened, she already owned a piece of him, and she had the power to destroy him as well. "It's not corny. Corny is how often I practiced lines in my mirror trying to get up the nerve to talk to you. I was pretty sure my scientific pick-up lines wouldn't go over well."

She gave him a slight smile. "I don't know about that. I'm kind of into science nerds. Try me."

"Okay, well, my personal favorite is 'do you have eleven protons because you're sodium fine.'"

She giggled. "Yeah, you're right. That's pretty bad."

He sobered. "But truly, you aren't corny. I respect you and any choice you make."

She cleared her throat and looked him in the eye again. "That's why I need us to take this slow. It's so fast. It feels like we've gone at the speed of light toward something I've wanted so badly for so long that I don't trust it to be real. It scares me."

He threaded his fingers in her hair, loving the silky feel of it. "I know it's fast, but it's also not. Imagine if we hadn't been in those cryostats for ten years and we'd simply discovered our mutual attraction with each other suddenly this week after tiptoeing around for three years. We would be in this same position."

She gave him a coy grin. "Except you would have the strength to tempt my resolve."

He grinned. "Okay, there is that. You're probably right. My lack of stamina and our situation is buying you all the time you want, but I would never rush you anyway."

She cocked her head to one side and shot him a look. "You've done nothing but rush me."

"Emotionally, maybe. I'll admit I'm anxious for you to admit you're so into me that it makes you flustered. It's nice not being the only one who feels this way all the time, but I would never rush you physically."

"Every time you touch me, my body lights on fire and I start to panic."

"I know." He grinned. "That's why I want you to admit we're already a couple. The rest will fall into place."

"You haven't even kissed me. What if there's no spark? What if one of us doesn't like how the other kisses?"

His grip in her hair tightened and he set his other hand on top of the one she'd rested on his chest. "You've been reading too many romance novels."

She groaned. "Give me a break. When have I had time to read romance novels?"

"Okay. Okay. But you have it all backward. The spark is already a given. You seriously can't fuck up a kiss with someone you're head over heels for."

"Yeah, well…" Her voice was filled with that doubt again.

This, he could fix. "Come here." He gave her head a nudge forward.

"Why?" She gave him that narrowed skeptical eye again.

"Because I'm going to kiss you and put that fear at ease."

"You've only been awake three days. You need more rest. You're getting ahead of yourself," she hedged.

"My lips are working fine." He slid his hand to the back of her neck. "Lifting my head to come to you or flipping you on your back so I can hover over you are currently not options, though, so I need you to come to me."

She licked her lips and glanced at his. And then painstakingly slowly, she smoothed her hand up his chest and lowered her body over his.

He grabbed her arm with one hand, still cupping her neck with the other. Every inch of her delectable body against his was heaven. And then she kissed him.

It started out as a simple peck, but he took control, angled her head to one side, and teased her lips with his own, tasting her, luxuriating in the feel of her soft, full mouth against his. When he drew his tongue across her bottom lip, she moaned into his mouth and parted her lips.

Oh yes. This was heaven on earth. He was definitely not dead or dreaming. He was kissing the woman he'd lusted after for three years. And it was perfection.

CHAPTER 12

Kate wasn't sure if she was more nervous or less after having her entire world spin in circles from that kiss. She couldn't stop thinking about it or touching her lips as if she could still feel him against her hours later.

Luckily, he gave her space after that and stopped hounding her for an emotional commitment. They spent the rest of the day in the great room with their amazing hosts, Graham proving once again how strong he was by sitting upright and engaging in conversation as if he hadn't emerged from a coma just three days ago.

He also insisted Kate set him up with her computer so he could start nosing around in it and get himself up to speed with technology. Naturally, he buried himself in the laptop for hours. Every time Kate glanced at him, she found his brow furrowed and his fingers moving fast over the mouse pad and the keyboard. He didn't ask questions. Instead, he figured things out on his own. This was the man she knew. The one she'd fallen for. Serious. Dedicated. When he occasionally shifted his attention to her and shot her a quick smile, she melted a little more. He was the entire package.

Kate helped Eliza with dinner and pushed thoughts of later that night out of her mind for the entire day. It wasn't until Jerry helped Kate support Graham to get him back to the bedroom that she let her insecurities seep back in.

She knew they weren't going to have sex. That wasn't the problem. The problem was she also knew she didn't have to have sex with him to tumble completely under his spell. It was already too late. Sleeping in the same bed with him holding her against his body would draw in deeper.

She worried about Graham's ability to make rational decisions so quickly after being reanimated. What if he was suffering from some sort of emotional overload or something, and now he felt the need to seize the day without thinking his decisions through?

What if he regretted having sex with her...?

They took turns using the bathroom, Kate leery about leaving Graham in there alone, pacing outside the door until he was finished and let her back in to lean on her as he made his way toward the bed. His strength was noticeably better by the hour.

She joined him ten minutes later wearing her usual soft shorts and a tank top. Today she felt self-conscious about it, but it would be weird to climb into bed in her scrubs. Obviously, even though she'd done so on the cot at the clinic, he would never buy that she slept like that when she was alone.

"You've been awake for a long time," she pointed out conversationally as she turned off the lights.

He was on his back, sheets drawn up to his waist, hand reaching out to her as she climbed onto the other side of the bed. "Maybe tomorrow I can make it all day."

She was nervous and excited and aroused as she lined her body up with his, pressing into his side for the night.

He wrapped his arm around her and held her close as she set

her cheek against his shoulder. "Relax," he whispered. "We're just going to sleep."

She sighed. "You're certifiable if you think lying next to you with you touching me all over is *just* anything."

He chuckled and kissed the top of her head. "We could kiss again," he suggested.

"Oh, that'll help," she responded sarcastically.

He laughed and hugged her tighter. "Yeah, it's probably a bad idea. The next time I kiss you, I don't think I'll be able to stop things from escalating. I only did that earlier to prove to you there were amazing sparks. It worked. I'm good."

"You're conceited and a lot cocky. Was this always hiding behind the shy, slightly geeky side of you?"

"Maybe... I don't know. I still feel the same inside, but I also know I'll do anything to ensure you realize I'm serious. I won't kiss you again tonight if it makes you nervous. I took a gamble. You had doubts. I didn't want you wandering around for days on end thinking there's even a slight chance sex between us won't be good. I mean, I'm no expert, obviously, but I think what we have is real. Did I or did I not prove my point with my lips alone?"

"You did. That's what scares the hell out of me."

"It was meant to calm you, not make things worse."

She lifted her face toward his. There was enough light coming from the nightlight in the bathroom to make out his expression. "It backfired. I kinda lost a few brain cells during that kiss." She was shocked by how bold she felt with him.

A huge smile spread across his face. "Excellent." His hand went up into her hair, and he pressed her face back down to his chest. "How about if I tell you one of my winning jokes to lighten the mood and help you relax."

She chuckled. He truly could be just as nerdy as the day she'd met him at times. "Go for it."

"An infectious disease walks into a bar..."

She groaned. "The bartender says, 'We don't serve your kind here.' And the disease responds with, 'You're not being a very good host.'"

Graham laughed. "Guess you've heard that one."

"Who hasn't?" But he had accomplished one thing—she felt more at ease.

"Go to sleep."

It took a long time to force herself to relax. Her mind wouldn't stop wandering to all the future possibilities between them. She was not kidding. She was both anxious and nervous about taking their new relationship to a level there would be no turning back from.

Eventually, his even breathing and steady heart beat lulled her to join him in sleep.

The following morning Kate took them through a routine of showering, eating, and exercising. As they were finishing, Dade showed up, and he was not alone.

Kate had settled Graham on the couch in the living room when they all heard the SUV pull up. Kate went out front with Jerry to find not just Graham and Blair but Grayson and Bianca too. Kate rushed down the steps of the porch to greet them.

Before anyone got to Bianca, Kate closed the distance and opened her door. She immediately pulled her friend in for a hug. When she finally released her to hold her at arm's length, she found herself emotional. "You look great. I'm so glad you're here."

Grayson set a hand on Kate's shoulder. "If you move, I'll get her out of the car," he teased.

Kate ducked back out of the way, but she also gave Grayson a hug on the way by. "Haven't seen you in a month either."

He stared down at her indulgently, a half grin on his lips. "It is nice to reunite. I wish we weren't all scattered."

"You need help?" Dade asked Grayson.

"Nope, I've got her." He unbuckled her seat belt and bent to scoop her into his arms. Bianca was a petite woman anyway, but Grayson made her look like a rag doll as he carried her toward the house. Her long dark hair was as radiant as it had always been. Her skin was just as tanned. And her big brown eyes were alive.

As Grayson carried her inside, Kate watched the way Bianca held on to him and wondered if there were sparks between them like the ones Kate had with Graham. It was all in her head, of course, but based on verifiable evidence, many of the members of the original team were finding love soon after reanimating. Maybe it made perfect sense if everyone else had the same feeling Kate did that life was short and should be embraced. But was that the right reason for her to have sex with Graham?

It also shouldn't be surprising that any one of them would find love among their group. They had a lot in common. Most of them were near the same age. They'd devoted their lives to science. And, most importantly, they'd been through the same crisis together. Even those among them who worked in the bunker with the second team or as support staff had a much better understanding of what it was like to be revived than the average human.

It was also possible that some members of her team had hooked up before they had all succumbed to AP12 and been preserved. Kate hadn't specifically known that to be true, but there were twenty-one of them. Anything could have happened during those last few months.

She shuddered as she considered the possibility since the team was now scattered all over the state or even farther.

Perhaps some of her coworkers had been sent to undisclosed locations without someone they loved.

Graham sat straighter and twisted toward Bianca as Grayson settled her on the loveseat. Kate watched his face light up. "It's so good to see you guys."

Grayson spun around and gave Graham a firm hug. "You look fantastic." Grayson stepped back and settled on the loveseat next to Bianca. Protective. Not surprising. Kate felt protective of Graham.

Graham shrugged. "According to Kate, I'm moving along faster than most others, but I'm impatient, so it's not fast enough for me. I can't stand not having full mobility because my muscles are weak and my brain won't fire messages fast enough."

"Tell me about it," Bianca complained. Her head rolled back against the sofa, but then Grayson stood up and situated her on her side so that she was curled up lying in the corner instead of trying to sit.

Kate intentionally did not sit next to Graham because she wasn't in the mood to have her relationship dissected, and she knew him well enough to know he would give them away in an instant by putting his hands all over her. Instead, she pointed at the couch and looked toward Dade and Blair. "You two, sit."

As they took a seat, Kate lowered into the armchair.

Graham shot her a knowing look and raised his brows. He was onto her. Of course.

Jerry and Eliza excused themselves and went out the back door, rightfully assuming serious plotting was about to commence in their great room, though the idea of kicking the kind older couple out of their own house unnerved Kate.

She had noticed Dade speaking to Jerry before they came inside, though, so surely they were on the same page.

Dade slapped his hands against his thighs. "So, here's the deal."

Everyone turned their attention to him.

"I still don't have a flipping idea what's going on in the inner circle of DEEP, but I don't like it. I've been moving people around for days now. No one knows where any of you are, and I'd like to keep it that way. Colton, Josiah, and Khloe are all with Dalton. He's armed. They're in a safe house. They're going to stay there for the time being."

"Where the heck is everyone else?" Grayson asked.

Dade nodded. "Tushar and Trish are at the bunker with the last two people who came out of their cryostats."

"Did Mina and Shelby stay back with them?" The two women were both medical doctors from the second team put together by Ryan.

"Yes. In addition, Ryan, Emily, Zeke, Michelle, and Damon Bardsley are at another government bunker in New Mexico. There are a few people preserved there also.

"No idea how many yet, but I do know Temple moved two of the reanimation chambers to New Mexico for the purpose of reviving people there. Damon is working on that. It's his specialty for anyone who doesn't know."

"So, what can we do to help?" Graham asked. Kate imagined he would leap off the couch and save the world if he had the strength.

Dade shot him a smile. "Funny you should ask. When I mentioned the other day that I needed you, it was because of an idea Spencer has."

"Of course. Anything." Graham glanced at Kate, determination on his face. He was stronger than her.

She wanted this insanity solved as badly as anyone else, but how far was she willing to go to make sure they all came out of this unscathed? It was exhausting.

"Yeah, hold off committing until you hear the idea."

Kate tipped her head to one side and watched Graham, who was staring at Dade with an eager expression.

Dade continued. "We could use a mole ourselves. I'm hoping it could be you. I need someone to get back into the bunker and do a job." He shifted his gaze to Kate. "This involves you too."

She flinched.

"No way in hell is Kate going back to the bunker if you think it's dangerous," Graham retorted quickly. *Great.* She might not be overly excited about getting back into the bunker or even being involved in any of this mess, but she didn't need him to make decisions for her or speak for her.

Dade shot Graham a grin as he set his hand on Blair's thigh and squeezed. Blair chuckled and crossed her arms. "Told you."

Graham shot Blair a look too. She was sitting right next to him, close enough to touch. Next, he glanced around the room at everyone else, and Kate knew without a doubt that he was two seconds from outing them.

Suddenly, she didn't care. It didn't matter really. There was no reason for their weird relationship to be a government secret or anything, and she sensed Graham was eager to publicly commit.

Her palms were sweating, and she wiped them on her thighs as she considered a new fact—no way would Graham claim her in front of so many people if he wasn't all in. He was too shy in spite of his newfound courage to take that kind of risk. He wasn't the sort of man who would sleep with her and then dump her anyway, but outing them meant a lot.

When his wide gaze landed on hers, she shot him a smile, giving him silent permission to finish what he'd inadvertently started.

He was persistent, she would give him that. He also seemed to be in a hurry to solidify their relationship as if he were afraid if he didn't do so quickly, she might get away or someone else would grab her. It was comical since she'd managed to live twenty-seven years without falling for another man—the last three of which had been spent pining after the very man with the pumped chest.

The honest truth she had to admit to herself was that she liked the fact that he so obviously wanted to proclaim his feelings to the group. It meant he was committed to making this thing work. It was sweet, and her heart beat faster knowing what he was about to say.

Graham watched her intently while he spoke to everyone else. "Kate and I are together. We seemed to have missed the cues between us before we were preserved, and we're still ironing some things out, but we're...together," he repeated, as if it were important to emphasize that one word.

Kate blushed, but she couldn't keep from smiling wider. Graham might have been quick to flex his muscles and go public with their precarious relationship, but she was falling harder for him every day.

Before their preservation, she had been infatuated with him from afar with not enough details about him as a person to really know what he was like. For the past month while she essentially held a vigil over his comatose body, she had willed him repeatedly to be okay, promising herself she wouldn't squander a second opportunity.

So, no. She wasn't upset with him. She was so enamored with him that she had to force herself to stay in her seat and not leap across the room to throw her arms around him. That would be a little too much. Especially after everything she'd said to him last night. Mixed signals from her were unnecessary.

Everyone turned toward Kate, smiling broadly.

Bianca's hand covered her mouth. She looked like she might cry from emotion. "I'm so happy for you."

Blair smiled warmly. "Congratulations. That's so exciting."

Dade shook his head, smirking. "So, as I was saying...I, well, the hacker we're working with, had an idea. Between the six of us, we can surely suss it out and make it workable."

"Tell us," Kate encouraged. Whatever it was, she needed to figure out a way to get on board and help the team. Now wasn't the time to balk and run. She was a member of a twenty-one-person team, a team that was actually twelve people larger if she included the second team.

"I don't have any way to get in touch with Tushar, nor would I if I could because I don't trust the security of any form of communication inside the bunker. Tushar also doesn't know I'm alive. I'm in contact with Ryan, but he can't give his parents any information or request help over the phone either.

"I'm certain Tushar and Trish will help from the inside, but they don't know it yet. You'll have to feel them out and bring them into the fold discreetly. I can't imagine there's any possibility in the world either of them are involved, nor would they do anything to jeopardize our efforts. You two will have to use your best judgment about what information to give them."

"What exactly do you need us to do?" Graham asked, tacking himself onto the plan readily, even though his brow was furrowed skeptically as he glanced at her.

She smiled warmly at him. It made her squirm in her seat that he was so blatantly worried about her.

"For one thing, I'm very concerned about the decades' worth of data stored at the bunker. We need to duplicate it and get it out of there, download it onto a separate hard drive."

Kate gasped. "You're afraid it could get deleted?"

"I *know* it's going to get deleted."

Kate gasped. "The hacker?"

Dade nodded. "Yep. He's trying to buy us time to get in there and download everything, but he can't stall forever."

Kate was confused. "You think this Blue Cell group is trying to stop us from curing diseases and healing people? Why would anyone do that? Project DEEP was created by the government for the express purpose of eradicating disease."

Dade inhaled slowly while he shrugged. "All things lead to

that conclusion. All of us—both the first team and the second—have experienced setbacks every step of the way for many years. Broken beakers. Scrambled data. Kidnapping. Bombs. Mandatory relocation. At this moment, we're scattered all over the place. Very few of us are doing the job we were hired for. Advances are not being made. Why?"

He had a good point. Kate wrapped her arms around herself and shuddered.

Graham ran a hand through his hair. "How do you propose we get an invitation back into the bunker? It would seem Temple is keeping everyone out."

Dade nodded. "Here's my plan." He turned toward Kate. "I think you should call in and tell Temple you're worried about Graham because he isn't getting stronger as fast as the others."

Kate widened her eyes. "I'm a doctor, not an actor. Besides, that's comical. He's breaking records by the hour."

"It's perfect," Graham stated. "I assume Temple has no idea where we are, and Kate can use that to our advantage, telling Temple she got nervous because I'm still so weak and she felt exposed, so she moved us to a hotel somewhere."

"Exactly," Dade agreed. "Make her believe you're scared and you need help. You haven't thrived well since waking up, and she's scared out of her mind hiding you in a hotel."

"That would work."

Grayson cleared his throat. "Do you really think Temple's involved? I can't wrap my head around that."

Dade shook his head. "I don't know what to think. Maybe she's involved. Maybe she isn't. What I do know is that information that gets to her always becomes our enemy. So either she's directing an inside job, or someone she communicates with is undermining all of us. Either way, she might know. She might not."

Blair sighed. "I'm personally praying she has no understanding of what happens when she gives updates to her superiors, but somewhere along the line, someone feeds information to Blue Cell and they use it against us."

Grayson wasn't the only one who hated to think Temple could be behind any scheme to slow down the advance of science. It made Kate sick to her stomach. She'd known Temple for three years prior to being preserved. Some of them had known and worked with Temple for twenty years.

"We'll do it," Kate said. She knew Graham would agree, but she wanted to be the one to verbally express their consent.

Graham added to her agreement. "I assume you also need us to poke around and figure out what the fuck is going on."

"That's the idea," Dade said. "And you're going to have to do all this while pretending you're very weak and sick. I'm hoping you can maneuver yourself into getting assigned to one of the suites where you can pretend to convalesce while spending the days working frantically to download and preserve data."

"Suites?" Graham asked. "Has the bunker turned into a Holiday Inn?" he joked.

Kate laughed. "Yes. As soon as they realized they were going to reanimate twenty-two people, the government added living quarters to one side of the bunker. Ryan's team also stayed in them so that no one needed to trek back and forth to town anymore."

"Makes sense." Graham was slowly nodding. "Nothing else makes sense, but at least someone somewhere gave a shit about the team enough to provide housing finally. Working long hours and then driving into Falling Rock just to sleep in an unused apartment was illogical."

Dade looked at Graham again. "How are your computer skills?"

Graham gave a wry chuckle. "I'm catching up fast, but you aren't kidding about the changes in technology in just a decade. The internet is a whole new world."

Dade laughed. "That was the weirdest part for me. It took

me a while to get up to speed. But you've got just a few days to accomplish it. Don't waste a single moment. You're going to need to be a computer god when you get to the bunker, though Spencer will get in touch with you and provide detailed instructions on what we need and how to get it."

Graham inhaled slowly, tipping his head to one side with a wince. "I'll do my best."

Bianca, who had remained mostly quiet for a while, finally spoke. Her gaze was on Graham. "How are you so chipper and alert and upright? No way in hell could I learn a new skill this week. I'm still trying to figure out how to get myself to the bathroom, and you're going to learn computer programming?"

"I'm wondering the same thing," Grayson added. "None of us were as far along as you on the fourth day after reanimation."

Graham shrugged. "Determination?"

"Even your mind is sharp. It's disconcerting," Bianca complained.

Graham grinned. "I can remember all the science jokes I ever knew too. You want to hear one?" He didn't hesitate before continuing, "Where does bad light end up?"

"In prism," they all responded simultaneously on a groan.

Kate couldn't keep from smiling. He might be dorky, but he was her dork.

Dade stood, Blair following him. "I hate this, but we need to leave. I want to get to Montana as soon as possible. That's where we have our base set up. Everyone is heading that direction as soon as they're able. Blair and I will head there now. Grayson and Bianca will stay here until Bianca is strong enough to travel that far."

He glanced at Kate and then Graham. "Graham needs more time to recuperate, but the clock is also ticking. I'm hoping you can make your way back to the bunker in about three days. It helps that Graham is seemingly stronger than any of the rest of us were on day four. He can easily fake being far weaker than he is. Call Temple from a phone along the way somewhere. Don't tell her where you are, just that you're scared and heading toward the bunker. There's no way she'll turn you down. Even if she is working against us, it would look too suspicious for her to leave you sick and scared and alone."

"Good point," Graham agreed. "I'll make sure I'm ready in a few more days."

Bianca was pushing to sitting. "Graham, I say this in the kindest possible way—fuck you." Her voice was sweet and syrupy.

Graham chuckled. "I don't know what to say. Maybe I'm a superhero now with extra powers."

Bianca rolled her eyes. "If you figure out what those powers are, please let me know because I'm already tired of playing the invalid."

Dade set a hand on Blair's shoulder. "I'm sorry we have to hurry out of here. I wish we could stay."

Kate was still trying to wrap her head around the fact that Dade was even alive. She also hated for him to leave. But she rose to see them out. "You'll stay in touch with us?"

Blair responded. "We will until you go back into the bunker. It won't be safe to contact us from inside. Either Dade or Spencer will reach out to you and establish contact through a computer."

Kate nodded, swallowing back nerves. The idea that the bunker was compromised, or more specifically Temple, didn't sit well with her.

After a round of goodbyes, Dade and Blair left.

"Well, that puts a new spin on things," Kate said, still staring out the front window.

Graham sighed behind her. "We probably need to double up the physical therapy sessions. I can pretend to be a sick as you want me to, but there's no way I'm going back into that bunker without the ability to get the fuck out easily if the need arises."

"Agreed." She turned toward him, taking a deep breath.

How had their entire world gotten so twisted and turned upside down?

CHAPTER 13

Three days later...

Graham shut the trunk of the car and turned around to head back into the house. They had gotten a rental, or rather Dade had gotten them a rental. They needed to turn it back in when they got to Falling Rock. He'd also provided Kate with a driver's license. It was even in her real name.

When he stepped back inside to say goodbye to Grayson and Bianca, he found Bianca's head cocked to one side and her eyes on him. "As soon as I'm strong enough to fully lift my damn head, I'm going to kick your ass," she stated.

Graham chuckled as he leaned over her on the couch and gave her a hug. "You couldn't have kicked anything of mine even before we were preserved. You weigh about a hundred pounds soaking wet."

She swatted at his arm as he released her. She was exaggerating. She was getting stronger every day, apparently right on track with the rest of the reanimated.

Leaving Bianca in the living room, everyone else followed

Graham and Kate to the car. While Jerry and Eliza spoke to Kate, Graham turned toward Grayson. "She'll be fine," he assured his friend.

Grayson nodded, his expression serious. "I'm sure she will. A few more weeks of physical therapy will help. She's impatient."

"I understand that."

"We all do." He sighed.

"Is everything else okay?" Graham asked, reading from Grayson's expression—the same look he'd had on his face for three days—that something was bothering him. Or perhaps Bianca.

Grayson ran a hand through his hair. "She's headstrong."

Graham chuckled. "This is news?"

"Not really. She always was, but things are different now. I've been trying to talk her into taking off instead of going back. She won't have it. She wants to head for Montana as soon as she can walk and join the fray."

"Yeah, that sounds like Bianca. She may be small, but she's no weakling. Why does that bother you? I would think you'd want to get to Montana too."

"Yes and no. If it were just me, I'd get in the car with the two of you right now. But Bianca...she's..."

"No longer just a coworker and friend?" Graham supplied. They had not discussed the chemistry between Grayson and Bianca. It was palpable, but Graham and Kate had stayed out of their business.

"Right. At least that's my opinion."

Graham laughed again. "Headstrong." He sobered. "But seriously, I've seen the way she watches you when you're not looking. She's into you."

"Yeah? Try telling her that." He rolled his eyes and slapped Graham on the shoulder. "Speaking of coworkers and friends looking at you..." He lifted an eyebrow. "I'm happy for you. I've seen a side of you I never knew existed."

Graham shrugged, feeling slightly embarrassed. It was one thing to talk to Grayson about Bianca. He still wasn't going to win any awards in the relationship department himself. Every day he was winging it. Sure, he'd held his head high and let everyone in the room know he was into Kate, but that didn't make him a new man. It just made him determined to seize the day.

Grayson smiled. "Look, I think it's great. You were always so timid. I'm happy to see you out of your shell a bit. Kate's a great woman. Anyone can tell your feelings are reciprocated."

"Yeah, well, as long as she continues to find my geeky jokes cute, it's all good."

Grayson laughed. "She will. Don't worry. You two drive safely. And be careful inside that bunker. Watch your back."

"I will." Graham turned to face Jerry and Eliza as they stepped to his side of the car. He hugged them both. "Thank you so much. For everything."

Eliza smiled warmly. "Be safe."

Moments later, Kate was behind the wheel with Graham in the passenger seat, and they pulled away from the mountain home that had welcomed them when they most needed it.

"How far is it?" Graham asked.

"About two hours. We'll be there by noon." She glanced at him. "You ready for this?"

"Ready as I'll ever be." He'd learned everything he possibly could about the latest computer software in the past three days, most of which had come from Eliza and Jerry since everyone else in the safe house had only existed in this decade for either three days or three months.

Once he'd gotten reacquainted with the newest technology, he'd also gotten in touch with Spencer-the-hacker several times. Spencer had given him instructions about how to download the data once he arrived at the bunker.

"I hope you can act like a sick man, because you're not remotely sick." She visibly shuddered.

He smiled at her profile, knowing she'd been growing increasingly nervous around him over the past two days as he proved more and more capable of getting around on his own. He was walking almost normally. He wasn't quite ready to run a marathon, but he could shower and take care of himself without any assistance.

Graham hadn't pressured Kate at all in the past three days. They shared a bed, and she let him hold her during the night, but he never let his hands stray over her body the way he ached to do. He hadn't kissed her so passionately again either. That part was hard.

He wanted to. Badly. But he also didn't want to stress her out. So he kept things chaste. Small pecks on her lips. Often, so he could remind her frequently how he felt, but he didn't linger too long or skim her lips with his tongue.

They hadn't mentioned their conversation from the other night in the last few days either. It wasn't necessary. What Kate needed was assurance from him that he truly cared deeply about her, would do anything for her, and was in it for the long haul. Words wouldn't accomplish that task. Actions would.

At the same time, he recognized that toying with her heart was out of the question. He needed to be equally certain beyond a shadow of a doubt that they could last a lifetime before he made a move. He'd be an asshole to do otherwise.

Kate had made it clear that her biggest concern was giving up her virginity before she was certain about their staying power. Or rather before *he* was certain about their staying power.

As much as he ached to get more intimate with her, he had to respect that. He had no doubt he was physically capable of moving forward. Maybe he wasn't ready to flatten her to a wall with her legs wrapped around him, but he was certain he could manage any number of supine or prone positions.

In any case, there hadn't been time for flirting and reassurances. They had been busy getting him stronger and reacquainting themselves with Grayson and Bianca—two people who obviously had their own friction. The two of them had moved into the room across the hall from Graham and Kate. Graham suspected Grayson was as reluctant to leave Bianca alone as Kate had been when Graham first awoke.

It was more than that. He knew. He didn't doubt Bianca had balked. He'd heard them arguing under their breaths through the door a few times, but he hadn't wanted to pry.

Graham had his own problems to deal with. His own woman and their impending plan to return to the bunker essentially as spies.

About an hour into their drive, Kate pulled into a gas station and left him in the car to find a phone she could call Temple from. She was only gone about three minutes.

"Do you get ahold of Temple?" he asked as she slid back into the driver's seat.

"Yep."

"You think she suspects anything?"

Kate shook her head as she returned to the highway. "No. She seemed sympathetic. Worried about your health and understanding of my concerns. It's weird lying to her, though. I hate it."

"I know what you mean. I can't wrap my head around it, but I keep telling myself she has nothing to do with any of this. Spencer has told me she's clean. He's dug around in her communications and can't find any evidence she is anything except above board. That does not, however, eliminate anyone she reports to, so we have to remain diligent."

"Yeah. I repeat that in my head over and over also, but how the hell is she so totally oblivious to this much mayhem?"

"It's not that she doesn't realize there's something wrong. I'm just hoping she's as in the dark about who's causing it as any of us."

"I'm not looking forward to the day when we have to come clean and tell her we all went behind her back and lied to her."

Graham agreed. It brought goose bumps to his skin.

When they got close to the bunker, Graham climbed into the back seat and lay down, curling on his side with a blanket over him as if he didn't have the strength to sit upright.

Kate was quiet for the last few miles, and he worried about her. He hated her being in this position, one where she had to lie for both of them. He was also panicked about the prospect of being separated from her, even for short periods of time.

They'd been together now for a week, and he didn't consider the bunker to be very safe, so he wasn't excited about her leaving him alone somewhere in a "sick" bed while she dug around in the bunker for explanations and information.

"You ready?" she asked. "I'm pulling up to the gate."

"I'll never be ready for this," he muttered.

He listened from the back seat while Kate spoke to a few people at the gate, and a few minutes later she pulled up to the bunker.

Tushar was the first person Graham saw. He opened the door near his head and leaned in, a crooked smile on his face. "So damn good to see you," he said, not mentioning the obvious fact that Graham was not well.

The other passenger door opened and Trish leaned in. She set a hand on Graham's leg. "Let's get you inside. We'll have you up and running in no time."

Two women Graham hadn't met were at the entrance to the bunker with Temple as Tushar rolled Graham inside in a wheelchair. They would be Mina and Shelby. He knew they were both career military and medical doctors.

Graham worked hard to hunch over as if it took too much energy to hold his head up and he was cold.

Temple set a hand on his shoulder. "Welcome back. Let's get you a room."

Kate stepped forward. "Put him in my suite. I assume it's still available?" She glanced around as if wondering how many people were inside the bunker when they all knew good and well hardly anyone was.

It was operating on a skeleton crew of mostly the people standing in front of them and support staff.

"Doesn't he need to be in the medical wing?" Temple asked, frowning.

Kate rolled her eyes dramatically as they'd practiced. "Try talking him into that. He's been cooped up on a medical bed for a long time. He's tired of machines and lights and wires and IVs. It's only because he's so weakened that I managed to convince him to come back to the bunker."

Graham lifted his head, wincing as if it hurt to move. "I just want to sleep. If everyone would leave me alone, I'll get better."

Temple's brow was furrowed as she looked at him. "I guess he would be more comfortable in a regular bed. Shelby or Mina can come check him out and see what he needs from there." She turned her gaze toward Kate. "There are plenty of suites available. You don't have to carry the entire burden anymore. You look exhausted."

Graham made the predetermined growling noise he'd rehearsed. "Kate stays with me, and if anyone says a word, I'll kick all your asses as soon as I'm on my feet."

When he lifted his gaze to Kate, he found she had no trouble blushing. "Seriously. Do you have to be so damn blunt?"

"Yes."

"Oh." Temple's eyes were wide, and she set a hand on her chest. "I didn't realize…"

Tushar's mouth fell open, but he said nothing. Trish grabbed her husband's arm and leaned into him. She was fighting a grin.

Mina and Shelby were from the new team. Graham had never met them. They didn't react except to glance away as if they were inadvertently intruding on a private moment.

"'Kay, I'm officially mortified. Can we please move to the suite? I'll help Graham get settled. He's been awake longer than usual. He's probably going to sleep half the afternoon." She looked toward the two women. "Maybe one of you can come check him out. I've run out of ideas. Bumping heads would help."

"Sure." The woman with the brown curls and chocolate eyes smiled at him. "Shelby Markham." She reached for his hand in his lap and gave it a squeeze. "We'll get you up and moving in no time. Your body is probably just taking longer to come around than some of the others."

Oh, the irony. "Let's hope," he growled. "I'm over this stage."

"It's only been a week," the other woman stated, setting her hand on his shoulder and smiling. "Mina Reese. Welcome back." Her long straight hair was so dark it was almost black. Her eyes were a gorgeous shade of green.

Temple clapped her hands together. "Okay, I'll let you get settled."

Trish reached behind the front desk and grabbed a keycard. She handed it to Kate. "This is for the same suite you were in a month ago. No one has touched it. Whatever you left behind should still be in there."

No one was working at the desk. Graham wasn't surprised. With a skeleton crew and no visitors, there wasn't really a need for full-time front desk help.

Trish excused herself to go back to the lab. Mina and Shelby followed her.

Tushar led the two of them to the side of the bunker that hadn't existed last time Graham was alive and kicking. As soon as they entered the room, Tushar pulled a wand out of his back pocket and without a word wandered around the suite swiping it back and forth.

Kate waited with Graham just inside the door. Was he sweeping for bugs? The idea gave Graham the chills. Since when did the bunker have bugs? He truly had stepped into a new world. The suite alone was shocking. When he'd been working in the bunker ten years ago, he'd had an apartment in town. They all had. It was quite an improvement to add the suites.

Granted, the space was nothing to get excited about. Neutral brown and khaki everything. The room they'd entered was a combination living room/kitchenette. Couch, chair, television, table for two, microwave, fridge. No oven or stove. It looked a lot like a hotel suite. A doorway to the right had to lead to a bedroom. The bathroom must be inside.

"Okay." Tushar lowered the wand. "Just being safe. Now"—his gaze landed on Graham—"I'm not buying for a second that you're sick or weakened. So, someone tell me what the hell is going on."

Graham should have known better. If anyone could see through his façade, it would be Tushar. Ryan's parents had always been the leaders of their group, and Tushar in particular was sharper than a tack. Nothing got by him.

Tushar continued, plopping down on the armchair. "Don't get me wrong. I'm sure everyone else was convinced. But I know you. And I also know you two weren't an item before you were preserved. So, start explaining."

Graham hesitated a beat while Kate squeezed his shoulder from behind. Finally, he stood and walked to the couch to sit. He reached out a hand toward Kate. She joined him without argument, lowering herself onto the sofa next to him. He took her hand and pressed it against his thigh.

"Hmmm," Tushar made the noise while rubbing his chin and glancing back and forth between the two of them.

"You're right. We weren't together. But apparently only because we were both too nervous and timid to make a move." He couldn't keep from smiling as he spoke of their awkward new relationship to the man who had essentially been his boss. "This part isn't a ruse."

"And you figured this out in less than a week?"

Kate gave a slight grin. "We figured it out in less than a day."

Graham's heart swelled. He loved when she smiled. He also loved that she felt giddy about being with him.

Tushar slowly smiled also. "Well, fuck me. That's great." He leaned forward. "Now tell me what's going on. I assume my son is involved in this. You didn't come here to convalesce." He glanced from Kate to Graham.

Graham lifted his brows. "You're quick. Long story short, the bunker is compromised."

Tushar was already nodding. "That's a given."

"We have to get every bit of data downloaded onto separate hard drives before someone deletes years of hard work and sets the medical community back two decades."

Tushar's eyes widened. "You're serious?"

Kate nodded. "Very. And we have only a few days. My thinking is that we set Graham up with a computer in here and insist everyone leave him alone to rest. He'll work his ass off to download everything while the rest of us seemingly go about our business."

Tushar didn't move for several seconds, and then he blinked. "Shit."

"Yeah," Graham agreed.

"And let me guess. No one can know about this."

"Right."

Tushar narrowed his gaze. "And why aren't we reporting this to Temple?"

Kate spoke up next. "Because someone she reports to is the mole, as far as we can tell, and until we know who it is, we don't want to say anything to her."

Tushar was nodding slowly as if he were processing everything. Finally, he stood. "Let's make it happen." He narrowed his gaze at Graham. "How the hell are you so recuperated?"

Kate chuckled as she stood and headed toward the door with Tushar. "We've all been asking the same question. Several of us would like to stab him."

Tushar set his hand on the handle and turned back around. "I'm not even going to ask who all knows about you or how you know the data is compromised, but I can't wait for this to all be over so you and everyone else can fill me in on about a thousand secrets. Starting with my own son."

"Thank you for understanding," Kate stated as she leaned in and gave him a hug. "You know we wouldn't keep anything from you if we thought there was another way, but it's safer. For now."

Tushar smiled at her, and then he left.

Graham leaned back against the sofa and sighed. "Better get me a computer lined up and send Shelby in to check on me."

Kate shoved off the door where she'd been leaning and came to sit beside him. "I hate keeping secrets from Shelby and Mina. I know in my soul no one in this building is involved."

"Regardless, someone is inadvertently feeding information to another person who *is* involved," Graham pointed out, reaching for her hand and tugging her closer. He lowered his voice when he spoke again. "I'm glad we don't have to pretend we're not an item. That would have driven me mad." He closed the distance and pulled her into his embrace.

When she tipped her head back, he kissed her lips gently.

He'd stuck to light touches for days, reminding her he wasn't changing his mind. She let him, and she'd relaxed more every day. He just needed to be patient and remind himself that Kate was used to a Graham who could barely speak to her, let alone kiss her.

With every passing day, he grew more confident what they had was precious. He would get this right. There was no other option.

She cupped his face and stared into his eyes. "I don't deserve you."

Graham grinned and tapped her nose. "Don't forget, you're way out of my league. I'm the lucky one." He would tell her that often for the rest of her life, partly because it was true and partly because he liked the way it made her smile.

She lifted his hand to her lips and kissed it before standing. "I'll get our stuff from the car and then find Shelby."

"I'll go lie in the bed and pretend I don't have the energy to lift my head."

CHAPTER 14

Graham kept a sharp ear out for the door to the suite as soon as he was left alone. He would need to every minute of the day. Tushar brought him a computer within the hour, and Graham familiarized himself with it as fast as he could, already downloading and duplicating data from the main server; but it was time consuming, and he constantly worried someone would walk into the suite.

Luckily, he had Kate running interference. No one else would pop into the suite without knocking. They had agreed that every time she came through the door, she would make as much noise as possible to warn him she was not alone.

Shelby came soon after Tushar to check on him. He was worried about her visit because she couldn't find anything wrong with him. Of course.

By the end of the first day when Shelby returned and it became obvious she was too perplexed for him to pretend he was legitimately ill, he realized he needed a new angle. He didn't have a fever or an infection or any problem with his heart or lungs.

Finally, he had a lightbulb. He spoke very little to her,

feigned exasperation, and rolled onto his side to face the wall before she left the room.

Bless Kate because she caught on immediately, and he heard her quietly speaking to Shelby outside the bedroom door, wondering aloud if perhaps he might be depressed, and it was manifesting as illness.

Shelby agreed it was certainly possible, especially if he was often as despondent as he'd been for the last fifteen minutes. She'd seen it in others from their team. He wasn't the first person to wake up and slide into a depressive state.

"Ever since we got here, he just wants me to leave him alone," Kate explained. "Seems like he wanted me to bring him back here so he could unload me."

Graham smiled as he listened. *Perfect.*

Shelby hesitated a moment and then spoke again. "You think he was telling you he didn't feel well so you would bring him back to the bunker?"

"Maybe. It's certainly an explanation. He's hardly spoken to me since we got here. He seems only interested in sleeping and staring at the wall. I'm surprised he didn't insist I have my own room if this was all some plan he had."

"Yeah. That sucks. I'm sorry."

"The worst part is that now I'm questioning whether he's as interested in me as he seemed when he woke up or if he just pretended so he could get rid of me."

Graham thought she was taking things a bit too far with that, but he gritted his teeth and vowed to demonstrate just how *uninterested* he was when he got her alone. "Uninterested, my ass," he muttered.

"Oh, Kate, surely not. Graham's just in a funk. He'll come out of it. I saw the way he looked at you this morning. Give him time. He's probably wrestling with a lot of things. I can't believe he faked being weak and sick so he could break up with you. That's so convoluted. He could have just told you he was no longer interested if that were the case. Coming back here would be hard for anyone. Maybe he got nostalgic from seeing the bunker after so many years."

Graham scrunched up his face as he listened to Shelby's possible explanations. First of all, as far as he was concerned, he'd been here last week. Second of all, he wasn't a nostalgic sort of guy. But her story was working. That was all that mattered.

Kate had Shelby believing she and Graham had been an item before preservation. It seemed Temple had bought that possibility also. He hadn't been sure if it was a good idea or not to insist on sharing this room with Kate. It could backfire on them. But there was no way in hell he was going to sleep in separate suites. Plus, he needed to keep an eye on her if she was going to put herself at risk digging around in the bunker.

They hadn't fooled Tushar into believing they'd been an item before preservation, but Temple hadn't worked directly in the lab with them, so she wouldn't have seen how painfully shy Graham had been around Kate. And certainly Shelby and Mina could fall for the idea. They hadn't even been there ten years ago.

Kate sighed loudly. "I don't want to see him checking out of life. I'm worried I should have kept him away. He just…wasn't thriving. I was scared." Even though intellectually Graham knew Kate was acting, her wobbly voice on the verge of tears tore at him.

"Stay close to him. Make sure he knows you care and you're here. He'll come around. Most of you suffered from some depression after being revived. It's not surprising. Maybe his is just worse than others."

"Let's hope so." Kate's voice trailed away, and then he heard the door open and close, the deadbolt snick into place. A moment after that Kate was back in the bedroom.

143

Graham climbed out of bed immediately and stalked toward her. He nailed her with his gaze.

She looked confused, eyes wide, backing up. "What's the matter? I thought I played into your hand rather well."

He continued to approach until her back hit the wall and then he closed the distance between them entirely, flattening his body against hers and setting his hands on the wall at the sides of her head. It was hard not to laugh. "How uninterested do I seem to you?" he asked, but he heard the lilt of humor in his voice.

Her face went from concerned and serious to light and fun in a heartbeat. She set her hands on his hips. "Do I get an Oscar?"

"You get payback. That's what you get." He lowered one hand to her neck and stroked her chin with his thumb.

"Hey, you wanted her to think you were depressed. Good thinking, by the way. I was impressed enough to award *you* an Oscar. Though I'm sure everyone is going to be confused about why you insisted on sharing this room with me if your goal was to break up with me when we got here. Sorry about that. I was flustered and started rambling. I probably went a little overboard." She tipped her face into his touch.

He loved when she did that, subconsciously wanting more from him. "The depression angle will totally work. It's perfect. It also keeps people from wanting to run a bunch of tests. But you didn't have to tell her you thought I wanted to get rid of you."

She turned her face into his palm and kissed him there. "I was ad-libbing. It worked. She bought it."

"So did I, but I didn't like it."

She shrugged, grinning. "Well, at least now everyone will think I should stay near you more often. They're all going to feel sorry for me if you dump me."

He decided to take a risk and let his hand trail down her back and around to the middle of her waist. His thumb landed precariously close to her breast, and he stroked her skin through her pale pink scrubs.

Since her eyes fluttered and a soft sigh escaped her lips, he took the opportunity to lower his lips to her neck and kiss a line to her ear. "Let me *show* you how uninterested I am," he whispered.

She leaned into him for a moment as if she'd forgotten herself, and then she righted and stiffened. "You've been awake a week, Graham..."

"Do I seem like an invalid?"

"No. That's what scares me."

He lifted his face and met her gaze, his hand at her waist, roaming to her back again. He was dead serious when he responded to that. "I never ever want you to be scared of me."

"I'm not scared of you. I'm scared...of me."

He frowned.

She swallowed. "Sex is new for both of us. I want us to both be sure so that neither of us ends up regretting it. I'm not strong enough to survive it if we fuck this up."

"You're the strongest person I know. You even agreed to come back to this bunker to sneak around without hearing the details. You're incredible. I envy you."

"I know that's how I present myself to the outside world. It's intentional. I would never want anyone to think I had a weakness. I was this way before I was preserved too. I like people to see me as outgoing, friendly, and totally put together.

"But inside, I'm not as solid. Friendships, I can handle. They grow slowly and don't usually implode. But dating is something else entirely. I don't have the ability to do casual or half-ass."

"Kate, nobody is doing casual or half-ass. It feels fast because we laid our cards on the table when I first woke up. But, we were both already interested in each other before we were preserved. You know that. I know it. There's a lot happening around us. It's intense. But when it's over, we're going to face this thing head on." His heart squeezed. He wanted her in every humanly possible way. He wanted her as a friend, a lover, and a life partner. The way he felt about her hadn't been casual before they were vitrified, and nothing about that had changed during their ten-year hibernation.

"I know. I know. But I'm still scared. Bear with me. I need more time to trust myself." She gave him a slight shove. "And you need more time to recover."

He gave her a slight half grin. "At some point you'll have to recognize you can no longer use my weakness as an excuse. Which is fine. I'm not going anywhere. Stall all you want. I want you to be sure."

"And I want *you* to be sure," she added before slipping under his arm and putting space between them. "I don't care how physically strong you are, nor do I care how sharp your mind is, you can't possibly be in a place emotionally where you can make heavy life decisions yet. So yeah, the speed at which this relationship is moving scares the hell out of me." She smoothed her hands down her waist as if she were disheveled and needed straightening.

He suspected the dishevelment was in her head, not in her scrubs.

"How is the downloading going?" she asked without meeting his gaze.

"Slow. I don't see how the hell I can save all the data in this bunker in just a few days, but I'm working as fast as possible."

"I brought another computer," she stated, rushing from the room and then returning moments later with it in hand. "I can help while people think we are sleeping."

"You can't stay up all night. People will notice."

"*You're* planning to," she pointed out as she opened the laptop and set it on the bed.

He came up behind her, pinning the front of her thighs to the mattress as he surrounded her with spread legs and his arms at her waist. "Everyone expects me to look tired. I'm supposedly depressed and sickly."

"Well, they can also easily believe I sat up long hours worrying about you."

"Which isn't far from the truth," he added.

She threaded her fingers with his and drew one of his hands to her lips to kiss his knuckles. "Your patience means everything to me."

"It's never-ending," he assured her, knowing definitively that even if she held him at arm's length for ten years, he would wait.

He hoped she wouldn't hold out that long, but he wouldn't care if that's what she needed.

He also knew they had a lot of work to do and they were treading in dangerous territory. They needed to keep their heads in the game and get this data downloaded and transferred as fast as possible. If they got caught, there was no telling what might happen. Though he still didn't understand who might unintentionally give him up to Blue Cell if they caught him.

Shelby?

Mina?

Temple?

Those were the only people besides support staff in the building who could possibly care, and it disturbed him greatly to imagine a world in which any one of those people would sabotage Project DEEP. He'd known Temple for many years. Shelby and Mina were new to the project, but they'd been vetted by Ryan.

Granted, Graham had not seen Ryan yet. He'd spoken to him on the phone in the last few days, but he hadn't met the thirty-year-old adult Ryan, the genius son of Tushar and Trish who had made it possible with the help of Dr. Damon Bardsley for all of them to be reanimated.

What Graham knew in his soul was that Ryan would never undermine his life's work and put his own parents in danger. In addition, Dade trusted Ryan. Neither Dade nor anyone else on the first team could have been involved in this disaster. It had started while they'd been preserved.

Or had it?

According to Dade, every mishap in the lab and elsewhere had been the work of either Spencer or someone from Blue Cell. If that was true, what about the broken beaker that shattered into a million pieces nearly eleven years ago to put all of them at risk in the first place? Was that incident included in the insanity? Or was it truly an isolated accident?

If Graham allowed himself to consider that for even a moment, his mind would explode. He didn't want to voice the thought out loud even to Kate. Though surely she'd pondered the same possibility: that a member of their own team had intentionally put them all at risk and succeeded in essentially killing them all for some unknown, unfathomable reason.

Kate turned around in his arms and faced him. Her eyes were filled with concern as she met his gaze. "You okay?"

He nodded and took a deep breath, realizing he'd been resting his head on her shoulder from behind for far longer than he'd intended. He needed to snap out of it and get back to work. "Yep. Do you think we'll be left alone for the rest of the night?"

"Yes. I'm pretty sure Shelby will report to the others that we're concerned about you being depressed, and then no one will think it's odd that I stay here and hold vigil over your gloomy self." She smiled.

He closed the distance and kissed her lips. He could do that all day every day. She melted into him as usual, solidifying his belief that she was on the same page as him.

When her mind was clear and she wasn't touching him, she seemed capable of convincing herself she wasn't ready to take their relationship to the next step, but when he held her in his arms at night or kissed her, she relaxed against him every time.

The battle was in her mind. The fear. The uncertainty.

Eventually she would let it go. He had to believe that. There was no other way. Time to make her smile so they could get back to work. "Did you know they found a gene for shyness?"

She rolled her eyes. Good. At least she didn't know this one yet. Finally.

"They would have found it sooner, but it was hiding behind two other genes."

CHAPTER 15

Three days later…

Kate smoothed her hand over the expanse of Graham's chest, loving the feel of his warm skin under her palm. She did this often: lay beside him, her head on his shoulder, her body snuggled close, her fingers toying with his pecs.

It was late, or early. Three in the morning. They had just moments ago decided to take a break and sleep for a few hours. It always took a while to wind down, though. The fast-paced scramble to download data was stressful. Kate trying to snoop on every conversation in the bunker was even more stressful.

"How much more time do we have?" she asked, drawing circles around his pecs with a finger. His chest was bare. Loose pajama pants were the only thing he had on. She wished for a moment that her own thin T-shirt could poof out of existence so she could be closer to him.

Graham's hand moved along her hip, smoothing over the skintight material of the black leggings she wore. The clothes were comfortable, and ordinarily she thought nothing of them while working long hours in the night. But suddenly, the tight, stretching Lycra drew attention to the ever-building need she felt when she was close to him.

She cleared her throat, shaking that thought from her mind. "Did you communicate with Spencer today?" Spencer had hacked into the computer Graham was using on the second day and made contact with him. They trusted Dade and by default Spencer and did as he said even though they'd never met him.

"Yes. He says he can hold off two more days at most. We have to get this done. It's making me so nervous that I'm not sure I can sleep at all."

Kate tipped her head back to see his face. "You have to rest, Graham. You'll get sloppy and be useless if you don't take a break."

Graham sighed. "I know, but I also keep reminding myself about the repercussions of not getting the job done in time. Lives are at stake. So many of them. Countless. There's no way to be sure what would happen if that data were all deleted with no backup in place."

"Have you spoken to Ryan?" she asked next.

He nodded. "Yes. He's been downloading the research from his facility in New Mexico to the main cloud so I can access it also. Spencer created a hidden chat room for the two of us. Without speaking to Ryan out loud, I can tell he's worried. He and his current staff are so close to a breakthrough with Myasthenia Gravis."

Kate understood the stress they all must feel in the New Mexico bunker. It was crazy to think some government conspiracy was jeopardizing not only the lives of ordinary citizens, but more specifically the lives of the two people preserved in New Mexico who had mysteriously contracted Myasthenia Gravis.

Graham continued. "I'm certain Ryan isn't sleeping at all. Nor are Emily, Zeke, or Michelle. And I still can't picture our

Emily in a relationship with Tushar and Trish's son. He was so young."

"Yeah, I know it sounds weird, but when you see them together, you'll understand. They were made for each other. I wouldn't be surprised if they were already planning a wedding and four kids." Kate smiled at Graham in the dim light coming from the bathroom nightlight.

"Sounds to me like every one of us has woken up horny and ready for a relationship. It's going to be a race to the finish line. By the end of the year, there will be ten weddings to attend."

He didn't specifically mention the two of them, but Kate knew he was thinking it. She prayed all the cards fell into place and the perfect path opened up for her and Graham. One in which she found a way to trust her instincts and relax.

She stared at him, pondering his words. There was no doubt he was a different man from the one who'd gone into the cryostat. He was still an introvert, figuring out something in his head before he talked about it. But he'd also changed. Everyone had to an extent. Waking up to find out they'd defied the odds had a tendency to make people decide to live life to the fullest. Carpe diem.

She wanted him. So badly. Especially right now, pressed against him, their entire bodies in line. But she also wanted to get this job done and get the hell out of this bunker. Until then, she couldn't fully let her guard down. No way could she drop everything and have a wild night of sex while so many people were counting on them.

In a way, this pit stop to save the world from some unknown organization called Blue Cell was also buying Graham time to get fully healthy and her time to calm her damn nerves when it came to sleeping with him.

So many concerns. It didn't matter which one she focused on. The important thing was she didn't want to sleep with him right now while their lives were at risk. She wanted them to be together for the long haul and not rush out of a sense of danger. She couldn't take the chance that he might walk away when things went back to normal. Her feelings were so strong for him, they scared her.

He gave her a squeeze. "You slid into your head again."

She lifted her cheek and kissed his neck, nuzzling against his warm skin and inhaling his scent. "Sorry."

"We're going to be okay, you know. You and I and everyone else."

"I hope so." She jerked her thoughts back to the work Ryan was doing, the discussion they'd been having before jumping to the anticipation of a rash of weddings. Getting married wasn't something she could begin to ponder. Disease eradication, though, she could dive into any day. "Do you think it's possible we were all intentionally infected with AP12, and likewise that the two preserved in New Mexico were also intentionally infected with Myasthenia Gravis?"

Graham sighed. "I have to admit the thought has crossed my mind, but I can't come up with any reason why."

"Maybe some faction of the US government doesn't want Project DEEP to succeed. Or perhaps some enemy slipped into the bunker to sabotage us."

"But why?" he asked. "Who the hell wouldn't want to cure disease and prevent the spread?"

"Some radical survival-of-the-fittest supremacists or something, I guess." She didn't have answers, just questions.

"I'm sure there are plenty of religious zealots out there who think we're playing God every time we even immunize people. Their voices have been loud and clear for decades. A substantial number among us thinks nature should take its course and we should leave it up to God to decide who should die and when it's their time.

"However, what I can't figure out is how the fuck some of those people infiltrated our government. And, if this thing is a big as it seems, the implication would be that whoever is manipulating us has been doing so for over a decade. That part makes no sense. How are they getting away with it? Why is there no system of checks and balances stepping in to help us?"

Kate closed her eyes and held on to Graham a little tighter. She didn't have answers to any of his questions, and he wouldn't expect them.

When he ran his hand up and down her back and then settled it on her hip, his fingers on her ass, her breath hitched. Conflicting emotions took over. She wanted him to stop before she got carried away, rose to straddle him, and threw caution to the wind. She also willed him to continue, reach lower, do something to ease the growing ache that never received gratification.

She could feel the stirring need to go there every time he touched her, held her, kissed her. Hell, a tight ball of need built in her belly even when she watched him from across a room. Honestly, it had existed for three years.

She realized rationally that part of her was preventing herself from having a normal life, a normal relationship, normal sexual experiences, all because she was afraid to find out the fairy tale in her head couldn't exist. Some crazy notion of having one true love who would have the power to melt her.

Rationally, she knew that spark existed with Graham even when she was alone thinking about him. She would face all of her concerns. After she and Graham got the hell out of the bunker and life was a little more normal.

The bunker gave her the creeps. This facility had been her life ten years ago. Ten years that seemed like three months since that was how long she'd been awake. The idea that the place was no longer safe stole a piece of her soul.

She assumed even though her mind was racing, Graham had fallen into much-needed sleep, but suddenly his hand moved again, trailing up her back and down again to cup her butt.

Every nerve in her body came alive again. "Sleep," he whispered. "I can't rest while your mind is running all over the room."

She smiled. "How do you know what's in my head?"

"Because I know you. I can feel it in the tension that holds your spine rigid. I'll know when you've finally fallen asleep when your fingers are no longer gripping my chest, your breathing evens out, and your face nuzzles fully into my neck. Until then, I wait."

Damn, his words were powerful. He had a way of making her feel so very loved, even in the most dire situations. She wanted to be closer to him, so she lifted her leg and wiggled it between his. Bold.

He gave her ass cheek a squeeze. Maybe he intended it to be playful or some sort of rebuke for not letting her mind shut down, but the pressure inadvertently pressed her clit against his thigh. A soft moan escaped before she realized it had come from her.

His grip froze. His erection stiffened against her thigh.

She took a deep breath, not moving an inch while her body continued to demand more.

Suddenly, his hand slid slowly from her butt to the back of her thigh, hitching her leg higher.

Wetness pooled between her legs. She'd never been so aware of her sex before in her life. With her thighs spread open like this, she felt exposed. Needy.

She lifted her head, gazed into his eyes, and then lowered her face to kiss him. Her hand smoothed up his chest until she was cupping his face. Her heart raced as she tipped her head to one side and deepened the kiss.

She'd never been this forward, but it felt good, and he responded by groaning into her mouth while his fingers slid higher up her thigh until she could swear the tips were inches from her sex. She wanted more. Now. And she thrust her tongue into his mouth, mimicking what she craved between her other lips.

When his hand slid back up to her butt cheek, she almost moaned out a protest, but then his fingers slowly eased down the center of her bottom, the tips growing increasingly closer to the one spot demanding contact.

Through her tight leggings and panties, he finally touched her, his fingers finding her wet heat, and then he reached farther until he pressed them against her clit.

She gasped, breaking the kiss. Her vision swam, so she closed her eyes, but she kept her lips hovering over his.

He nibbled on her bottom lip as he dragged his middle finger over her swollen, sensitive clit.

The breath whooshed from her lungs, and he reached with his other hand to thread his fingers in her hair. He took her lips again, lifting his mouth to capture hers while pressing against her neck at the same time.

The kiss switched from her control to his as his fingers stroked her again. And then again. Suddenly, he was devouring her mouth while he pressed his palm hard against her channel and flicked his finger rapidly over her swollen nub.

Oh my God. The pressure built. The need. The intensity.

She lost the ability to return the kiss, her brain cells focused on one spot. And then she was flying. With no warning, she had her first orgasm against a man's hand. Her entire sex clenched over and over, while her body shook from the aftershocks.

She gasped against his lips, suddenly feeling self-conscious as she came back to reality. What the hell had she just done? She wasn't sorry, but she was stunned. And his erection was still pressing against her thigh.

Slightly embarrassed and chagrined, she blinked at him, easing her hand down to his chest. Her goal was to wrap her fingers around his length, but she didn't get that far before he

156

removed his hand from between her legs and clasped her fingers in his, pressing them against his chest.

His eyes were closed, and he took several breaths before he met her gaze. "Damn, that was hot."

Her heated face flushed further. "Let me touch you," she whispered, tugging on her hand.

He shook his head. "Not tonight. I'm barely holding on to a thread of control here."

"Who says you have to?" she asked, trying to sound coy.

"I say so." He lifted her fingers to his lips and kissed her knuckles. "Thank you for giving me that gift. I'll never forget this moment as long as I live. But I don't have the willpower to let you reciprocate. Not tonight."

She nodded slowly, set her head back on his shoulder, and eased her knee from between his thighs. "Seems a little unfair," she murmured, feeling even more embarrassed. She'd come so hard, exposing a piece of herself to him.

"Not unfair at all. We're not keeping score here. That was gorgeous." He stroked her hand with his thumb as he pressed her palm against his chest again. "Now, you really have to go to sleep, or neither of us is going to be on our game in a few hours."

She twisted her head to kiss his neck, inhaling the familiar scent of him. "You and your *game*," she teased. "Hey, I've got a joke for you."

He chuckled. "Go for it."

"What's a tornado's favorite game?"

"Twister."

"Darn. Thought I might have you."

"Not a chance. You can't compete with the nerdy joke master."

She smiled as she closed her eyes, took several long deep breaths, and blew them out slowly. It took a while, but she finally succumbed to sleep.

~

Kate jerked awake. She bolted to sitting, glancing around to look for Graham who was no longer pressed against her body.

"I'm right here," he soothed, inches away from her side, his hand reaching out to grab hers. "Take a breath."

She blew one out instead, already having sucked in a deep breath the second she woke up. "What time is it?"

"Eight. You slept four hours."

"How long did *you* sleep?" she asked as she pushed more fully to sitting and took in the fact that he was wearing a T-shirt and shorts, the laptop on his thighs, his back against the headboard. His fingers were already racing across the keys once again.

"Long enough. I'm refreshed. Trying to get as much of this downloaded as possible before Shelby makes an appearance to assess my depression, and then I'm sure we'll be seeing Temple soon after."

Kate arranged her pillow at the headboard and pushed herself back to sit next to Graham. She forced herself to focus on the urgent task at hand instead of the way he'd made her come a few hours ago. "How do you imagine this going down? You think we're going to pretend you're miraculously feeling better and walk right out of here?"

"Maybe. I haven't worked that out in my head yet. Let's take this one step at a time. I'd like to have all this data downloaded in about twenty-four more hours. If I work hard and don't have too many interruptions, I might be able to get it done early enough that we can pack it up and remove it sometime tomorrow."

"'Kay. Guess I'll take a shower and then venture out and see if I can overhear anything suspicious, and grab some breakfast for us from the cafeteria."

"Sounds good. I'm starving. I need you to find another hard

drive too. The two you brought are almost full. I'm hoping I can fit everything on one more."

"I'll see what I can do." She started to crawl away from him to head for the bathroom, but he reached out with one hand and grabbed her forearm, pulling her back until she landed across his chest. He set the computer on the nightstand and rolled the two of them so fast she lost her breath, blinking at him above her.

With one hand on her waist and the other woven into the hair at her temple, he had her full attention. "We're going to get out of this mess by tomorrow afternoon at the latest, and then we're going straight to a hotel where we can relax and be alone. And then we're going to explore this thing between us." He lifted a brow suggestively.

She stopped breathing and nodded.

She couldn't disagree with him because she knew he was right. A slow fire had been burning between them until they crossed into new territory during the night. She wanted to be with him more fully. His feelings for her were all over his face every time she looked.

What was she waiting for? She didn't need him to get on a knee and proclaim his undying love. Asking for more than he was already giving her was absurd. Keeping herself at arm's length from him at this point had nothing to do with needing to be certain.

She *was* certain. And he couldn't do more than he'd already done every day to prove he was too. So the only thing holding her back was her own reluctance to move their relationship to another level, a reluctance based on fear. Once they got out of this damn bunker, they would have more time to explore their attraction without the constant sense of urgency.

But no one had the kind of guarantees in life she wanted. She, above nearly everyone alive, should know life was fragile. Hesitating out of some irrational concern that a life with

Graham wouldn't be perfect was nonsensical. Nobody's life was perfect.

But this thing between them was damn close. It didn't have any holes she could see. At this point, she needed to take a deep breath and let him all the way in. Literally and figuratively. Take a risk. Her heart was his already anyway.

She lifted her face to make eye contact with him and saw exactly what she'd always dreamed of in his eyes. He cared about her deeply. Deep enough to respect her wishes while she worked through her doubts.

It was time to stop the charade.

The first opportunity they got, they were going to explore this thing burning between them and see where it went. For better or worse, she would be all in. "Promise?" she whispered.

His smile was fast and huge. And then his lips landed on hers and he kissed the daylight out of her, angling his head to one side, holding her where he wanted her, and delving his tongue between her lips until she couldn't think of anything except eliminating the clothing between them and making his vision a reality. "Promise," he responded when he finally pulled back. His voice was husky with lust. "Go take your shower before I lose my resolve."

Her legs were shaking as she padded into the bathroom. She could feel his gaze on her the entire time. When she shut the door and leaned against it, she finally managed to draw in a breath. Her nipples were standing at attention under her tank top, and her sex was throbbing with desire.

Until just hours ago, Graham had never touched either of those parts of her body. Probably intentionally. His thumbs had come close to grazing the underside of her breasts a few times, but he'd never covered one with his palm and caressed it the way she longed for. He'd never let his hand trail down between her legs to cup her sex either. Now that he had, she craved more with an intensity that was palpable.

Whatever her doubts were about their future didn't matter, because she knew these feelings trumped every one of them. She wouldn't be able to deny herself the chance to find out what could be between them. If things went south and they didn't make it together in the long run, at least she'd never have to look back and wonder what could have been.

It was time to stop hedging and go for it.

And she would.

Tomorrow.

Every inch of her skin tingled with excitement.

CHAPTER 16

Dade paced the entire length of the small office he occupied in the basement of the enormous country house he was using as a home base in southwest Montana. The place was large, but it was jammed with his team members. Every day more of them trickled in from wherever they'd been hiding.

He'd made contact with each member of the original team and Ryan's team. With the exception of those who were living in the bunker in Colorado and those who were with Ryan at the second bunker in New Mexico, everyone was working their way toward Montana.

Chaos reigned as everyone did their part to help by either scouring the internet for information or keeping the house running.

Thank God for SURVIVE. The underground group had provided this home set far away from the main road on several acres of ranchland. It was a godsend. Without the help they were receiving from SURVIVE, Dade wasn't sure where everyone would be. The looks on everyone's faces when they found out he was alive were priceless.

Currently, he was holding his phone waiting for Ryan to pick up. "Comeoncomeoncomeon..."

"Hello," Ryan finally answered, sounding winded. "Sorry. I didn't want to answer in front of anyone."

"Have you made contact with Graham today?" Dade asked, not bothering with formalities. The clock was ticking.

"No. But he's been in communication with Spencer. He knows he only has hours to finish."

Dade rubbed his temples with the fingers of one hand spread across his forehead. "I hope he and Kate have a plan. I'm concerned."

"I know. Trust me, I'm pacing my office."

Dade glanced around and stopped walking. "You and me both, then."

"You at least got to see Graham firsthand. Is it true he's recovered at an extraordinary speed, or is he pushing himself too hard?"

"Oh, it's true. I wouldn't have believed it if I hadn't seen him. He had far more stamina than I had at one week. And that was before I even knew I technically wasn't going to live. I was still tired and far too weak to walk. Graham left us all in the dust."

"If anyone could do it, it would be Graham. I trust him and Kate to get the job done and get the hell out of there. They know the stakes."

"I hope you're right." Dade turned around as the door to his office opened. Blair stepped inside, closing it behind her. "Please let me know if you hear anything."

"I will. You do the same."

The line went dead, and Dade set the phone on his desk and hauled Blair into his arms, nestling his face in the thick hair at her neck. *Please, God, let this work out.*

Kate stood in the bedroom, running both hands through her hair while Graham stuffed everything in a backpack. "I don't know how we're going to get out of here."

Graham sat on the edge of the bed and reached for his shoes. "Tell me what happened with Temple."

"I told her I thought you would benefit from some fresh air and better scenery. That it might help you snap out of your funk. I suggested I take a car and we go for a drive. She was adamantly opposed to the idea. She doesn't think it's safe for us to leave the bunker. She suggested we go for a walk around the perimeter instead."

"Shit." Graham glanced at the clock. "We need to come up with something. I want to get these hard drives out of here, but more than that I'm seriously concerned about what's going to happen when everyone on staff realizes the mainframe has been compromised and someone has deleted all the data. I don't want to be inside when that happens. We could really be trapped here then."

"I agree." Her hands were shaking, and she rubbed them together. "How long do you think we have before they force Spencer to delete the mainframe?"

"Not sure. An hour maybe. Tops."

Kate fidgeted. "I didn't expect Temple to balk at my plan."

Graham rubbed his temples and pushed to standing. "Maybe we should pull the fire alarm."

Kate pursed her lips, thinking. "That could work. It would get everyone out of the building, but it won't get us off the government grounds. We'll never be able to walk out the front gate."

"Perhaps in the mayhem, we can get the guards to let us out. Lie our way out. Tell them we're going to get more help or something." He grabbed the backpack and tugged it onto his shoulder, and then he approached her, cupped her face, and met her gaze. "We can do this."

"This is the craziest thing we've done yet. People are going to be suspicious as soon as you walk out of this room on foot. You're going to attract attention."

"I'll go out the side door on the south end of the building past the living suites. You need to go pull the alarm, then I want you to head out the front door with everyone else."

"Someone will be able to see me pulling the alarm on the security camera."

"Eventually, but by the time they analyze the video, it'll be too late. We'll be gone." He slid his hand to the back of her neck and squeezed. When his lips touched hers, she calmed marginally. "We can do this because we have no other choice."

"Where will I meet you?"

"Come around to the side after you leave the building. I'll meet you there. You should beat me if you move fast enough."

She nodded slightly as he spoke. "'Kay," she breathed.

A few seconds passed while she stared into his green eyes. "We're out of time, babe," he pointed out, and then he released her. "Meet you outside."

She backed up, taking a deep breath, but before she could turn around, alarms started blaring. She jerked to a stop, eyes wide. "What the hell?" she mouthed over the deafening sound.

"Fuck," he mouthed in return.

Someone pounded on the door to the suite.

They stared at each other for several seconds. Kate's heart was racing.

Graham lowered to sit on the bed, looking defeated. He pinched both temples with the fingers of one hand and nodded toward the door, the only way he could communicate that she was going to need to answer it.

She spun around and rushed to the door, looking through the peephole first. Two security guards she didn't know stood outside. She opened the door. "What's going on?" she shouted over the roar of the alarm.

"You need to come with me." The taller bald man reached for her arm and pulled her into the hallway. The second man, shorter, stockier, with dark hair went into the suite.

"Is there a fire or something?" Kate shouted.

The blood drained from her face when she saw the guard's expression. There was definitely no fire. He was nearly dragging her down the hallway. The alarm was sounding because of them. Because of what Kate and Graham had done. She could feel it in her bones. They'd been caught.

When people rushed past her, heading toward the entrance, Kate began to panic. The man was holding her arm too tight. He knew something. Who the fuck was he? When she glanced at him, his expression was serious, brows furrowed, lips pursed. He didn't care a bit that the alarm was blaring.

He also wasn't leading her out of the building. He was heading toward the medical wing and the hallway with the lab. What would he do with her?

She had to get away from him. She knew in her gut she would be doomed if she let him take her wherever he intended. Graham was also in serious trouble.

Two people from the cafeteria rushed past her. And then Shelby came out of the lab. Her gaze was wide as she spotted Kate and then glanced at the tall, bald man. "Is the alarm for real? I assumed it was an accident."

The man scowled at Shelby. "Get out of the building, you stupid fool."

Shelby's eyes widened further. "Where are you going?" she shouted as the bald man attempted to drag Kate past Shelby, heading deeper into the bunker in direct opposition of his advice to Shelby.

Shelby stepped in front of Kate, blocking her from passing.

Kate took the opportunity to jerk free of the guard while he was struggling to maintain his grip. She needed to get out of the building.

The guard shouted at her, but she ignored him and Shelby as she turned around and ran toward the front door.

Even though the medical staff was operating on a skeleton crew after the relocation of most of the Project DEEP team, there were still dozens of other personnel. Guards, kitchen help, cleaning, and front desk staff.

The guards were the people Kate should have been paying closer attention to for the last several days. Even though Tushar had swept their suite looking for potential bugs, he could have missed something. Or perhaps Spencer had done this. Was it possible he wasn't trustworthy after all? No, that made no sense. If his end goal had been to delete all the data, why go to all the trouble helping Graham and Kate download it first? Unless his plan had been to trap Kate and Graham all along.

As soon as Kate burst through the front doors into the afternoon sun, she glanced around, wondering what the hell to do next. She decided to rush toward the side of the building where she and Graham had intended to meet. Perhaps he would have somehow managed to get to that exit.

People were milling around outside, speculating about what the alarm was about. Kate noticed Mina talking to Trish, but she turned away quickly and raced for the south entrance.

As she turned the corner, nearly jogging, she ran straight into Temple Levenson, who grabbed her biceps with both hands as if to stop her or steady her. "Where are you going?" Temple asked.

"I didn't see Graham out front. I thought he might have made it out the side door."

Temple's brow was furrowed. "He's not going to exit from any door."

Kate swallowed the bile that rose in her throat. "What do you mean? I need to go back in and help him."

"It would seem you've helped him enough."

"Pardon?" They were both shouting over the continuous

loud blare of the alarm that was still sounding. Kate was going to have to think fast on her feet.

Temple gave her a shake. "I don't know what you two have been doing, but security is questioning Graham now. I thought they were questioning you too."

Kate tried to breathe. This was not good. "Temple, I have to get back in there."

"Not a chance. If you want to be useful, you can start by telling me what the hell you've been doing and who you're working for."

How much did Temple know? How did she find out? *And whose side is she on?*

Kate searched her boss's face. She'd known her for three years. Had worked for her closely all of that time. It was so hard for her to imagine Temple undermining the work being done by the team, but she couldn't risk the very real possibility. She was going to have to ad-lib. "What has he done to cause such suspicion?" Kate decided it might be best if she answered questions with questions for now.

"We know he has a computer. We also know he's been lying about the state of his health. So, you can stop the charade now and tell me what's going on, or I can call the guards, tell them I've found you, and turn you over to the government."

This was way past bad. It was awful. Did they have surveillance in the suite? That didn't make much sense since they would have been caught days ago if that were the case.

Her thoughts returned to the possibility of Spencer. Had he set them up? All the blood drained from her face at the thought that the hacker had something to do with this.

Temple released Kate's arm with one hand and reached behind toward her back pocket to pull out a phone.

"No," Kate shouted. "Temple, you need to listen to me."

Temple lifted one brow. "Start talking. I'll give you about thirty seconds." She palmed the phone, but didn't put it away.

Kate was out of options. She had nothing to lose. If Temple was in on the ruse to undermine the team, it no longer mattered if Kate called her out on it. "Graham is not the bad guy here. He's been trying to help. We need to get to him." *We need to get the hard drives out of the building.* Though Kate imagined it was probably already too late for that.

"If Graham has done nothing wrong, then security will figure that out."

"Who is holding him? What does security have to do with anything?" Something was missing here.

"Two people from the government are here. They arrived this morning when they got a tip that Graham was logging into the system and snooping around. They found out he's been stealing data."

Fuck. Goddammit. Kate's mind raced around, trying to come up with the possibilities. Spencer was now her top pick. Had he sold them out? Had he been lying to Dade and Ryan and all of them the entire time? But why would he let them almost escape before sounding the alarm. He could have had them captured at any time.

It suddenly seemed less likely Temple was involved. She was as confused as Kate, plus she was convinced Kate and Graham were the moles.

"I see this doesn't surprise you, which tells me I need to turn you in also." Temple lifted her phone again.

Kate reached out and swiped it out of her hand. It went flying across the grass. Kate wasn't a violent person, nor had she ever done anything this bold in her life. Especially not to her superior. But desperate times called for desperate measures.

Temple's eyes flew open wider. She glanced at the phone and then at the grip she had on Kate's arm, undoubtedly trying to decide if she should release Kate to retrieve the phone. Too bad it hadn't landed on concrete and busted in half.

Kate turned the tables. She needed to shake sense into

Temple. If Temple was on the right side of things, Kate would force her to see reason. If not…well, Kate didn't know what the hell she might do if Temple proved to have fooled everyone for three decades.

Kate shook herself free from Temple's grasp—partly to prove she could and partly to gain the upper hand. She grabbed Temple's elbows with both hands and shook her slightly. "You need to listen to me. I don't know what the hell is going on, and I swear to God if I find out you're involved, so many people will hunt you down that no corner of the universe will be far enough for you to hide."

Temple's eyes widened again. "Me? What the hell are you suggesting?"

"You heard me. Someone is undermining the entire project. You know that. So, yes, Graham and I snuck in here under false pretenses in attempt to salvage what we could. No, we didn't tell you or anyone else because frankly we don't know who to trust. Someone listens in on you or else they use information you provide them. You're compromised, Temple.

"And, I've got to tell you, you're at the top of nearly everyone's list as the guilty party. So, it's time for you to shut up and listen. If you're the one who undermined three decades of work, then may God have mercy on your soul. But if not, then stop talking and hear me out."

Temple's mouth fell open. "I am most certainly not involved. Right now, you are, though. And so is Graham, and it doesn't matter what you say or do, the two men inside the bunker who are questioning Graham will get to the bottom of his involvement."

Kate was scared out of her mind about what might happen to Graham if the two men in question worked for Blue Cell and wanted to shut him up. Permanently. Not to mention the fact that they would come after Kate next.

"Who the hell are these two men, Temple? Talk fast. We don't have much time."

"How should I know? They showed up, briefed me, and set off the alarm."

"Dammit. What did they say?"

"That's none of your business," Temple shouted. The roar of the alarm was still blaring annoyingly, making them shout louder to be heard anyway.

"Temple, this is serious. You have to trust me."

"Like you trusted *me*?" she screamed.

"You're in charge of this bunker. You have been for three decades. For more than ten years someone has been undermining the work you direct. Forgive me if I'm not inclined to give you a free pass while you disperse two teams of scientists all over the Midwest, causing years of work to halt and science to stall out."

Temple gasped. "I've been doing everything in my power to protect all of you."

"Why? Why do you think you're protecting everyone by stopping the progress of scientific development and sending everyone away to hide for over a month?"

She pursed her lips and inhaled through her nose, and then she spoke again. "Just because your team has been dispersed doesn't mean we've halted progress. Project DEEP continues to work on diseases. None of you could be doing that, even if you wanted. You're too far behind on the latest scientific developments. Nothing is holding back science. I'm doing everything in my power to keep the bunker safe and protect all of you. I've guarded that data with my life. You each obviously have targets on your backs. My job is to protect my people and this bunker."

"I sincerely hope that's the case. I hope to God you have innocently been following the direction of your superiors, blindly though it seems. Even if you are innocent in this mess, I will always question why you would follow the directions of your superiors when time after time it would seem you should have questioned them."

"You're talking about jeopardizing my career for a hunch that you all have that no one bothered to tell me about."

"Your *career*? Is that all you care about? Retirement?" Kate was screaming.

She noticed people had gathered behind her at a distance, but someone pushed through the crowd to approach. Tushar.

It probably killed her, but Trish stayed behind, holding everyone else back as her husband jogged toward Temple and Kate. "What's going on?" he asked as soon as he reached them.

Kate caught him up without looking his direction, her gaze still pinned on Temple. "Two government officials are inside holding Graham. I don't trust them, and I'm trying to shake some sense into Temple to get me back inside." Kate knew Temple had access to enter the building. Kate did not. In fact, it wasn't as simple as a key. Temple would need to use her thumbprint to get the door opened.

"Let's calm down and discuss this rationally," Tushar implored.

Kate jerked her gaze to him. "You think we have time to calm down here? Graham is probably in serious trouble as we speak. Every second is another one closer to his death. I have no doubt those motherfuckers will shoot him in the head and then make up a story about him going postal and trying to kill them."

"She's right," Tushar said, his attention directed at Temple.

Temple jerked. "You too? What the hell is wrong with you people?"

"The entire project is compromised, Temple, and you know it," Kate repeated. "Someone doesn't want us alive. Someone doesn't want us researching disease. That someone might be above you, but whoever it is, they've been using you as a puppet for years."

Tushar stared at Temple, probably hoping she would see reason.

Temple's shoulders fell. "What has Graham been doing? Are you sure he isn't the mole?" she asked, her voice calmer.

Kate said a silent prayer that she could get Temple to see reason fast. "He's been downloading all of the data and copying it to hard drives."

"Why? It's backed up. In triplicate. Nothing can ever happen to the data in any of the bunkers. Is he trying to steal it?"

"Fuck no. He was trying to *save* it. And it's no longer backed up anywhere. Surely you're aware of that. Someone wiped it all out about thirty minutes ago."

"How the hell could you know that?"

"She's right," Tushar added. "I saw it myself moments before the alarm went off."

Temple shuddered. "That's impossible."

"It's true," he added.

"Did you know about this? About Graham?"

Tushar nodded. "I gave him the computer and the hard drives."

"Which we need to retrieve before they're destroyed. Three decades of scientific research, Temple. Your entire legacy. It's on three hard drives inside this bunker where two men with bad intentions are hoping to destroy it."

Temple hesitated. "It's very hard to imagine the world you two are painting."

"You know we're right," Tushar said. "And you also know we're running out of time. Open the door, Temple."

She stared at him for a moment and then nodded. Seconds later she turned around and ran toward the side entrance.

Kate followed. As did Tushar.

Temple typed in a code on the door and then set her thumb on the pad. A moment later, the door snicked, indicating it was unlocked. She pulled it open and then reached toward her back and grabbed a weapon, which she handed to Tushar. "You better be right. My job is on the line. As is yours."

Tushar grabbed the gun and stepped inside. Kate followed him. She could hear Trish screaming behind them and knew Tushar's wife would be seriously pissed when they next saw her, but Tushar didn't stop.

Temple grabbed Kate's arm and tugged her back. "You guard the door. I'll go with Tushar."

Kate shook her head. "Not a chance in hell." It was Graham they were after. No way was Kate going to stay back and wait. Temple was out of her mind.

Temple took a deep breath and nodded. "Be careful." She held the door open while Kate rushed to catch up with Tushar.

The alarm was so much louder inside the bunker, and Kate cringed, hating the sound. Suddenly the shrill noise stopped.

"Where was he when you last saw him?" Tushar asked as he reached under his shirt and pulled out a second weapon from a holster strapped across his chest. He set Temple's in Kate's hand. Naturally. No way would Tushar have fled the building unprepared.

Kate kept her voice low. "Our suite. One man grabbed me. The other went inside. I shook free and ran from the building. I assume that man returned to help the first. I've never seen either of them before. I thought they were with the bunker's own security when I first saw them. Didn't occur to me they had come from outside."

"Did Graham get everything downloaded before it was erased?" He shot her a glance after peeking around the corner to the next hallway. The inside of the bunker was totally silent. No sign of anyone.

"Yes. We were just about to get out of here when the alarm went off."

Tushar nodded and rounded the corner, gun raised. "When was the last time you shot a weapon?"

"Before." She didn't need to add to that. He would understand.

"Then let me lead. I got a lot of practice while we were in Montana."

Tushar and his wife had been the leaders of their team. They had been with Project DEEP for twenty years when they succumbed to AP12 and had to be preserved. Kate would never forgive herself if anything happened to him. He was only forty-five. He'd just been reunited with his wife and son. He didn't deserve this. He hadn't asked for it.

She grabbed his arm. "No." It wasn't that she believed her life was more expendable than his, but in a way it was. She didn't have a husband. Kids. She had been too pigheaded to let any of those things happen for her. If she didn't make it through this, at least she wouldn't be leaving behind people who counted on her. Her parents and sister would be devastated all over again, but they weren't the same as a spouse or kids.

Holding the weapon in one hand, she reached into her pocket to pull out her keycard, praying she would find Graham and the two assholes in the suite. If not, she and Tushar would then need to scour the building.

In a quick motion, she swept the keycard over the pad above the handle and opened the door. Silence. Shit. She spun around and shook her head.

"Dammit," Tushar muttered. He turned around, and she followed him away from the living quarters. If they weren't in the suite, the two men had most likely taken Graham to the medical end of the building. That's where they'd been heading with Kate.

Kate closed her eyes when they reached the hallway that led to Temple's office and a few others. She heard voices. Good sign.

Tushar continued forward even though Kate wished he would trade places with her. He eased along the wall, holding his weapon at the ready. When he reached the first door, he glanced at Kate and nodded across the hall. They couldn't be sure where the voices were coming from yet. Left or right?

They waited. Kate held her breath, offering a silent prayer to whoever might be willing to help them.

Something crashed.

She jumped in her spot, itching to rush forward. Tushar reached out and grabbed her arm, stopping her.

Someone screamed. Graham?

Then she smelled smoke. She yanked free of Tushar and ran down the hallway toward the smoke. Gun raised, she stepped into the doorway of the conference room. The two men from earlier had their backs to her. They were standing over a huge metal trash can dousing it with lighter fluid. She knew in an instant they had burned the hard drives.

Graham was tied to a chair, shouting. Neither man paid any attention to him, though Graham was bouncing the chair forward as if he could stop the madness.

Kate knew the moment Tushar was next to her. He lifted his gun and took a shot. The first man's knees buckled slightly as he grabbed his thigh.

Kate took the second shot, aiming for the other man's leg and hitting her mark, even though she hadn't shot a weapon since being reanimated. Both men spun around, guns drawn.

Kate jumped out of the doorway as shots were fired. She searched for Tushar, but he hadn't been as fast. He'd gone down.

Panic swallowed her whole, causing her to reach around the corner without regard for her own safety. If Graham hadn't been behind the men, she would have fired off the entire chamber and been done, but she couldn't take that risk, so instead, she glanced around the doorframe, exposing her head.

Before she could do anything else, several more rounds went off inside the room. People screamed. She couldn't tell who, but she didn't waste another moment. She spun fully into the doorway.

The two men who'd been holding Graham were on the ground now. Tushar was in front of them, gun lifted as he shifted it back and forth between them. Graham was still sitting in the chair, eyes wide. "Tushar's been hit. Get help, babe."

"I'm fine," Tushar said from the ground. "Flesh wound. Get Graham untied."

Kate kneeled in front of Tushar first, ignoring his command and checking him out. He had dropped the gun and was holding his left arm with his right hand. Blood was oozing between his fingers.

Kate peeled his hand back and winced. "More than a flesh wound." She grabbed the base of his shirt and yanked it over his head, and then she wrapped the dark blue scrubs around the wound and tied it off. "Hold it tight with your hands."

She jumped up and rushed toward Graham. His gaze was on the fire. "Put the fire out first," he exclaimed.

She spun around, grabbed the fire extinguisher from the wall, and doused the already dwindling flames. Dropping the canister, she rounded Graham and worked the tight knots at the back of the chair.

Tears stung her eyes from the smoke.

Someone appeared in the doorway, and Kate jerked her attention that direction to find Trish behind them.

"Oh my God," Trish exclaimed, kneeling at her husband's side. She was shaking, her eyes wild.

"I'm fine," he reassured her.

Trish took a look at her husband's arm and then frantically touched him everywhere as if to ensure herself he hadn't been hit anywhere else. "I can't believe you did this. You could have been killed." She batted his hand away and applied pressure to the wound herself.

Tushar set his hand on her forearm. "Trish," his voice dropped lower, "I'm okay."

She shook her head, her face flushed and tears streaming down her cheeks. "Don't try to placate me. I'm pissed. You ran into a dangerous situation without thinking. Of me. Of us. You scared the hell out of me. You could have been killed. I nearly died when I heard the shots."

Tushar didn't try to argue with Trish, but he did pull her head into the crook of his neck. He gripped her tightly, holding her close, mouthing something Kate couldn't hear into her ear.

Trish was still breathing heavily, but she nodded.

Kate returned her attention to the ropes. Finally, she managed to free Graham, whose gaze was locked on the trashcan.

Tushar stood, staring at the same spot.

No one said a word. They didn't need to. The damage was obvious.

Kate knew better, but it didn't matter at the moment.

What mattered was two men had infiltrated the space that should have been the safest place on earth and tried to kill her man. What mattered was that the bunker where she'd spent three years of her life didn't feel safe.

What mattered was that nothing in her life felt safe anymore. She could run, hide, lie, change her name, color her hair, leave the country, or even pretend to be homeless and sleep under a bridge. Whoever was trying to take down DEEP, and everyone involved, would find her. The only way she could be safe again would be to leave DEEP, leave the project. Leave town. Leave this life. The message was received loud and clear: Anyone meddling with this project would be hunted.

None of them were safe, and she was tired. She wanted out. She wanted to go home, see her parents again, meet her niece, sleep, live life. She couldn't do this for much longer. Living on the run was not in her blood.

Tushar kneeled to check the pulse of both dead men. "Who are they?" he asked.

"No idea," Graham responded as he shook the ropes free, pushed off the chair, and grabbed Kate, hauling her into his arms and dipping his face into her hair. When he seemed satisfied that she was okay, he lifted his gaze to everyone else, but he didn't release her. He probably had no idea he was holding her so tight it hurt.

"What did they say?" Kate asked him, tipping her head back to look up at him. She was numb. She wanted to get out of this bunker. This city. This state. Her ears were ringing from the alarm and the gunfire.

Her energy was zapped.

"Not a lot. They came here to do a job, and they did it." He shifted his gaze to Temple as she appeared in the doorway.

Temple's face was red with some emotion Kate couldn't read. Fear? Shame? Remorse? Guilt? She dropped her gaze to the floor, her shoulders drooping. "I swear I had no idea."

"Why did you let them inside?" Graham shouted. "Why would you let two strangers question us? If Tushar and Kate hadn't entered when they did, I would be dead."

Temple ran a hand over her face. "They convinced me *you* were the mole. They even had evidence to prove you'd snuck in here and logged into the system. They showed me how many hours you've spent downloading the data." Her voice rose. "They convinced me you had stolen the data and then deleted it from the system." She stood taller. "Not to mention the fact that all of that is true."

Graham flinched. His voice rose again. "*To save it!* Not to destroy it. I put it on those hard drives to save it. And I'm not the one who deleted it. I've been working day and night to save it before it would be deleted."

Temple glanced at the trash can and cringed. Her hand went

to her forehead again, rubbing back and forth. "If you're not the one who deleted the data, who is?"

"How the hell should I know?" Graham asked. He was still holding Kate, his body shaking.

"How did you know someone was going to delete it?" Temple asked.

"Inside tip," was all Graham gave her.

Temple rolled her head back to stare at the ceiling, hands on her hips. "I'm the one in charge here, Graham. Not you. If you don't give me all the information, how the hell am I supposed to help? Are you telling me that you and other members of your team have been hiding things from me?"

Tushar stepped forward, holding his shirt over his arm still. So far, he hadn't gotten involved. Now he looked fit to kill. "Temple, you're compromised. You might not like to admit that, but it's true. Information that comes to you gets dispersed to someone who misuses it every time."

Temple jerked her gaze to Tushar.

The room was silent for long moments before she finally relaxed her shoulders and nodded. "Okay, you might be right. It's happened far too many times to be a coincidence."

While everyone spoke, Kate stood next to Graham shaking. She wanted to get out of this bunker. Now. Run as fast and as far as she could.

Temple's voice was calmer when she spoke again. "I assume you have more secrets than just this one."

"Yes," Tushar readily agreed. "Though I'm not privy to them. I've been here with you. But yes. I can assure you there are people working to solve this problem."

She nodded slowly again and glanced at everyone in the room. "Then you have my support. I don't want any member of your team in danger. Whatever you know, keep it to yourself. Because you're right, it would seem any information I'm privy to gets used against your team. This conversation stays in this room, though. If my superiors find out I'm helping you, I'll be implicated."

"You have our word," Tushar agreed.

Kate wanted to scream that she was done, that she didn't want to know another detail either. She glanced at Graham to see a determined look on his face. He was staring at Temple. "We will get to the bottom of this if it's the last thing I do on this earth."

Temple nodded.

Kate nearly swallowed her tongue. Of course Graham would be committed to seeing this through. That was the kind of man he was. Dedicated. Devoted to the job, to the bunker, to the team.

But Kate wasn't with him anymore. They weren't on the same page. He was furious, shaking, anger fueling him into action. He looked like he might personally sprint across the room and rip these two men into ten pieces even though they were already dead.

She was done. She wanted out.

CHAPTER 17

"Do you believe her?" Kate asked Graham three hours later as they drove away from the bunker.

"Yes. I don't see how she could be lying after everything we went through today." He'd considered everything Temple had said from several angles. "If she's lying, she's a damn good actress, and she's been at it for at least eleven years. Probably longer."

Kate gripped the steering wheel of the silver Toyota Corolla they'd borrowed from Blair. It turned out Blair had left her personal vehicle behind months ago, so it worked out perfectly that Graham and Kate could use it. After all, they were headed for Montana anyway. It provided transportation and reunited it with its owner.

Tushar had given them the keys.

Kate kept licking her lips. Graham knew she was stressed. He was too. Even hours later, his blood was still pumping with the adrenaline rush, but he hadn't wanted to spend another night inside that bunker, and he hadn't wanted Kate inside either. So, they'd left. No one even tried to stop them.

But something more was going on with Kate. She'd changed.

Her shoulders were low in defeat. She hadn't said much in the last few hours, instead letting everyone race around her as if she were in shock. She also hadn't met his gaze in a while. She was distant. Detached.

She sighed. "Do you think it's possible someone actually sabotaged our work from the beginning? Causing our exposure to AP12 in an effort to kill everyone and put an end to our research?" Kate's words were expected. Her tone was filled with defeat, however.

"I can't even begin to come to grips with that." He rubbed his thighs with both hands. "It would destroy my faith in humanity." *Though I'm losing that faith right now as I try to read you.* She was making him nervous. He needed to reach her.

She nodded, biting her lower lip before releasing it to continue. "Someone sabotaged us today. Do you think Spencer was involved and he's duped everyone we know?"

"I don't know. Hopefully, someone can get to the bottom of it. If we've been compromised as far back as eleven years ago with the broken beaker that put all our lives in peril in the first place, Spencer couldn't have had anything to do with it. He would have been eleven. But we don't know how long this Blue Cell organization has been in operation, nor do we know how many employees they have."

"How do you suppose those two men found us?"

"The ones with no identification and fake uniforms?" he asked, dripping with sarcasm. He was furious to find out no one would be able to track down where the two men came from. It pissed him off more than anything else that had happened that day. "I don't know, but I hope our assumption is true, that this Blue Cell group tapped into my computer and saw what I was doing. If Spencer knows anything about it, though, I'll personally hunt him down and kill him with my bare hands."

"I keep worrying he set us up." She shuddered.

Graham gritted his teeth. If they'd been fooled by this

Spencer guy, as was certainly possible, Graham would lose his shit. So would Dade and Ryan and about a dozen other people who had fallen for the man's story. All of their lives were in jeopardy.

"You think Tushar is going to be okay?" She frowned, her expression worried.

"He'll be fine. No bone was hit. Clean shot. Shelby stitched him up."

Kate blew out a breath. "Trish was frantic. Out of her mind."

"Yeah, I noticed that. I was kind of surprised. She and Tushar have been through a lot. I've never seen her that unhinged before, though. Trish has always been a rock under pressure. Even when we were all facing death." Graham frowned. Something was going on with them. That was for sure.

Kate shot Graham a glance. "Not one person mentioned the elephant in the room."

"Which elephant, babe?" There seemed to be a dozen.

"The lost data." Kate shivered. "When I saw that fire…"

Graham smiled. "Do you think Temple and Tushar truly believed the data was totally lost?"

She shook her head. "They can't be that stupid. Surely, when they stop to think about it…"

"Well, it's done now. The hard drives would have been nice, but I'm sure someone is creating new ones as we speak. Assuming Spencer isn't a total fuck and didn't stab us all in the back. It's easier for now if everyone believes the data is gone. Or at least for Temple to believe it. And tell her superiors. As long as we don't specifically tell her the data is safe, she has no choice but to report its total loss to her bosses. I'm sure that's why she never asked and never brought it up."

"You think someone above her did all this? Someone working for this Blue Cell? It's so incomprehensible."

"I don't know what to believe." He pointed at the next exit. "Pull off. Let's get a phone and touch base with Dade."

She took the next exit, easing the car up to a gas station before cutting the engine. The next moment, she sighed heavily, her hands dropping, her head leaning against the headrest, her eyes closing.

Graham reached across to grab her hand. "You okay?"

"Nope." She didn't open her eyes.

He needed to get her someplace where she could unwind as soon as possible. "I'll run in and grab a phone."

"'Kay."

He hated leaving her, but there weren't many choices. He jogged into the mini-mart attached to the station, grabbed a burner phone and two bottles of water, and was back in the car in less than three minutes.

Kate hadn't moved. Her eyes were still closed. She was breathing heavily.

Graham ripped open the phone and dialed Dade's number. Luckily, Dade answered on the second ring.

"It's Graham."

"Thank God. You two safe?"

"Yes. Have you heard?"

"Yes. Tushar spoke to Ryan. Ryan called me. Listen, I know you have Blair's car. I'm going to text you an address. Go straight there so someone can sweep it."

"You think the car could be bugged?" Graham asked.

Kate flinched and then wrapped her arms around herself and rubbed her biceps. Her eyes were still closed. It felt like she was hiding from him. And it was starting to scare him to death.

"Who narced on us, Dade?" Graham asked, forcing himself to focus on the call when what he really wanted to do was shake Kate and make her look at him.

"I don't know yet."

Graham sighed. "You sure you trust your hacker? Because I've gotta say, I'm incredibly suspicious."

"I do. We'll talk more later. Get the car swept before you do anything else."

"Okay. And then we're going to find a hotel. We're both too shook up to drive very far tonight."

"Put some miles under you after the sweep first. I don't want it to be easy to find you. I'm not fond of you stopping at a hotel where you might be recognized. Let me see if I can line up a safe house between there and here. I'll text you that also."

"Sounds good. I don't like anything about this. We need to figure out what the fuck is going on and fast before someone gets killed."

"I agree. You sound strong. You able to make the trip here without an issue?"

"Of course. I've been almost full-speed for days. Hell, I've been awake for nearly three days straight downloading the data. Please tell me you've verified it's safe." He cringed. If this car was bugged, all of Blue Cell knew too much already. Hell, Graham and Kate had discussed the data even before this call.

"It's safe. You succeeded. We all owe you, man."

"You don't owe me anything. I'm one of the team. But I'm anxious to get to Montana and help get this resolved as fast as possible."

Kate still hadn't looked at him, but she turned her face toward the driver's side window and seemed to be staring out at nothing.

"Listen, we need to get moving. I'll call you if we have any problems." Graham opened his door and climbed out of the Toyota as he ended the call. He rounded the car, opened the driver's side door, and reached for Kate's hand to pull her out.

"What are you doing?" she asked, finally meeting his gaze.

He stared down at her for a moment, trying to read her. Yeah, she was checked out, though he wasn't sure why or what to do about it. "Driving. Trade seats with me."

She nodded and left him standing there without argument.

As soon as they were both buckled in, he pulled away from the gas station and headed for the address Dade had texted him. It was about twenty minutes north, and when Graham pulled off the road, he found a beat-up older model Chevy waiting for them next to an abandoned barn.

"What is this place?" Kate murmured.

"No idea. Probably just an easy spot to meet someone without getting caught. Wait here." He climbed out of the car, left the door open, and headed for the man who shoved off his vehicle as Graham approached.

The guy nodded at Graham, but he didn't say a word. Instead, he took quick strides toward the Toyota and started examining the entire body. He pulled a device from his pocket and scanned the exterior along the bottom. "Can you pop the hood and the trunk for me?" he asked.

Graham reached inside and did as the man requested. The only reason why Graham didn't bolt was because he trusted Dade. But this guy was an odd bird.

He looked like he'd been working on cars for his entire life without taking frequent showers. His fingernails were black. He had on worn coveralls that might have been khaki at some point. His hair was long, but pulled back in a ponytail at the nape of his neck. Graham guessed him to be about sixty.

After about two minutes, the guy reached under the hood and lifted something out, holding it up for Graham to see. "Tracker. You're good now," he stated matter-of-factly, as if he found GPS devices on cars every day and didn't even feel victorious about it.

Graham shuddered. "Jesus. Did it record us?"

"Nope. Just a tracker." The guy shut the hood. "I'll dispose of this for you." He tapped the hood with his hand. "Get moving before someone tracks us here."

Graham nodded and slid back into the driver's seat. He pulled out without a word and drove a bit faster than he normally would to put some distance between them and that fucking tracker.

Kate had pulled even further into herself, her arms wrapped around her middle, her lips pursed.

Graham drove for half an hour before he got another text from Dade. Another address. He didn't even question it or speak. He simply typed it into the car's GPS and took the next exit to head in the direction of the address.

Kate didn't ask what he was doing or where he was going, and she was making him more nervous by the minute.

There was nothing he could do but drive and get them to this address as quickly as possible, and then he intended to pin her down and figure out what the hell was going on in her head.

It took another hour to get to their destination. They had left the highway several miles ago and turned about four times, each road getting progressively sketchier until at last they were on a gravel drive that led to a lodge.

Kate spoke for the first time since they'd left the gas station. "Where are we?"

"No idea. I'll go inside and figure it out." As he stepped out of the car, he decided it might be a vacation spot for fishermen or hunters or something. The lodge was large enough to have at least a dozen rooms inside. Like a hotel.

He entered the front door and headed for the check in area. An older woman behind the desk met his gaze and smiled. "Graham?"

He startled. "Yes."

She held out a key. "You're in cabin six behind the main lodge. If you head around to the left, you can't miss it. It's been stocked with food for a few days."

For some reason, he was stunned. "Thank you." He took the key, still looking at her, surmising she was the owner of this lodge and the outbuildings and also worked for SURVIVE. "We appreciate it."

She nodded and turned to help the next customer who'd entered behind him.

Five minutes later, Graham had steered them around the building and down a winding road until he found the marker for cabin six. It was isolated enough between the trees that each cabin was rather private.

Kate climbed out of the car and helped him grab their meager possessions from the trunk, and then they made their way onto the quaint front porch and into the cabin.

"Wow. Cute," she whispered as she dropped the bag she was holding.

He set his down next to hers as he shut the door behind them and flipped on the lights. The cabin was nestled in the trees, so the lighting coming in the windows was dim. It was also getting close to evening, the sun dipping low in the sky. "You really have to enjoy the company of whoever you stay with in this cabin," he joked.

She ignored him as she took several steps toward the center of the room. One room with a bathroom off to the right. Queen-sized bed. Kitchenette. Loveseat. Armchair. Fireplace. That was about it. But it was decorated by someone who loved trinkets and wall hangings. The owners had a lot of pride in their cabins.

Kate sighed. "I'm exhausted. I think I'll take a shower if you don't mind." She turned around to grab her bag without looking at him and padded toward the only space in the room where anyone could get privacy.

He watched her, itching to grab her arm and dig into her brain, but deciding against it and letting her spend some time alone first.

For several minutes, he stared at the closed door, listening to the shower run, his heart in his hands as he feared what she would say when he finally shook it out of her.

He was head over heels for this woman. The last several

hours had stressed him out more than he could imagine possible. He'd spent the time driving in silence, imagining the worst scenarios. All of them ended with her telling him to take a hike. That she'd changed her mind and didn't want to be with him after all.

He was scared. Out of his mind.

Forcing himself to move, he finally checked out the refrigerator to see what kinds of provisions they had and then tucked his bag of clothes next to the bed. There wasn't much else to do, so he was pacing the small space when she emerged.

She wore a tank top and shorts. Normally she dressed similarly for bed, but this time she had on a bra. And he wanted to read her thoughts. "How's the shower?" he asked, instead of the dozens of other questions running through his mind.

"It's good. I left you some hot water if you want."

What I want is for you to look me in the eye and tell me what the hell is going on...

He was quick. Less than ten minutes later he stepped back out wearing nothing but his jeans. He hadn't taken the time to shave, but she'd never seemed to mind in the past. In fact over the last ten days together he had only shaved a few times. After that first day when Kate had shaved him, he'd gone several more without and then done so himself. He hadn't wanted to take the time tonight either.

He headed straight toward her where she stood at the sink in the kitchen area staring out the small window at probably nothing.

This had to end. Whatever was going on in her mind, he wanted to be let in. So he wrapped his arms around her and pulled her back against his front. He angled his head around to kiss her temple. "Talk to me."

She sighed, her chin dipping. "Sorry I've been so quiet."

"You're allowed to be quiet. It was a stressful day. I get it."

He felt her swallow as she lifted her head and tipped it

toward his cheek. "It was more than stressful, Graham. It was too much."

"I get that. I've never been tied up by two madmen waving guns in my face before. It was intense."

She twisted in his arms, giving him a bit of a shove so that he had to step back. "Intense doesn't even begin to describe this day. Those men could have killed you."

He held her biceps even though several inches separated them now. "I don't think they intended to kill me. They wanted the data."

"They had *guns*," she shouted. "They shot at Tushar. They shot at me. I had to shoot one of them. Tushar had to kill them."

He nodded. "Okay. I mean, you're right. It wasn't the sort of day I want to repeat."

"Yeah, that's just it. I don't want to repeat it either. Ever."

Where was she going with this? That morning she had been soft and smiling and seemed eager to take their relationship to the next level. Now? It was as if she blamed him for what happened and didn't want anything to do with him. "Kate? What's going on?" Fear crawled up his spine, the kind of fear anyone would feel when they suspected the person they loved was about to break up with them.

"Nothing." She squirmed free. "I just realized this isn't going to work. I'm sorry. I thought…" She bit her bottom lip and turned back to face the window. "I'm sorry," she repeated, softer.

He struggled to speak, his mouth opening but no sound coming out because he didn't know how to respond. He only knew he needed to get this back on the tracks before she destroyed him in exactly the way she'd worried he had the ability to destroy her. "What's not going to work?"

"Us." One word. One horrifying word that made his knees buckle. What the hell had he done today to change her mind about them?

"Kate…" He fisted his hands at his sides, still standing right behind her but not touching her. "Did I do something?"

"No," she blurted, spinning toward him again, her head shaking. "No. God, no. You didn't do anything. I just realized we aren't on the same page."

He felt faint. "How did you decide that? We've been on the same page almost from the moment I woke up. The same page. The same paragraph. The same sentence. What changed?"

She blew out a breath, and he knew everything between them was about to implode.

CHAPTER 18

Now that the dam was open, Kate needed to get this all out before she got weak and caved. "I saw how furious and determined you were today. And you have every right to be. I don't disagree. But I lost the will to keep going when bullets started racing past my head. I don't want this life anymore."

The expression on his face made her resolve weaken. Shock. Confusion. Pain. She was hurting him in exactly the way she'd hoped to avoid feeling herself. Hell, she felt exactly the way he looked too. This wasn't supposed to happen. She'd intentionally guarded her heart so that this could never happen.

Taking a breath, she continued to explain. "You obviously need to get to Montana and help Dade and the rest of the team fight the bad guys and save the day. I thought I could do it. I thought I wanted that too. But every day feels like a game of Russian roulette. I'm tired. I want out. Maybe that makes me disloyal to the team, but I want to go home.

"I want to see my parents and my sister and my niece. I want to sleep for two weeks and eat my mom's cooking and watch old movies and read those romance novels I've never had time for."

She stepped around him, trying to put a few feet between them. His proximity was killing her. She forced herself to meet his gaze. "I don't want to duck from bullets and hide and worry and stress and chase after bad guys. I'm a doctor, not a secret agent."

"So what? You're just going to leave?" His words slammed into her as he took a step forward. "Walk away from me because you're scared?"

She licked her lips. "Yes."

He shook his head. "Yeah, see, it doesn't work like that."

Her eyes widened in shock.

He continued. "I understand you're scared. Fuck, I'm scared. I have no idea what tomorrow will bring. Or the next day or the day after that or next month. But we still have to get up in the morning and face each day." He inched closer to her, making her nervous.

She'd spent the last several hours convincing herself they couldn't continue this farce because he needed to go to Montana and fight the bad guys, and she needed to get out of this situation and hide from the world. They weren't on the same path.

His proximity made her want to slam against his body instead and absorb his strength. His scent. She wanted his hands on her back, holding her. Making things feel right.

But it was a bad idea. She needed to break this thing between them off so they could go their separate ways. He could take his newfound strength and determination to Montana. She could take her fear and exhaustion to Georgia and hide from the world.

Graham rubbed his forehead with his thumb and forefinger. "Kate, you have every right to be scared."

She stood taller. "I also have every right to head in a different direction. I don't want to go to Montana and fight bad guys. You do."

He shook his head. "And you get to singlehandedly make this decision for the both of us without talking to me?"

She jerked back a step, feeling like she'd been slapped. "I'm not making any decisions for you. I'm simply pointing out our differences."

"Kate, you're standing there telling me how I feel. You're not giving me an opportunity to respond. You didn't even ask me how I felt. You decided several hours ago to end this relationship based on something you didn't ask me about."

"Fine. Do you want to go to Montana?" she asked with as much snark as she could fit into those words, hands on her hips.

His shoulders dropped and he ran a hand through his hair, but she had to give him credit for not losing his temper with her. "That's not the point."

"Isn't it?"

"Not even close." He dropped his hand and reached out to grab her around the waist before she knew his intention. And then he was holding her against his body. Bad idea.

She couldn't think when he held her. She opened her mouth to protest, but he set a finger over her lips. "Just listen to me. Please. If you still want to walk away from us after I finish, I won't stop you, but I want you to hear me out first."

She pulled her bottom lip between her teeth, his fingers still distracting her against her lips. Finally, she nodded subtly.

"Thank you." He backed her up so that her butt rested against the counter, trapping her. Her resolve crumbled when he crowded her like that. She wanted to pull his face down to meet hers. She wanted him to kiss her. Which was totally irrational while she was trying to end things.

Graham's hands slid to her waist, his hips pressing against hers. "I think you're trying to sabotage this relationship because you're scared."

She flinched. "Of course not. As I've told you before, the reason I didn't let things escalate into a relationship was because I wanted to be certain we were compatible in every way before I took that leap."

He chuckled, which annoyed her. "You're saying this isn't a relationship? Because that's horseshit. And you know it. You think just because we haven't had sex it's not a relationship? I've never in my life been this deeply involved with a woman. We don't have to have sex for me to be as dedicated as humanly possible to this *relationship*.

"I know it was fast and intense, but I'm in love with you. So, don't try to convince yourself we aren't in a relationship."

She stopped breathing. *Did he just say he was in love with me?*

He grinned. "You heard me. I'm in love with you. And furthermore, you're in love with me. I see it in your eyes every time you look at me. Even today, for as hard as you've tried to back away from me, you haven't hidden your feelings. You just avoided looking at me. But when you do, you can't hide your emotions."

She swallowed. He was right. She was in love with him. But that didn't mean they could make things work if they wanted two different paths.

"You're scared. Hell, I'm scared. I'm not an expert with women as I've made more than clear. I don't want to fuck this up. I want to get it right as badly as you do. I want it to be perfect. I want you to have that fairy tale you're determined to live. And I will spend my entire life making that happen because you're worth it."

Holy shit. "But…"

He shook his head. "I'm not done. You don't get to step away from me just because we got shot at. We're a couple. We have to talk things out and help each other through the difficult times. We may not always have the same ideas, but we'll work things out."

"We have very different ideas this time, Graham. Too different."

He shook his head. "You're wrong."

"How the hell am I wrong?" Her voice lifted. "I don't want to go to Montana with you."

His hands slid up her body until he held her shoulders. "You're wrong because you matter more to me than a destination or a job or even another person. And I know I matter that much to you too. So we're going to discuss this difference of opinion as a couple and make a plan we can both live with. Together.

"We're not separating over something as ridiculous as geography or a job. I love you more than any job or any state. Don't you get that?" His hands moved up to her face now, cupping her cheeks. Holding her steady as he stared into her eyes.

"Yes," she whispered at last. Because he was right.

He lifted a brow, another slow smile forming. And then he blew out a breath. "Okay. Progress." His fingers smoothed up the side of her face and brushed a lock of hair off her forehead. "You're scared."

"Petrified." Her bottom lip trembled. "People shot at us."

"They did."

"We could have died."

"I know, Kate."

"I already died once. I want to go home." Her voice was weak. Exhausted.

"I get that."

She was shaking now, but she set her hands on his waist and gripped his jeans. "Your adrenaline was pumping hard afterward. There were two dead men on the floor, and you were hell bent to get to Montana to fight a war while I was standing there thinking I wanted to get as far away from Montana as humanly possible."

He kissed her forehead. "I know. I did get a little GI Joe there for a while, but you have to believe me when I say that everything in this relationship is negotiable for the rest of our lives. We talk. Share. Discuss. Argue sometimes. But we're not splitting apart. Because at the end of the day the only thing that matters to me in the whole world is you and making sure you're happy."

A tear slid from her eye. Why hadn't she discussed this with him hours ago?

"Am I right?"

"Yes," she breathed. "I'm sorry. I didn't trust you to be as deeply committed as you obviously are."

"Well, now you know." That grin again.

She hesitated. "Are you sure you even want to consider other options? I get how important the job is."

He lifted a brow. "Did you get how important *you* are? Did you miss that part?"

She swallowed. "How did I get so lucky?"

He shrugged. "I'm pretty sure I'm the one who got lucky. I was in a coma while you worked your ass off night and day for a month to make sure I survived. That's devotion." He tipped his head to one side. "I don't think I've properly thanked you for that."

She gave him a smile even though a few tears were still falling. "Maybe you could kiss me again?"

"Yeah?" He lifted a brow. "Do my lips have to stay in the range of your mouth?"

She flushed but shook her head. "No. I think I'd like it if they didn't, actually." Yeah, it was time. She might have spent most of her life waiting for the perfect man, but it didn't get more perfect than the man she loved telling her he loved her back before ever having sex with her. That was dedication.

His mouth descended on hers as his hands slid into her hair, tipping her head to one side so he could angle her just how he wanted.

She melted against him, instantly craving the world. His tongue slid along her bottom lip, urgent, demanding, hot.

She opened her mouth to him and met his tongue with her own, tasting him while her body came fully alive. Every nerve ending made itself known. Her skin crawled with the need to get closer to him. She wanted to be naked in his arms. She wanted the promise of his lips on her skin. Everywhere.

She moaned into his mouth as she visualized what she needed.

He stepped closer, as if that were possible, his legs parting so that she stood between them, pressed against his erection.

An ache formed between her thighs, demanding attention more than ever before. There was no reason to be scared or panicked because there was no way anything could go wrong. She might flounder around a bit as she figured out all the mechanics, but she knew he would be right there with her.

I love you. His words rang in her mind.

When he finally released her lips, he set his forehead against hers and stared into her eyes, breathing heavily. He searched her gaze.

"What?" she whispered.

"Just memorizing this moment."

Another flush stole up her cheeks at the romantic gesture. "How long do you intend to memorize before you undress me?"

He smiled. "As long as I want." His hands slid down to her waist again and then he grabbed her hands and backed up, tugging her with him toward the bed.

Yes.

This was it. This was right. This was the time and the place.

This was her fairy tale.

~

Graham was nervous but only because he wanted to make this special for her. He understood the mechanics of this perfectly, but executing it might be trickier. Two virgins trying to have sex without the awkwardness. He wanted them both to remember and enjoy it. Starting right now, she was his. Forever. For a lifetime. For an eternity.

When he reached the side of the bed, he sat on the edge and pulled her between his legs. "You sure about this? If you'd rather wait, we absolutely can. If you want to be married first, we can make that happen."

"God, no." She shook her head vehemently. "Unless there's a minister staying in the cabin next to ours, I'm not waiting."

He chuckled. "Kate, I'll find a minister if that's what you want. I don't want you to have sex with me if you'd rather wait. It's not a deal breaker. It never will be."

"No." She set her hands on his chest and then eased them down his bare skin. "It was never about being married. I don't care about weddings and ceremonies. It was about commitment. About me not being willing or able to give my heart away to someone until it was the right person."

"Yeah, well, your heart is mine. But that's not the same as your body."

"It is for me. They're connected. The man who took my heart would get my body at the same time." She slid her hands up to his pecs.

He was watching the way her gaze roamed over his chest, her fingers following in the same path. Goose bumps rose on his skin. And then she shocked him by crossing her arms at her waist, grabbing her tank top by the hem, and drawing it over her head.

He was shaking with nerves, while his sweet, loving, devoted Kate was all in. She inched closer, confidently.

He fought to control his racing heart and the hard-on that scrambled his brain. *Shit. Condoms.* He licked his lips. "I don't supposed you're more prepared than me and have condoms in your bag?"

She gave him a sweet smile. "We don't need them. I've been taking birth control since I woke up."

Sweet Jesus. In order to give himself a moment, he scooted back on the bed, propped himself up on one side, and patted the mattress next to him. "Come here." His voice cracked a little.

She surprised him again by stepping out of her shorts first and then climbing up next to him in her bra and panties. A matched set. White. Lacey. And destined to land on the floor soon, he hoped.

He set his hand on her cheek as she settled against his side. The fact that she'd stripped down to her underwear and climbed up to snuggle against him spoke volumes.

He set his gaze on her lips and then stroked her bottom lip with his thumb. He struggled to control his anxiety.

She parted her lips and then licked them, the tip of her tongue teasing his thumb. Her voice was a low whisper when she broke the silence. "I love you."

He scooted his body closer as his hand slid down to her shoulder, and then he eased her onto her back, keeping his hand flattened on her arm so she wouldn't see him shaking. This was seemingly more nerve-wracking for him than it was for her.

She smiled as she lifted a hand to his waist and smoothed it up his side. "Take a breath," she whispered.

He drew in air long and slow, and then he smoothed his hand around to her belly. "I'm nervous."

She cupped his face. "I know, but there's no need. We can't screw this up, remember? It's physically impossible."

He wanted to be strong for her, but inside he was a mess. What if he came too fast or fumbled and came before he even slid inside her? It seemed like a real possibility. "We're not doing anything you aren't ready for, are we?"

"No. I'm ready. Waiting won't change my feelings."

"I want it to be perfect," he admitted, holding her gaze.

"It's already perfect. Can you feel the electricity between us?"

"Yes. All the time." She was right. There was an electricity between them, and they would get this right, though maybe not the first time.

"Those sparks are gonna explode." Her hand slid down his back and she smoothed her fingers under the edge of his jeans. The boldest Kate he'd ever experienced, her gaze never leaving his.

His erection threatened to bust the zipper down the front. She'd seen him naked, probably dozens of times while he'd been unconscious. He intended to even that field right now. His turn to see her completely naked.

He moved his hand to her breast and cupped it through the lace. She arched her chest, gasping. Yeah, he was going to come in his jeans.

Before he got completely caught up in loving her, he wanted to fully see her, soak her in, so he lifted onto his knees and popped the front clasp on her bra. As it fell to the sides, she shivered. He slid the straps down her arms and tugged it out from under her, dropping it so that it joined her other clothes on the floor.

For a moment, he continued to hold her gaze while she pursed her lips, her body rising and falling with every breath. And then he lowered his face to take her in visually for the first time.

Her skin was several shades darker than his, the contrast mesmerizing. Her breasts were full, the nipples tight buds that stood at stiff peaks even before he'd touched them.

He eased his hand up from her waist to cup her breast, molding his palm gently around the globe and marveling at how damn lucky he was that this amazing gorgeous woman was his.

She held his forearm, but the moment he swiped his thumb

over her nipple, she arched her chest again, inhaling sharply. *Yes.* "You like that?"

Her voice was breathy. "God, yes."

He leaned down and kissed the pointy bud and then flicked his tongue over the tip.

She moaned. "Jesus."

He smiled against her chest and then lifted his gaze. Maybe this wasn't so difficult after all.

She was flushed. A moan escaped her lips when he brushed his thumb over her nipple. Every tiny reaction gave him the confidence to keep going.

She grabbed his arm, gripping so tightly her knuckles were white. "Graham…" She squirmed. "What are you waiting for?"

He smiled broader. "Savoring the moments." *Trying to keep from coming in my pants.*

She rolled her eyes. "That's cheesy. And how the hell are you so calm?"

"I'm not. I'm just hiding it. Inside, I'm freaking out a bit." He lifted one hand so she could see the tremble.

She reached for his fingers and drew them to her lips, kissing the tips. "Okay. At least I know you're human."

"I'm human." He cocked his head to one side and then lowered his face again to suck her nipple into his mouth.

She moaned, her fingers digging into his arm, undoubtedly without her knowledge.

While he continued to torment her nipple with his lips and tongue, he slid his hand down her waist to her thigh. He let his thumb caress the sensitive skin at the top of her thigh, inches from her sex. Her legs fell further apart, a sign that he was on the right track.

He released her nipple with a slight pop and eased farther up her body to claim her lips. They were parted and waiting for him, and she eagerly joined the kiss, tilting her head to one side and then sliding her tongue along his teeth.

The sweet sounds coming from her made him harder by the second, but he wanted to keep every ounce of his attention on her until she fell apart in his arms. He wanted to make her come before he did anything else. For one thing, he wanted to watch her orgasm, this time naked and open to him. For another thing, he was growing increasingly certain he wouldn't last two seconds inside her.

As soon as she started to relax, he released her lips and quickly slid down her body, grabbing the sides of her panties and pulling them away.

Jesus. She was perfection. While he stared at her body, absorbing his good fortune, he unbuttoned and unzipped his jeans. He removed them, along with his underwear, in record time.

For a moment, they stared at each other, her lying on her back with her legs spread open, him on his knees memorizing her from above. Her gaze roamed up and down his body, making his erection bob.

When she finally moved, it was to shudder and lick her lips. "You're making me feel self-conscious staring at me like that," she whispered as if she weren't ogling him in the same fashion he was her.

Before she could focus on her nudity, he returned to her side, his lips lowering to hers again.

While he devoured her mouth, he lifted his leg and situated it between hers, parting them wider. His thigh pressed against her sex, and he nearly groaned into her mouth at the feel of her warmth and the wetness that coated his leg. Apparently he was doing something right.

Still kissing her, he slid his hand higher up her thigh to her stomach, and then he turned his wrist so that his fingers eased down her belly until the tips hit their mark.

Kate moaned into his mouth, and then she pulled her head

to one side, sucking in a deep breath. "Graham..." Her gaze came back to his.

He held it while he pressed a finger against her clit. "How's that?" She was so wet that it was easy to gather some of her arousal and swirl it around the tight nub. Damn, she was hot, and she responded to him like a firecracker. Would she always be this ready for him? This eager? Hot and aroused? Thoughts of rubbing her to completion through her clothes the other night increased his confidence.

"There are no words," she whispered. She tried to lift her hips, but he held her down with the weight of his leg between hers, trapping her thigh and making it difficult for her to squirm away from him. When her mouth fell open and her eyes widened, he knew he was hitting every mark just right.

Now he just needed to make her fall apart. Totally. The look on her face was enough to make him press his erection against her thigh. Again, he was afraid he might come before he entered her. She melted him with that shocked look of awe.

The desire to taste her was palpable, but he didn't want to break his gaze from hers, so it would have to wait for another time. Right now, he intended to watch her face as she came.

Easing his knee away from her wet heat, he pulled her legs farther apart and slid his hand lower.

She licked her lips as he ran a finger between her lower ones. She was so wet. And her face was mesmerizing. He could grow addicted to watching her if she was always this expressive. When he pressed one finger slowly inside her, her mouth fell open again and her eyes rolled back. She tipped her head back and moaned, lifting her hips.

Her hand jerked up to grab his shoulder. "Ohmygod."

Damn, he loved her. So much his heart was pounding. This experience was all his. No one else had ever seen her like this. No one ever would. For the rest of his life, he would own this piece of her. Thousands and thousands of times he would watch her unravel for him. It was humbling and exciting.

Her breaths came in sharp pants, her chest rising and falling. When she lifted her free leg and dug her heel into the mattress to help lift her hips higher, he glanced down. She was so unencumbered.

He eased his finger out, curving it forward to draw it across the front of her channel in the way he'd researched, and she nearly shot off the bed. No amount of Google searching had prepared him for how responsive she was.

She pressed on his shoulders. "Graham..." she whispered. "Oh God."

When her breath hitched, he added a second finger, thrust them into her tightness, and pressed his palm against her clit. Her entire body stiffened, hips off the bed, foot digging into the mattress, hand on his shoulder.

He ground his hand down and pressed against her G-spot with both fingers. Her leg started shaking, a low moan coming from her lips, and then she cried out, an unintelligible noise that didn't include words.

Surprising him, he felt the pulse of her orgasm against both his palm and inside her. The walls of her channel milked his fingers hard.

When the pulsing stopped, her hips dropped to the bed and her leg fell to one side, knee bent to leave her wide open. Her eyes were squeezed shut, but they gradually relaxed until she blinked them open and met his gaze. "Holy shit."

He grinned huge. It didn't matter that his length was throbbing with the need to be inside her. This was so much better. He continued to slide his fingers in and out of her, not wanting her to float all the way back to earth.

She sucked in air. "I had no idea." Breathing heavily, she loosened her grip on his arm and glanced at where she'd held him. "Shit. Sorry."

"You can squeeze my arm anytime you want." He leaned down and kissed her breasts, first one and then the other.

She shuddered, and then she reached for his hip. "Do it again. Use something thicker and longer this time." Her cheeks pinkened as she made the cute demand.

He finally removed his fingers, climbed between her legs, grabbed his erection, and stroked it through her swollen folds. "So bossy," he murmured. His arm was shaking as he held himself above her. The mechanics were simple. Now that he'd touched her so intimately, he knew how easy it was going to be to slide into her. It would be tight, but the only way he could fuck up would be if he came before he got fully inside. And that couldn't be helped.

Her hands were on his waist and then down over his ass and then climbing up his back. She held him tight as if she feared he might escape. He would never escape. Not in a million years.

Holding himself aloft with one elbow, he met her gaze and lined up with her entrance before pulling his hand out of the way. He settled his other elbow at her side, tucked his hands under her shoulders, and rubbed the tip of his erection against her.

She squirmed, either in anticipation or arousal. "Graham, do it."

He didn't want to hurt her, but her eyes were wide with desperation, and he couldn't hold back any longer. So, he eased an inch or so into her.

Holy shit. Holy shit.

His eyes slid closed and he gritted his teeth, willing himself not to come too fast. But she was so tight. Warm. Wet. And her hands were racing up and down his arms. This was so much better than he ever imagined.

"Graham…" Her voice was barely audible. "Just do it," she demanded a second time. As she spoke, she lifted her hips, forcing him deeper.

He couldn't resist a moment longer, so he drew almost out and then thrust into her all the way.

She sucked in a breath, held it a few beats, and then blew it out. Her fingers smoothed down to his ass and gripped him. "Again."

He lowered his forehead to the pillow beside her, fighting for control, holding his breath. Stars would have been swimming in front of his eyes if he could open them, but he was afraid to move an inch for fear he would break the spell of perfection or come.

Her fingers danced up and down his arms. "Look at me," she whispered as one hand rose to his head and tugged.

He lifted his forehead and met her gaze, knowing he was out of control and looking at her would send him over the edge.

"You okay?" she asked.

He swallowed and gave her a lopsided grin. "Me? You're worried about me?"

She flushed, shrugging. "Well, you're the one not moving."

He held her gaze. "I want to remember this, and the moment I move, I'm going to come."

"That's the idea," she teased lightly, her sweet hands stroking up and down his back and arms again.

"Yeah, I would have preferred to last a bit longer." Maybe if he talked to her, he could control his erection and stretch this out.

"Next time," she urged, wiggling her hips.

That shattered his resolve. He pulled almost out and then eased back in fully, watching her closely as her face switched from the slightly pinched sign that he was filling her too tightly to the one he wanted to see—sheer bliss.

Her eyes fluttered shut as a smile spread. "I was so missing out. Move."

He obliged her, gritting his teeth while trying to focus on anything but the unbelievably amazing sensation of being inside her. She looked so damn sexy with that contented smile and rosy cheeks. He concentrated on memorizing that look while he thrust in and out of her heat a few more times. She wasn't just tight, she was gripping him to death.

And it was heaven.

When her smile fell and her lips parted again, her head tipping back and her fingers pressing into his ass, he knew she was going to come again. Amazing.

She was holding back. He could see it in her stiff expression. He lowered his face to her neck, nibbled a path to her ear, and when she shuddered, he whispered, "Can I get you to do that again?"

Her orgasm was immediate and powerful. He thrust harder and fast, not wanting to miss a moment of her euphoria. But he was only able to hold off for a few more seconds, and then he poured his love into her with the most powerful release of his life. There was simply no comparison between her tight channel and what he could do with his hand.

His arms were shaking as pulses of his come filled her. He pressed his forehead into the bed at the side of her face again, unable to lift himself until he was fully spent.

In order to avoid smashing her against the bed, he eased out and slid to her side, resting his head in the crook of her arm, one leg still between hers, gasping for breath.

She smoothed her hand up and down his arm, humming softly, perhaps not even aware.

When he was finally able to lift his face to meet her gaze, he nearly swallowed his tongue at her expression. He forced himself not to blink. She was so sated and gorgeous and sexy and happy and relaxed.

And he vowed to make her look like that every day for the rest of their lives.

CHAPTER 19

Kate couldn't stop touching him. Everywhere. It had taken her a minute to regain control of her arms, her hands, and her fingers, but then she pushed him onto his back and lifted to her side, her gaze roaming boldly all over his body.

He was fit and built. His skin was lighter than hers, typical of someone with his shade of strawberry-blond hair. So sexy. She leaned over his chest and flicked her tongue against his nipple.

He moaned, his hand running up and down her body.

Her gaze wandered lower to fully take in his length. Maybe it had been slightly less erect for a moment after he'd pulled out of her, but now it was back to being completely full. It bobbed in front of her eyes.

He ran a hand up his side and clasped it while she watched, his fingers gently easing up and down the shaft.

When she lifted her gaze to his, she found him staring at her. He released his length to reach for her breast, cupping it, molding it, flicking his thumb over the nipple. "You okay?" he asked, his voice throaty.

She smiled. "Perfect." Wetness coated her thighs, and she wanted to clean up a bit so they could repeat the performance.

As she started to push off him, he grabbed her arm and pulled her down for a kiss. "Stay here," he murmured against her lips. He flattened her onto her back with his hands at her shoulders and left her lying on the bed.

Thirty seconds later he was back with a washcloth in his hands.

Maybe she should have been embarrassed to have him clean her off, but she wasn't. It was so intimate and personal the way he gently parted her legs and wiped the evidence of their lovemaking away. Next, he stroked the washcloth over his shaft too.

When he was done, he climbed up beside her again and pulled her against his chest.

The sun had almost disappeared from the sky, leaving them in the dim light bathing the room. Soon it would be completely dark.

"We didn't eat," she whispered while dragging her fingers up and down his chest.

"Hmmm. I'm not ready to move yet."

She smiled against his chest. "We didn't resolve our disagreement either."

He chuckled this time and hugged her closer. "We were never having a disagreement. It was all in your head."

She lifted her chin to set it on his chest, frowning at him. "How do you figure it's all in my head?"

He lifted his face and kissed her lips before dropping back again. "Because I would never do something that makes you uncomfortable. Not in this bed nor in our lives. If you don't want to go to Montana, that's the end of the discussion. We won't go."

She flinched and pushed off him, wanting to more fully see his face even though they were quickly losing light. "You can't do that."

He lifted a brow. "Why not? Of course, I can."

She shook her head. "That's not a negotiation."

He chuckled again. "Okay, but it's me making my woman happy. And that's all that matters."

"Not even close. You said we needed to discuss things."

"We are discussing things." He was still stroking her back even though she was now sitting next to him, her hand on his chest. "You said you didn't want to go to Montana, and I'm saying, okay, we won't."

Her spine straightened. "That's ridiculous. It doesn't work that way. After you just gave me a long speech about talking things out, you're just going to roll over and let me decide everything?"

He started laughing now, and he pushed himself to sitting, grabbed her by the waist, and flipped her once again onto her back so he could hover over her. His fingers danced up and down her body from her outer thigh to the space between her breasts.

Her body came alive again at his touch. "It's still a negotiation, hon. I'm just using my judgment with regard to the level of importance of this topic to you. If you had asked my opinion about sausage or pepperoni pizza, maybe we could have learned each other's preferences and ordered half and half, but you were willing to break up with me over stepping foot in Montana, so that put a period on that sentence. In the event of one topic being a deal breaker, I'm not an idiot."

She rolled her eyes. "I might have spoken rashly."

He gave her a ridiculous grin, wagging his eyes. "Are you saying now that I have you naked and made you hum a few times, you aren't as inclined to break up with me?" he teased, his palm landing on her breast, his fingers toying with her nipple.

She moaned, her eyes rolling back. When she could find her voice again, she licked her lips. "You could probably convince me to do just about anything while you're touching me like that."

He lowered his face to suck her nipple into his mouth. When his tongue reached out to flick over the distended tip, she grabbed his arm. How could she be this aroused again so soon?

He released her nipple with a pop. "Perhaps I could convince you to let me taste more than just your sweet breasts."

For a moment, she wasn't sure what he meant, but while she was still making sense of his words, he climbed between her legs, spread them wide open, and nibbled a path down her belly.

She grabbed his shoulders. *Holy shit.* "That wasn't what I had in mind for dinner," she choked out. Was he really going down on her?

Oh yeah. He totally was. The second his lips landed on her clit, worshiping it with the flick of his tongue, she cried out. She had thought nothing could be better than the feel of his fingers making her come. And then nothing could have prepared her for the deeper orgasm she'd experienced with him buried inside her.

But now... Lordy.

His lips became more urgent, sucking her clit between them while lathing it with his tongue. The intimacy was so erotic she didn't have time to be embarrassed.

His hands were on her spread thighs, pressing them open while he devoured her most private parts.

Heaven. This was what heaven felt like.

When he thrust his tongue inside her, she gripped his shoulders tighter and moaned so loud it vibrated throughout the cabin. "Graham..."

He went back to her clit next, sucking urgently, flicking his tongue again and again while he drew her closer and closer to the edge of sanity. This may have been his first experience with sex, but the man was a medical professional, and he'd clearly spent some time studying the female anatomy.

In moments she was right there. So close. She held her

breath, tipping her head back, trying to hold off another moment so she could enjoy every second of this torture.

She couldn't win that battle, though. He sucked her clit hard, forcing her orgasm to rush through her body. Her ears rang as her body shook. Her brain was mush, every ounce of her attention on the pulses that seemed to flow from her entire body through her sex.

It wasn't until she shuddered that he released her. Somehow he sensed that she was too sensitive to take any more. As he climbed back up her body to hover over her sated form, he wiped his mouth with his fingers and smiled. "Now we can find something for dinner."

She giggled, unable to stop the emotion from erupting. "You just ate."

He shrugged. "Appetizer."

There was nothing in the world sexier than watching Kate wander around in the kitchen naked. They had turned on the lights, but he'd managed to convince her that clothing wasn't necessary.

For a moment, she'd glanced around at the windows, but then he'd reasoned with her that no one could see them in this cabin tucked between the trees.

There was a god because she got over both her concern about the neighbors and her modesty. If he wasn't mistaken, she was actually empowered by her ability to so easily arouse him, and flaunting her assets more than necessary to get a rise out of him. Literally.

He was not about to argue. Instead, he leaned against the wall next to the fridge and watched her make sandwiches. They didn't need words for that. She knew exactly how he liked his sandwich.

Everything about this night was perfect. She was his. She was no longer freaking out. She was calm and sated and happy and glowing. And he'd done that to her. If he could do that every day for the rest of their lives, he would be a happy man.

She finally pointed at a chair at the small table for two. "Sit. Eat. You're gonna need your strength so you can do that thing with your tongue again in a while." She flushed, but it was cute as hell that she'd forced herself to speak those words.

He shoved off the wall and sauntered toward her. He wrapped his arm around her waist and drew her close to plant a kiss on her lips. "You'll never have to work hard to convince me to eat you, hon. The reward was in the way you moaned and called my name. Music."

She flushed a deeper red, shoved him into the chair, and took a seat across from him. "Lucky for you it's summer, otherwise we'd be freezing right now and I'd be covered in a sweatshirt and leggings."

"Mmm," he said around his bite as he worked to swallow it. "Maybe we should move to California or Florida."

She swatted at him playfully.

"Or perhaps one of those islands with nude beaches."

She groaned. "I'm nervous enough walking around naked in front of these windows in the middle of the woods. You think I'm going to lie on a public beach with no bikini?"

"You're right. That wouldn't work. I'd have to fight off everyone who walked by. We'll get one of those little gondola thingies that are out in the water. A private one."

She giggled. "Okay. It's a deal. As soon as we win the lottery."

He reached across the table, cupped her cheek, and stroked her chin with his thumb. After searching her face and making sure he had her full attention, he spoke again. "How about we spend the next two days doing nothing but eating, sleeping, and fucking? After that we can discuss the future and make a plan."

She smiled. "I love that idea."

CHAPTER 20

"We have to go to Montana," Kate announced two mornings later, the day they intended to discuss their future and leave the cabin.

It was early. The sun was barely up. But a glance at Kate's face through the slits Graham managed to make with his groggy eyes, still half asleep, told him she'd been awake for a while.

She was propped on one elbow, staring down at him.

She was also naked and sexy as hell.

He wasn't sure what to make of her statement, but his brain was too foggy from sleep to respond. He licked his lips and then rolled to his side to pull her under him and kiss her senseless. He much preferred starting his days making out and then making love, than discussing important topics like where they were headed later today.

When he released her mouth, she patted his arm. "I'm serious."

"I'm not even sure what you said. I was still asleep. I think I misunderstood."

She rolled her eyes. "You didn't. You heard me. We have to go to Montana. Today."

He shook the cobwebs from his brain. "If I remember correctly, you told me not forty hours ago that we needed to break up because you weren't inclined to set one foot in Montana."

She sighed. "That was before."

"Before what?" He wasn't sure he wanted to hear the answer, but he was sure it would be convoluted.

"Before I realized what you meant when you said you loved me."

That got his attention. "Not following you, babe." He dipped his mouth to her neck and kissed the soft spot that always made her squirm.

"You knew. You knew before I did."

At that, he lifted his face to meet her gaze, blinking away the last of sleep. "I knew what?"

"What it meant to fully love someone."

"Mmm. What does it mean exactly?"

"It means you would do anything for them. Anything in the world. I didn't quite get that. Or I was hiding from it because I was scared. But now I understand. When you said you didn't care where we went as long as we were together, I thought you were crazy."

"Yeah, well, we aren't going to Montana." He pushed off her, hoping if he went to the bathroom and returned, she would have found her senses.

She grabbed his arm as he started to sit up. "Listen to me. I'm not crazy either."

"You are if you think we're going to Montana after the breakdown you had the other day." He tried to extricate himself from her if for no other reason than to find his own brain cells somewhere in the room.

She gripped him harder, sitting up at his side and then climbing onto his lap, straddling him with her naked body. She even scooted closer so that her heat pressed against his growing erection.

He set his hands on her hips to steady her. It did no good. He was doomed. Her fantastic breasts bobbed in front of him, begging him to cup them and bring them to his lips. Her core was wet and warm, making him completely hard in seconds.

So much for escaping.

And then she lifted her body a few inches, lined herself up with his erection, and thrust downward.

He nearly died. Under any other circumstances, he would have found this arrangement to be the most erotic sexy situation he'd ever been in, but the little nymph was manipulating him.

As soon as she was fully seated, stealing his last brain cell, she repeated her first statement. "We have to go to Montana."

"Why would we do that?" he asked through gritted teeth.

She lifted halfway off and then thrust back down, jarring his skull. "Because it's important to you, and I love you."

"I love you too, Kate. That's why we're not going."

"You said we should compromise." Again she lifted almost off, hovered above the head for several seconds while he held his breath, and then dropped back down. She had gotten really good at riding him.

"How is that a compromise?" he asked, gritting harder. The manipulative woman knew exactly what she was doing. Two could play at this game, though.

Graham slid one hand around from her hip to find her clit. He pressed his thumb against the swollen bundle of nerves, making her moan.

"You're not playing fair," she crooned.

"Me?" he nearly shouted. "Who climbed on top of me and started using her womanly wiles in order to get her way?"

She blinked at him, her lips forming into a half-grin. "Did you just say womanly wiles, you big dork?"

"Mm hmm." He pinched her clit and then started stroking it rapidly until she moaned.

"I can't think when you do that," she breathed. "You're ruining my seduction."

He chuckled. "Good. Maybe you won't try to use sex to get me to do something in the future."

She met his gaze, her eyes dancing with love and lust and teasing laughter. "I find it's useful. I think I'll be inclined to use sex to my advantage often."

Without warning, he grabbed her hips, lifted her off his length, and spun to set her on her hands and knees at his side.

"Graham," she yelped. "I was busy."

"Now *I'm* busy, my love," he informed her as he turned to kneel between her legs, lined himself up once again with her center, and thrust deep.

She rocked forward, a shocked gasp escaping her lips. "Oh God."

"Yeah. I thought you might say that." He held her hips steady as he pulled almost out and thrust back in, deeper this time. So deep he needed to hold his breath and concentrate on the wall in front of him to keep from coming prematurely.

"Graham…" she whispered, which didn't help his problem. He loved it when she called out his name. He loved it even more when she barely whispered it because she was lost to him.

"You like that?" he asked as he continued pounding into her.

Her gasps of pleasure were his answer. And then she started moaning softly in that way he'd come to realize meant she was about to come. "So good," she murmured. "I didn't know…"

He loved the way she responded every time they did something new. Shock filled her. He'd obviously done a bit more research on sex in his life than she had. She wasn't wrong. This was one of his favorite positions so far. Sliding one hand around from her hip to her clit, he stroked the little nub again as he continued to thrust in and out of her. Desperately. With an urgency that defied logic.

It was like he was in a hurry to claim her, to show her how much he loved her, to demonstrate his feelings with his body.

Suddenly, she cried out again, her head tipping back as she pressed herself more fully against his erection. Her body shuddered, and he couldn't stop himself from coming on the heels of her orgasm.

When he was finally spent, he wrapped one arm around her waist and lowered her shaking body to the mattress, landing half on top of her and half at her side.

She was breathing heavily, but she managed to say, "We're still going to Montana."

He chuckled as he brushed her hair from her face and then kissed her neck. "Neither of us is going to win any awards with these negotiating skills."

She twisted her face to meet his. "If you'll listen to me," she began, still gasping for oxygen. How she managed to form solid thoughts so quickly after coming hard around his length was amazing. "I'll finish telling you how we both benefit."

He narrowed his gaze. "I'm all ears."

"Good. Now that I've had some time to think more clearly about our future, I realize Montana is the safest place we could be right now. As much as I'd love to go to Atlanta and hide at my parents' home, there's a possibility we would be putting them in danger if we went there."

He watched her face closely as reason leaked out in the form of her words. He let her continue.

"I don't want to feel as out of control as I did two days ago ever again in my life. I don't like the man I love getting shot at while I can do nothing about it. I don't want to get shot either. But the best way to ensure that never happens again is to join with the rest of the team and fight for our future freedom."

He kissed her shoulder blade and then nuzzled her neck.

"Your logic is sound, as long as you're not making this sacrifice under duress because you think I won't love you if we skip town."

"I didn't decide we should go to Montana suddenly this morning. I've been thinking about it for two days. Putting an end to the insanity that follows us everywhere we go has to be our top priority. As soon as we're safe, however, I think I can guarantee you I won't want to return to the bunker. The idea of stepping into that facility ever again makes me cringe. I wouldn't be able to even breathe the air without hearing the echo of those shots in my ears."

"Deal," he agreed. "I promise we won't go back to the bunker. As soon as it's safe to move about the country, we will head for your parents' home for as long as you'd like. After that, we'll head for mine. When we're fully recuperated, then we can pick a spot to call home and get civilian jobs. Yeah?"

She wiggled out of his grip and rolled onto her back. She was smiling up at him as she spoke. "Sounds perfect."

"You're sure?"

"Yes. The only thing I'm more sure about is how much I love you."

He kissed her gently. "I love you too."

CHAPTER 21

Two days later...

Graham took a deep breath as he entered the main control room at six o'clock in the morning on his second day in southeast Montana. He'd left Kate sleeping in their room, kissing her temple as he encouraged her to stay in bed.

For Graham, sleep never lasted more than a few hours at a time, and from the moment they'd arrived at this makeshift office space, his stress level had escalated.

More than a dozen members of his team and the second team had already congregated at what was essentially a converted barn behind a large country estate. The main house had ten bedrooms, so there was plenty of space for everyone, and the structure behind the house, which looked like a barn to anyone approaching, had actually been turned into a high-tech office.

Already, at six in the morning, several of his team members were bustling around the room. It buzzed with activity and the hum of computers.

Dade caught his attention and waved him closer. He was standing next to a young guy Graham hadn't met yet. He looked far too young to be a member of the second team. Graham pegged him to be in his late teens or early twenties.

Dade leaned his butt against the desk next to the kid in the computer chair as Graham approached. "Graham, this is Spencer Casey."

Graham's eyes shot wide. "*The* Spencer?"

Spencer tipped his head back and chuckled. "The one and only."

Dade continued. "Yep. He's the guy who's been feeding us information and helped you get the data from the bunker preserved."

"What's he doing here?" Graham was confused. If the guy was working deep in the bowels of whoever the Blue Cell group was, how was he sitting in this secret office space in Montana?

"It got a little too hot inside Blue Cell's organization," Spencer provided.

Dade crossed his ankles and met Graham's gaze. "Suspicions rose among his superiors the day you were caught by another hacker in Blue Cell downloading data in Colorado. He realized he was going to have to bail fast before he got caught, so when he left for lunch that day, he never went back. He didn't even go home. He came straight here."

Graham nodded slowly. "And you trust him?" he asked, not giving a single fuck the kid was listening. "Our entire team is at risk. Are you sure it's okay to bring a guy who has a direct line to the enemy into our inner circle?"

Spencer smirked.

Dade smiled. "Trust me, I wouldn't have him here if I wasn't a hundred percent certain he was on the level with me."

Graham narrowed his gaze, his blood pressure rising. "I was caught four days ago by his people. I could have been killed. What was he doing then?" Graham jerked his gaze back to the kid with the messy hair wearing some sort of worn gray concert T-shirt. Ordinarily, Graham wouldn't be so distrustful, but as far as he was concerned, Spencer's organization had gotten him captured, and it could have been much worse.

Spencer spun his chair around and stood. He had on old canvas sneakers and jeans that were covered with intentional holes. He ran a hand through the hair on the top of his head that was too long, though that part of his appearance was also intentional because the sides had been cropped short. It was undoubtedly the latest style among young people.

Spencer also looked nervous, and he shuffled his feet as he spoke, tucking his fingers into the pockets of his jeans. "Listen, I know it's hard for you to believe, but I swear I'm on your side. The people who work for Blue Cell have lost their minds. The stories I can tell you will make you cringe."

Graham interrupted, well aware he was still growling skeptically. "Let's stick to the one about how you're here and why two men tried to kill me." Graham noticed several other people in the room had gathered closer to listen.

Spencer glanced around at everyone, swallowed, and took a deep shaky breath. "Look, Blue Cell is huge. They operate out of an underground facility in rural Kansas. I don't have the location." He rubbed his brow with two fingers, obviously stressed. "I've never been to the main building. They maintain pockets of employees all over the country, and it was another hacker in another state who discovered what you were doing. I was working out of an apartment building near Kansas City in a cramped space with four other people. My job has always been to hack into the DEEP system and keep tabs on your team."

"If you're able to hack so deeply into the DEEP bunker, then tell us how information is leaking out of that facility," Graham demanded. "What about Temple Levenson? Is she inadvertently feeding info up the chain of command?"

Spencer shook his head. "Temple is clean. I can't say what

she might be doing unknowingly, but I've never once found her to be aiding Blue Cell."

Graham narrowed his gaze, still unsure about this kid no matter what he said or did.

"Look, like I said, I'm honestly not the only hacker working for Blue Cell. God knows how many they have. Some other guy in some other location was assigned to monitor the computers inside the Colorado bunker that day. He caught the sudden activity on the one you were using to download data.

"I didn't realize a sting was going on until it was already happening. I overheard two of the guys working in another room where I was located discussing you by name." Spencer nodded toward Graham.

A hand landed on Graham's arm and he turned to find a very pale Kate pressing into his side. Her gaze was on Spencer.

"That's when I got worried." Spencer licked his lips, rocking back and forth on the balls of his feet. "I can't explain it, but there was a distinct shift in the air in the room at the same time those two men stopped speaking, and it got eerily quiet.

"When they wandered back in, they busied themselves nervously, and that's when I knew I needed to get the fuck out of that building as fast as possible. I left for lunch and never returned.

"I have no doubt someone was on their way to the apartment to get me. Hell, I probably would have passed them in the lobby if I hadn't taken the stairs at a run and darted out the back door."

Spencer ran a hand through his hair again, even though it fell haphazardly across his forehead seconds later. "I've been aware of other employees of Blue Cell disappearing before. I don't know what happened to them, but I didn't want to become a statistic. So, here I am."

The kid spun around and pointed at the computer behind him. "The good news is that I've restored all of the data you downloaded in the last week." He smiled at Graham over his shoulder. "You did a fantastic job retrieving it. Hopefully whoever wanted it to disappear believes the only copy was on those hard drives that went up in flames."

"Have you been able to ascertain why the hell this Blue Cell organization is working so hard to derail the work of Project DEEP or who their boss is?" Dade asked.

Spencer shook his head. "Not a clue. There are so many arms to that organization that it's impossible to follow any trail. Even the people who work for them don't know who they work for. I have no doubt that within minutes of my escape, the entire apartment we were using as an office was wiped clean and relocated. It wouldn't be the first time. We relocated every few weeks anyway."

Kate gripped Graham's arm tightly. She was leaning into him hard. He could feel her shaking against his side, and he wrapped an arm around her waist to support her.

Spencer glanced at Kate and then back at Graham. "I'm so sorry I wasn't able to warn you to get out faster. I would have if I could."

Dade shoved off the desk to his full height. "Yeah, your track record in that area sucks."

"What's that supposed to mean?" Graham asked.

Spencer turned his gaze toward Dade. "He's talking about Zeke and Michelle. I did manage to send them a text message to get out of the bunker several weeks ago before two men followed them, kidnapped them, and tried to get information out of them, but apparently I wasn't fast enough. They were trailed anyway. I had no way to follow up afterward either."

Graham stiffened. What a convoluted shit show.

Spencer continued when no one spoke. "I overheard someone talking about sending a pair of guys to follow them to wherever they were going. I hoped those two guys weren't in position yet. I was wrong." He glanced at Kate and then back at

Graham. "In your case, I was completely in the dark. I was so focused on making sure your data was secure that I had no idea anyone had found you out." He winced.

Dade cleared his throat. "The important thing is that the data is secure, Graham and Kate made it here, and none of the good guys were killed."

Kate nearly lurched forward. "Tushar was shot. I thought Trish was going to have a heart attack."

"Yeah, but he's going to be fine. Ryan touched base with his mom yesterday. Trish is still shaken up, but Tushar is healing."

"Do we have any way to make contact with them?" Kate asked.

Dade shook his head. "Sorry. It's not safe. I don't trust the security level of that bunker. But they know we're here, and they're doing their part from the inside to be helpful."

"Trish must be frantic," Kate murmured. "I've never seen her that upset."

"Her husband was shot," Dade said. "It's understandable."

Graham had to agree with Kate, however. Dade hadn't seen Trish that day. The woman had always been as solid as a rock when it came to the team. She had morphed into a frantic state right before Graham's eyes. Understandable? Yes. Characteristic of Trish? No.

As Kate sighed heavily, Graham turned her away from Spencer, threaded his fingers with hers, and led her to a work station across the room. Dade had assigned the space to the two of them.

"Do you think he's telling the truth?" Kate whispered.

"I don't know, but I can tell you he put his life on the line to help get the data from the bunker saved. That's enough for me."

She chewed on her bottom lip. "Yeah, you're right." She looked over his shoulder at the computer. "Did Dade assign us a task?"

"Several of them."

She set her hands on his shoulders. "Then I guess we better get to work. This place gives me the creeps. The sooner we save the world, the sooner we can get back to living."

He pulled her in close and closed his eyes. "I like that plan."

Now, he just needed to make sure it happened before Kate lost the will to stay in Montana in hiding.

Tushar awoke with a start, his heart racing as he reached across the bed for his wife.

She immediately set a hand on his chest. "I'm right here."

The room was dark, the only light coming from a lamp in the next room. Tushar licked his dry lips and turned toward the woman who made him a whole person. The woman he'd been married to for over two decades—three if he counted preservation. He wrapped his good arm around her and kissed the top of her head. "You okay?"

"Yes. I'm fine." She patted his chest. "We're fine..." she whispered.

He was breathing heavily from waking so abruptly, and he turned onto his side and flattened her onto her back. He cupped her chin reverently and kissed her lips, letting his mouth trail down her neck and shoulder and then lower between her breasts.

He continued nibbling a path to her belly, nudging her shirt up so that he could kiss the soft spot that would soon be impossible to hide.

Her hands went into his hair, and she started giggling when the shadow of his beard tickled her skin. He lifted his face and smiled at her in the dim light. "How much longer do you want to keep this a secret?" he asked.

She shrugged. "As long as possible. We can't very well tell anyone until we've told Ryan."

"We have to get out of this bunker." Tushar sighed as he climbed up her body. "We should go to your mom's first."

"She's going to freak." Trish's smile faded quickly as he watched her slide back into that dark place of doubts. She wasn't wrong to be concerned. They hadn't seen a doctor yet.

It was ironic considering nearly everyone they knew was a doctor and all the equipment they could possibly need was in the bunker. Even an ultrasound machine.

But they'd discussed their options at length and decided they didn't want to know anything. If the universe had blessed them with a child after ten years of hibernation and at the ages of forty-five, they would take whatever they got.

Trish hadn't even taken a pregnancy test for the first several weeks. It hadn't seemed reasonable that she could be pregnant, and she'd been in denial. It wasn't until Tushar grew concerned from watching her vomit first thing every morning that he came to her with the test and held her hand while they waited for the results.

He remembered that moment well as he stared down at his beautiful wife. She'd stopped feeling nauseous several weeks ago. Now she had that amazing glow that never left her. He was actually surprised no one had guessed.

Until a week ago, they had been tiptoeing around keeping things to themselves, but he'd seen the panic all over her face when he'd gotten shot. It was time to get out of this bunker. It was time to talk to Ryan. It was time to catch up with the team and get his wife someplace safe.

This bunker did not qualify as a safe place to fall. It should have been the safest place in the world, but it no longer represented that. Even though he felt much calmer now that they'd proven Temple was on their side and hadn't known about the source of the threats, the bunker still represented danger to Tushar. Either there were bugs he couldn't detect in the lab, or some advanced technology was spying on them, or someone who worked there was a mole. It didn't matter. He wanted out.

"I'll work on a plan," he told her as he leaned down to nuzzle her breasts. They were already filling out just like they had when she'd been pregnant with Ryan.

"You can use my mom easily as a reason we need to leave the bunker."

He nodded. "Yeah, convincing Temple we need to take a day trip won't be difficult. What makes my skin crawl is visualizing how disappointed she's going to be in us when we don't return."

Trish sighed. "I know. I hate that part. We've known her for over twenty years. I consider her family. I know in my heart she has nothing to do with whatever secret band of people is trying to undermine the work of Project DEEP, but I'm equally aware that she stands way too close to the enemy and we can't tell her anything."

"Yeah. At least she realizes that now and doesn't want to *hear* anything either. What she doesn't know, she can't inadvertently pass on." Tushar held her gaze for a long time, soaking in the love he felt radiating off her. "I hope it's a girl," he teased.

"I hope it's not born in a cave somewhere on the run," she responded.

He reached up to smooth a hand across her cheek. "I promise that won't happen. I'll move mountains to ensure you're in a safe place long before the delivery."

"I love you," she whispered.

"I love you too." He leaned down to kiss her lips, knowing their future was going to be full of happiness and excitement.

AUTHOR'S NOTE

I hope you've enjoyed the fifth book in the *Project DEEP* series. Please enjoying the following excerpt for book six in the series, *Reviving Bianca*.

REVIVING BIANCA

PROJECT DEEP (BOOK SIX)

Grayson Maston's nerves were completely frayed when his cell phone rang in the pocket of his scrubs, making him jump in his seat. He'd been tapping his foot nervously for over half an hour, keeping a close eye on the comatose woman on the gurney in front of him.

Bianca Serrano. Young. Hispanic. Petite. She'd been with Project DEEP for less than a year before the entire team had been cryonically preserved ten years ago.

They were in the back of an ambulance. An ambulance that had been sitting idle behind a strip mall for much longer than he would have liked.

He tugged the cell from his pocket, glanced at the screen, and connected the call. "Ryan. Thank God. What the hell is going on?"

"Sorry. Detective Pierce Titus is going to pick you up."

"Who the hell is Titus? And why?" Grayson needed answers, far more of them than he suspected he was going to get, judging by how fast Ryan was speaking.

"I'll explain later, but you can trust him. He's going to transport the two of you to a safe location."

Grayson's brows shot up. "A safe location," he repeated sarcastically. "Right." As far as Grayson was concerned, there were no safe locations on earth.

Ryan sighed. "As safe as we can manage right now. Titus will take you to a private clinic where Bianca can be hidden for the time being. We don't want your current driver to know where you're going."

That made sense, but why was Grayson on this trek with a woman he didn't know? He himself had only been awake for two months. He hardly had his bearings. "Why am *I* here?" Two hours ago the majority of the scientists and doctors working in the Colorado bunker for Project DEEP had been evacuated when an explosion compromised the front gate. In a mad scramble to get everyone to safety, Grayson had been randomly assigned to leave in an ambulance with Bianca.

"Temple did her best to pair people up in the most logical manner. You're a medical doctor. You'll be beneficial to Bianca along the way."

Grayson sat up straighter, his spine stiffening. "Wait. Whoa… Are you thinking I'm going to stay with Bianca for a month waiting for her to wake up?"

"Yes. That's the plan. Sorry. We need you."

Grayson glanced at his patient and cringed. He ran a hand through his hair. He couldn't think of anything more boring than guarding a woman he barely knew while she lay in a coma for another four weeks.

"Grayson, the reason I called is because you need to know something."

Hearing the concern in Ryan's tone, Grayson closed his eyes and rubbed his temples with his free hand. "There's more?"

"Yes." Ryan sighed. "Bianca's been abused. I seriously doubt very many people know this. Even Temple didn't know. It wasn't until Damon pulled her from the reanimation chamber a few days ago that he saw the scars on her."

Shit. "What kind of scars are we talking about?" Grayson understood the nuances of abuse all too well. He wondered what would have led everyone to assume Bianca had been abused just because she had scars.

"They look like whip marks up and down her back, her butt, and her thighs. They're old enough to have been endured when she was a child. I'm inclined to believe she won't like anyone knowing this since she never spoke of it. Temple is arranging for a nurse to care for Bianca while you're at the clinic."

Grayson's spine stiffened. *Fuck.* His gaze went to Bianca. His hand flew to her much smaller one where it rested against the gurney. He wrapped his fingers around hers instinctively, pain piercing his heart. Who would do such a thing? His mood switched from frustrated to concerned in a heartbeat. A moment ago Bianca had been a scientist he barely knew. Now, she was someone with a story. A story he did not like.

"Grayson?" Ryan interrupted his thoughts, making Grayson realize he hadn't responded.

"I'm here." He sighed. "I'll make sure the nurse is informed."

"Perfect. I'll get in touch with you again as soon as I can." Ryan ended the call without another word.

Grayson put the phone back in his pocket, returned his gaze to Bianca, and slid his hand to her wrist to check her pulse for the millionth time. She was fine. All the machines hooked up to her were working fine. Everything was fine. Except it wasn't, and he didn't think everything would ever be fine again. Not for any of them, and certainly not for Bianca.

Bianca didn't move. Of course. She wouldn't be awake for another three and a half weeks. That was how long she needed to remain in a coma so that her organs could fully become functional. No one came out of a cryostat ready to run a marathon.

For the first time since Grayson had been paired up with Bianca, he looked at her differently. He hadn't known her well before they were preserved. She'd been quiet and reserved. Kept her head down. Worked hard. She was a brilliant scientist with a specialty in research, specifically hematology. He knew that much about her, but he'd never known a single personal detail.

Did anyone?

He swallowed back the pain he felt on her behalf now and kicked himself for not recognizing the signs. He should have known better. Reserved. Quiet. Detached. She didn't open up to people. She didn't let anyone get close to her.

He thought back on her situation. Unlike most of the team, Bianca hadn't had an apartment in town ten years ago. She'd had a room inside the bunker. As far as he knew, she'd never left the bunker.

Fuck.

He had no idea how much time passed while he held Bianca's small hand, noticing the contrast between her darker skin and his pale complexion. He'd been raised on a farm in Nebraska to blond parents who didn't donate an ounce of melanin to either him or his sister.

Bianca's skin was the gorgeous tone he'd always wished for while he'd slathered himself with sunscreen every day even though he still managed to burn his face and neck every summer.

He cringed again when he thought about Ryan's words. In the time Grayson had worked with Bianca, he'd only spoken to her a handful of times, mostly because she'd never been outgoing or social with the rest of the group. A sign he should have wondered about.

Grayson was no stranger to witnessing trauma. He'd watched his sister go through years of abuse at the hands of her husband. She had married young and had two kids before she finally got away from the asshole. But in that time, she'd been beaten so many times, Grayson was sure she'd lost count. She'd taken the abuse and hidden it at first, doing so to protect her children. Her husband had threatened to kill them if she told anyone.

Grayson's heart pounded even now remembering the broken woman who'd shown up at his parents' doorstep one night, her small kids in the car, her lip swollen and bloody, her eye black, and her clothes ripped. She'd finally had enough and gotten the strength to leave him.

Grayson's parents had known. Grayson himself had known. But no matter what any of them said to her, she would deny it, and the longer she was with her husband, the less she'd seen of her family. She was twenty-three when she finally got away. Grayson was eighteen and about to go off to West Point.

He tried to shake the memory of that night from his mind, but it was never far away. He remembered the welts he'd seen on her back when their mother lifted her shirt to examine them.

Jerking his attention back to the present, Grayson set his gaze on Bianca once again. She was so small. So pretty. Her dainty features and silky hair made her seem younger than she was.

Granted, she was far younger than him. Twenty-seven if he remembered correctly, eight years younger.

He suddenly felt horrible for not paying attention to her or making an attempt to befriend her. Everyone had a story. Apparently hers was horrific. She deserved better. He hoped whatever asshole had struck this gorgeous woman was currently rotting in hell.

Bile rose to his throat as he squeezed her hand. Every ounce of frustration he'd felt an hour ago for being saddled with a stranger in a coma fled the ambulance. There was no reason for him to be angry. He didn't currently have anyplace else to be for heaven's sake. He would do Bianca a solid and befriend her when she woke up.

Every member of their team was in jeopardy. All twenty-one of them. They needed to stick together. Help each other through this crazy time while God-only-knew who would prefer to see them dead. Someone had obviously been very careless with her life at one point. That would not happen again. Not on Grayson's watch.

Suddenly the driver's door opened and Grayson lifted his gaze to find a man he didn't know climbing into the driver's seat in place of the original driver. The man twisted around and smiled. "Detective Pierce Titus." He held his badge and identification open for Grayson to see.

Grayson nodded.

"I'll have you settled in a much better location in no time. Hang tight."

Grayson wondered what the hell a *better* location was going to look like. Not for the first time, he doubted there was such a place anymore. Someone was securing information about the employees of Project DEEP, and that someone was wreaking havoc on all their lives no matter where they fled.

DEEP. Disease & Epidemic Eradication & Prevention. The acronym was absurdly long and tedious, but it was perfectly descriptive of what the members of the team did for the government. They researched disease. Every one of them had been handpicked from the finest schools in the country to join the team.

And every one of them was now in danger. Both the original team being reanimated and the new team who'd come on two years ago with the technology to bring back the first team.

Grayson relaxed his shoulders. For the time being, there was nothing he could do but hope Titus indeed got him and Bianca to a safe location where she could recover and rejoin the living.

Her first shot at life apparently hadn't gone so well. Grayson made a silent vow to ensure she fared far better at her second shot. In the course of his life, he'd done a lot to help the human race. Right now, one small woman needed him. He could at least keep her safe.

He knew his boss, General Temple Levenson, was offering relocation packages to anyone who wanted to start a new life with a new name. Perhaps that would be the best plan for Bianca. Anything would be better than waking up to find out that after the horrors of her childhood, she was now on the run from an unknown enemy who apparently intended to hunt her down.

For now, all Grayson could do was protect this petite woman with his life, and then when she woke up, help her gain enough strength to start over. He could do this. He had to do this.

~

Three and a half weeks later...

Something very heavy was weighing Bianca down. Too many blankets? She couldn't lift her arms, and her mouth was dry. She tried to lick her lips and found even that was difficult. Her head was pounding too. She'd never been drunk in her life, but she imagined this was what a hangover felt like.

Maybe she had the flu. She wracked her brain, trying to come up with the last thing she could remember.

Then her eyes flew open. Her heart was pounding as she glanced around the room. She was in a hospital. Machines were hooked up to her. One of them started beeping.

Seconds later a man rushed into the room from the hallway. His brows were furrowed as he approached, a smile forming on his lips as he leaned over her.

Wait, she knew him... She worked with him at the bunker. Grayson Maston. The last time she'd seen him, he'd been very sick. They all had been. Every member of her team had contracted a rare form of anemia. AP12. He didn't look sick now.

He set a palm on her forehead and then released her just as

quickly to grab something from the table at her side. "Welcome back," he said. "A few ice chips will help with the dry lips." He spooned a sliver of ice and held it to her lips.

The coolness soothed. She coughed to clear her throat, hoping she would be able to speak. "We weren't preserved?" she asked. Obviously not. The last thing she remembered was receiving a shot that would put her to sleep so she could be preserved. Had someone miraculously found a cure instead?

No. That made no sense. She'd seen Grayson go into the cryostat days before her. He'd definitely been preserved. Which meant she had been too. Holy shit.

He smiled. "We were. It's been ten years."

Her eyes bugged out. "Ten years?"

He set a hand on her shoulder and slid it down to her wrist. "Yep. I know it's shocking. I nearly choked when I woke up."

She glanced down at where he held her wrist and shuddered. It had been a long time since anyone touched her so intimately. Far more than ten years.

It wasn't that no one ever made contact with her. They did. She bumped into people in the lab. It was unavoidable. But not like this. Grayson was practically holding her hand.

She realized she was staring at the way he touched her when he suddenly jerked his hand free. "Sorry. You want some more ice?" he rushed to add.

She nodded, feeling a flush run up her face. He'd done nothing wrong. She hated making him feel bad about touching her. It wasn't intentional. It was a kneejerk reaction she'd always had.

She watched his face as he fed her a few more ice chips. His brow was furrowed and he swallowed several times. Suddenly, she froze, the last piece of ice running down her chin. *He knows. Fuck. He knows.* Her worst nightmare had come to life.

Of course he knows. Everyone probably knows. She glanced

around in a panic, wondering how many of her team were awake and when the sympathetic stares would begin. Pity.

She'd gone to sleep that day believing in her soul she would never wake up again. It wasn't conceivable to imagine she would ever be revived. Even if someone eventually found a cure for AP12, there had been no procedure to reanimate anyone yet. Apparently things had changed.

Shit. This was not what she'd wanted.

Something was different about this room. She didn't recognize it. "Where are we?"

"A clinic in southern Colorado. Safe."

Safe? What did that mean? Why wouldn't they be safe?

"Where is everyone else?"

"Scattered. Long story." He reached for her forehead again, set his hand gently on her skin, and then yanked it away when she winced. He straightened to his full height and wiped his palms on his thighs. "You should sleep some more. You'll be more alert the next time you wake up."

For a moment, she stared at him, her heart racing as she read the pity on his face. She closed her eyes to black out his expression. Sleep was a good idea. Maybe she'd never been awake in the first place. If she was lucky, this entire weird episode had been a dream. Or a nightmare. If she was lucky, she'd go back to sleep and never wake up again.

Because she'd never wanted to see that look on anyone's face. That was why she never spoke of her childhood to a living soul. It was why she never opened herself up to relationships with men. It was why she kept to herself and didn't even have close girlfriends.

Fear of seeing that look had propelled her to remain private for her entire adult life. And now it was here to bite her in the ass, mocking her with some insane level of scientific research that dared to bring her back from the dead to taunt her with horrifying looks of pity from her teammates.

Yeah, sleep was the best option.

Death had been her first choice to avoid confrontation, though. She'd been at peace with death when she'd contracted AP12. She'd worked hard and been happy with what she'd accomplished in life. She'd been ready for the end, knowing she'd survived trauma most people were never subjected to in her life and had still managed to make the world a better place.

She didn't want to be reanimated if it meant having to go through the nightmare of explaining her childhood to anyone.

ALSO BY BECCA JAMESON

Seattle Doms:

Salacious Exposure by Becca Jameson

Salacious Desires By Kate Oliver

Salacious Attraction by Becca Jameson

Salacious Indulgence by Kate Oliver

Salacious Devotion by Becca Jameson

Salacious Surrender by Kate Oliver

Danger Bluff:

Rocco

Hawking

Kestrel

Magnus

Phoenix

Caesar

Roses and Thorns:

Marigold

Oleander

Jasmine

Tulip

Daffodil

Lily

Roses and Thorns Box Set One

Roses and Thorns Box Set Two

Shadowridge Guardians:

Steele by Pepper North

Kade by Kate Oliver

Atlas by Becca Jameson

Doc by Kate Oliver

Gabriel by Becca Jameson

Talon by Pepper North

Bear by Becca Jameson

Faust by Pepper North

Storm by Kate Oliver

Blade by Pepper North

King by Kate Oliver

Rock by Becca Jameson

Blossom Ridge:

Starting Over

Finding Peace

Building Trust

Feeling Brave

Embracing Joy

Accepting Love

Blossom Ridge Box Set One

Blossom Ridge Box Set Two

The Wanderers:

Sanctuary

Refuge

Harbor

Shelter

Hideout

Haven

The Wanderers Box Set One

The Wanderers Box Set Two

Surrender:

Raising Lucy

Teaching Abby

Leaving Roman

Choosing Kellen

Pleasing Josie

Honoring Hudson

Nurturing Britney

Charming Colton

Convincing Leah

Rewarding Avery

Impressing Brett

Guiding Cassandra

Chasing Amber

Controlling Natasha

Provoking Camden

Surrender Box Set One

Surrender Box Set Two

Surrender Box Set Three

Surrender Box Set Four

Open Skies:

Layover

Redeye

Nonstop

Standby

Takeoff

Jetway

Open Skies Box Set One

Open Skies Box Set Two

Shadow SEALs:

Shadow in the Desert

Shadow in the Darkness

Holt Agency:

Rescued by Becca Jameson

Unchained by KaLyn Cooper

Protected by Becca Jameson

Liberated by KaLyn Cooper

Defended by Becca Jameson

Unrestrained by KaLyn Cooper

Delta Team Three (Special Forces: Operation Alpha):

Destiny's Delta

Canyon Springs:

Caleb's Mate

Hunter's Mate

Corked and Tapped:

Volume One: Friday Night

Volume Two: Company Party

Volume Three: The Holidays

The Complete Set

Project DEEP:

Reviving Emily

Reviving Trish

Reviving Dade

Reviving Zeke

Reviving Graham

Reviving Bianca

Reviving Olivia

Project DEEP Box Set One

Project DEEP Box Set Two

SEALs in Paradise:

Hot SEAL, Red Wine

Hot SEAL, Australian Nights

Hot SEAL, Cold Feet

Hot SEAL, April's Fool

Hot SEAL, Brown-Eyed Girl

Dark Falls:

Dark Nightmares

Club Zodiac:

Training Sasha

Obeying Rowen

Collaring Brooke

Mastering Rayne

Trusting Aaron

Claiming London

Sharing Charlotte

Taming Rex

Tempting Elizabeth

Club Zodiac Box Set One

Club Zodiac Box Set Two

Club Zodiac Box Set Three

The Art of Kink:

Pose

Paint

Sculpt

Arcadian Bears:

Grizzly Mountain

Grizzly Beginning

Grizzly Secret

Grizzly Promise

Grizzly Survival

Grizzly Perfection

Arcadian Bears Box Set One

Arcadian Bears Box Set Two

Sleeper SEALs:

Saving Zola

Spring Training:

Catching Zia

Catching Lily

Catching Ava

Spring Training Box Set

The Underground series:

Force

Clinch

Guard

Submit

Thrust

Torque

The Underground Box Set One

The Underground Box Set Two

Wolf Masters series:

Kara's Wolves

Lindsey's Wolves

Jessica's Wolves

Alyssa's Wolves

Tessa's Wolf

Rebecca's Wolves

Melinda's Wolves

Laurie's Wolves

Amanda's Wolves

Sharon's Wolves

Wolf Masters Box Set One

Wolf Masters Box Set Two

Claiming Her series:

The Rules

The Game

The Prize

Claiming Her Box Set

Emergence series:

Bound to be Taken

Bound to be Tamed

Bound to be Tested

Bound to be Tempted

Emergence Box Set

The Fight Club series:

Come

Perv

Need

Hers

Want

Lust

The Fight Club Box Set One

The Fight Club Box Set Two

Wolf Gatherings series:

Tarnished

Dominated

Completed

Redeemed

Abandoned

Betrayed

Wolf Gatherings Box Set One

Wolf Gathering Box Set Two

Durham Wolves series:

Rescue in the Smokies

Fire in the Smokies

Freedom in the Smokies

Durham Wolves Box Set

Stand Alone Books:

Blind with Love

Guarding the Truth

Out of the Smoke

Abducting His Mate

Wolf Trinity

Frostbitten

A Princess for Cale/A Princess for Cain

Severed Dreams

Where Alphas Dominate

ABOUT THE AUTHOR

Becca Jameson is a USA Today best-selling author of over 150 books. She is well-known for her Wolf Masters series, her Fight Club series, and her Surrender series. She currently lives in Houston, Texas, with her husband. Two grown kids pop in every once in a while, too! She is loving this journey and has dabbled in a variety of genres, including paranormal, sports romance, military, reverse harem, dark romance, suspense, dystopian, BDSM, and Daddy Dom.

A total night owl, Becca writes late at night, sequestering herself in her office with a glass of red wine and a bar of dark chocolate, her fingers flying across the keyboard as her characters weave their own stories.

During the day--which never starts before ten in the morning!-- she can be found walking, running errands, or reading in her favorite hammock chair!

…where Alphas dominate…

Becca's Newsletter Sign-up

Join my Facebook fan group, Becca's Bibliomaniacs, for the most up-to-date information, random excerpts while I work, giveaways, and fun release parties!

www.ingramcontent.com/pod-product-compliance
Lightning Source LLC
Chambersburg PA
CBHW070104280626
47159CB00016B/1179